Bigfoot

Tor books by Richard Hoyt

Cool Runnings
The Dragon Portfolio
Fish Story
Head of State
The Manna Enzyme
Marimba
Siege!
Siskiyou
Trotsky's Run
Whoo?

Bigfoot

Richard
Hoyt

A Tom Doherty Associates Book

New York

BIGFOOT

Copyright © 1993 by Richard Hoyt

This book is printed on acid-free paper.

A Tor Book
Published by Tom Doherty Associates, Inc.
175 Fifth Avenue
New York, N.Y. 10010

Tor ® is a registered trademark of Tom Doherty Associates, Inc.

Library of Congress Cataloging-in-Publication Data

Hoyt, Richard,
    Bigfoot / Richard Hoyt.
        p.   cm.
    "A Tom Doherty Associates book."
    ISBN 0-312-85278-9
    I. Title.
PS3558.0975B54   1993
813'.54—dc20   92-36535
                                                                CIP

First Edition: January 1993

Printed in the United States of America

0 9 8 7 6 5 4 3 2 1

For Avi and Kimi Feuer
and their uncle Herb Goldberg,
the Most Golden.

Contents

Chapter One

An Occurrence
at Ape Cave

Willie Prettybird and I had just finished a job at Coos Bay on the central Oregon coast and had returned to his cabin on the Nehalem River near Vernonia, about fifty miles northwest of Portland, when the first of the Bigfoot stories hit the news.

I ranked Bigfoot stories right up there with astrologists and faith healers, but Willie, perhaps in keeping with his allegedly being a shaman, took them more seriously.

"Sasquatch," he muttered.

Sasquatch was the name given the beast by Indians of the Pacific Northwest. Willie always said "Sasquatch," never "Bigfoot." "Bigfoot" was generic for "unidentified mountain monster," and better left to newspaper-checkout rags.

Willie didn't like Sasquatch being mentioned in the same breath with Yeti either. Yeti was Yeti. Yeti was said to live in the Himalayas. Willie wasn't concerned with Yeti or the Himalayas. He said if you wanted to know about Yeti, go to Nepal. But he did care about

Sasquatch, who was said to live high in the snow-capped Cascade Mountains—a range that ran from Northern California to British Columbia, in Canada.

When a Sasquatch sighting was reported, Willie paid attention. *"Reported* sighted, Willie," I said. "That's code. While the proles dream on, believing 'reported sighted' and 'sighted' are the same thing, rational people can smile to themselves and pour another cup of coffee. No harm done."

Willie groaned. "You'll never learn, will you, Denson?"

"Until we have proof, I'll remain skeptical."

"Three sightings in four days, Denson. Mount Baker, Mount Rainier, and Mount St. Helens. Count 'em. Three. From top to bottom of Washington State. When robins are migrating we see more of them, right?"

I shrugged.

"So they're moving around up there." Willie popped a tape into his VCR so we could view the St. Helens Bigfoot, er, Sasquatch sighting that was coming up on KATU-TV, Channel 2.

We watched the anchors report the news with the sound turned off. We both thought watching the newsreaders mouth the news in silence was more entertaining than actually listening to them.

They were saving the Bigfoot tape for last in order to keep us glued to the rest of the news. The pretty woman member of the team reported another item with great solemnity then said, "Coming up, a Bigfoot is taped on Mount St. Helens." It was easy enough to read her lips, but just in case we weren't the only Portlanders watching with the sound turned off, this was repeated in large letters at the bottom of the screen. Unstated: hurry up and pee, or you'll miss the fun.

Of course, that didn't mean Bigfoot was due up immediately after the ads exhorting us to buy tires from Les Schwab or groceries from Fred Meyers. Freddy's, as the chain was called by Portlanders, had advanced the cause of civilization by banning the straightforward word "sale" from its promotions in favor of the fancier "temporary price reduction" or TPR.

Finally, Bigfoot time.

Willie punched up the sound with his remote.

A Channel 2 photographer showed us the upper entrance to Ape

Cave on the southern slope of Mount St. Helens. As he did, a reporter explained in a voice-over what most Portlanders already knew, that a volcanic eruption in May 1980 had blown away the north face of the mountain, which was now a National Volcanic Monument.

She told us how Ape Cave, discovered by a logger in 1946—and now part of the Volcanic Monument—was the longest intact lava tube in the United States.

I had been to Ape Cave before and knew that it was not named for Sasquatch, but rather for some young outdoorsmen who called themselves the "St. Helens Apes" or some such. But KATU, either not knowing this, or not wanting to dirty the story for believers, did not report it.

We were told that the couple who blundered into Sasquatch had parked their car in the Ape Cave parking lot and gone for a hike up the mountain, planning to return via the upper entrance to the cave. It was late in the afternoon, and the sun was low, but still good.

They had turned on their flashlights, and were about ready to enter the darkness, when a departing beast nearly ran over them. They estimated this thing "to be eight or nine feet tall at least."

The man, one Ralph Mactan, an athletic trainer at California State University at Bakersfield, was carrying a videocamera that his wife had recently given him for his birthday.

He wheeled, dug the camera out of his daypack, and photographed the fleeing beast, getting a little over three seconds on tape before it disappeared uphill into the brush.

What we saw, when we at last got to see the tape, was a large, hairy beast hunkered over in an odd lope. It was big, although an officer of the Washington State Patrol estimated it closer to seven feet, not eight or nine. It had longish arms, but nothing to be confused with an orangutan or gibbon.

"Well, what do you think, Willie?"

Mmmmmmmm. Willie was noncommittal.

"You're supposed to be the hot-damn medicine man."

Willie gave me a look. Other Indians claimed he was Coyote in human form, never Willie. On the other hand, he never denied it either.

"A man like you. Name of Prettybird. A person would think . . ."

"Pay attention, Denson. They're running it again."

They played the tape once more, this time in slow motion. They stopped the frame as the beast appeared, momentarily, to look back at the camera. The boy-scout newsreader told us this was the best look at a Bigfoot since one was filmed at Bluff Creek, California, in 1967.

Willie closed his eyes in disgust. *"AAAGGGHHH!"*

"Say what?"

"I've seen that tape several times. The jackass thing was supposed to be female. It had a stiff neck and was hairier than hell with enormous breasts and a big butt. The boobs were hairy and the butt looked more like a load it couldn't shake from the bottom of its costume." Willie looked to the ceiling, pleading to whatever deities might reside there. "Californians! Spare us."

"Ah, well, then you are a member of the ranks of the sane."

"I didn't say that."

"Insane or sane, which is it?"

"I just said that I've seen that tape on television. Why do they have to keep dragging out a 1967 film of a bogus Sasquatch? What's the point?"

"The television people don't care whether anything's genuine or not. I'm surprised at you."

"You know, Denson, I've got friends who wonder just why it is, with all the white men I could have found as a partner, I wound up with you. Lately, I've been thinking. That's not a bad question. Why?" He tapped the remote on his VCR.

We watched the current tape again, three times. Each time it was the same, in my opinion: some moron in a Bigfoot costume having a good time.

"Which accounts for the other two sightings, I suppose." Willie opened the refrigerator and retrieved two bottles of Henry Weinhard's.

"More morons," I said. "It must be the season."

Willie gave me a bottle of Henry's.

"Gotta be something," he said.

Bigfoot didn't fit the system of ps and qs that I believed in. All ps are q. Some ps are q. Some ps are not q. No ps are q. If you knew how to mind your ps and qs, you should be able to figure anything out.

Well, the prime mover excepted. Original creation. That one had me stumped. Until the physicists traced out the chain of cause and effect, I had to be generous with such strange faiths as Willy's being a shaman, and there being a creature named Sasquatch roaming the high Cascades.

There was no hard evidence that I knew of to support the proposition that Sasquatch, p, existed, much less as a form of q, or hominid. But I knew there were plenty of people out there who believed most passionately that the beast did exist. The sightings and videotape would almost certainly bring the believers out in force.

I wondered what manner of large-footed beast this was that lurked in the shadows of alpenglow?

Chapter Two

Scarecrows of Fools

The next morning as Willie Prettybird and I and loaded up on cholesterol with bacon and eggs at the Huckleberry Inn in Vernonia, the circus was in full swing on the television set above the bar. Well, no, not full swing. This was just openers: the march of clowns.

The first star of the hour, because he was most qualified to give hope to Bigfoot believers, was Dr. Thomas Bondurant, director of primate study at the British Museum.

Bondurant, in his late fifties, was a small, bald man with bushy eyebrows and a preposterous, large gray moustache. Bondurant's left foot was in a cast, which he said was caused by falling off a stool trying to retrieve a book in his study. He said, in a proper southern English accent, that Sasquatch rather than Bigfoot should be used to describe the sightings reported in the Pacific Northwest. Large-footed, hairy creatures were said to live in many parts of the world, including the famous Yeti of the Himalayas.

"All right," Willie said. "My man. My main man. Listen to this guy, Denson."

I took a bite of killer egg yolk as Bondurant said the human capacity to believe in monsters is both inherited and learned. All people have the ability to believe in myths, but particular stories are learned.

"You don't say, Red Ryder!" I said. I took a bit of toast soaked in butter; it went straight to my veins, I knew, but boy, did it taste good. It could kill me, but I ate it anyway. Where was the learning there?

"Just pay attention," Willie said.

Bondurant said, "If we are fastidious about this matter, if we require cold, hard scientific evidence, then there is no Bigfoot . . ."

"Hah, see there," I said.

"Shush."

"We have no captives. No skulls. No films or photographs that can't be challenged."

"What have I been saying?"

"Dammit, Denson."

"We must remember our Dr. Johnson, 'All power of fancy over reason is a degree of insanity.' "

I said, "Yes, yes, give it to 'em, Tom."

Willie was silent.

Bondurant said, "And Thomas Henry Huxley tells us that 'logical consequences are the scarecrows of fools and the beacons of wise men.' "

"All right!" I went for some more egg yolk, to hell with it.

"Butt fucker," Willie said. Whether he meant me or Bondurant was uncertain.

I took it he meant Bondurant. "He's from the British Museum, what do you expect? They're taught to accept as evidence only that which you can see, feel, smell, or touch. Go talk to the animal people, Crow or somebody."

Willie caught the waitress's eye and motioned for more coffee.

Bondurant said, "Individual sightings may be rationally explained as the product of a drunk, say, or a joker, or the easily spooked. Was the witness lying? Was he after publicity? Was he hallucinating? If we are to be responsible, we have to be rigorous and consistent. We have to ask all these questions and require clear, unambiguous answers."

Willie said, "I thought this guy had an open mind."

"But . . ." This was a "but" pregnant with meaning. Bondurant waggled his finger at the interviewer. He was obviously ready to deliver a caveat that would likely put him in Willie's camp, the treacherous little bastard. I wanted to shout: hey, dork, pay attention to Dr. Johnson and Huxley!

"However, *consensus* opinions are another matter, and by consensus, I should stress that I most assuredly do not mean *group* opinion . . ."

"What? Hey there, professor, you want to tell us just what a consensus opinion is?"

Willie brightened, grinning like a rat in a garbage can. "He's your man, Denson. Mr. Science."

". . . You get group opinions in a pub or by a campfire. People reinforce one another by repeating things they've heard or seen. To a scientist, group opinions are of no value whatever. A thoughtful investigator can safely ignore them."

"I hope to hell so," I said.

"A *consensus* opinion is where the same details pop up repeatedly, again and again over time and from wholly independent observers. The consensus opinion of those who claim they have never read anything about Sasquatch, especially with regard to those who have seen footprints, is impressive, I have to say. Extraordinary, in fact."

"What?"

"Give it to us. Give it to us."

"Mind your *p*s and *q*s," I shouted at the set. "You can't trust those cheeky Brits."

"Quiet!" Willie was grinning so big his face had to be aching.

"It stretches the imagination to believe that every single Sasquatch footprint among the tens of thousands reported in the Pacific Northwest is a hoax. Some may be real. All may be fakes. But if just a single footprint is established as genuine, then one must jettison the explanation of the beast as a myth."

"What's this guy been smoking," I said. "And from the British Museum as well. Look at that stupid moustache of his. What do you expect?"

"If just one footprint is genuine, then we have to accept the fact that *Homo sapiens sapiens* are not the sole survivors of the hominid line."

"Sure, sure," I said.

"You heard the man."

I said, "We may as well hire witch doctors and call them scientists."

"Hey! White man!" Willie pretended to be offended. Medicine man was an acceptable term. Or shaman. But not witch doctor.

"Okay, I amend that. We might as well hire medicine men and call them scientists."

"We might do worse."

"Aw, Willie."

"Bondurant has an open mind."

"I guess so. It's so open it's got holes in it. Willie, those mountains are swarming with hunters and hikers and fishermen. If there's a population of Sasquatches roaming around up there, how come we haven't found them? Nobody ever sees a cougar either, but we know they're there."

The interview with Bondurant was followed by a few words from a man introduced as one of the writing Pollard brothers, Alford and Elford. The interviewer told us the energetic Pollard brothers had assembled "the largest collection of Sasquatchiana in the world."

Before I could ask what on earth "Sasquatchiana" was, the elder Pollard, Elford, in his late thirties, red of hair, large of beak, showed us.

Elford treated us to a tour of the interior of the Pollards' thirty-foot-long recreational vehicle, which served as a traveling Sasquatch museum. Pollard held dried turds in his cupped hands as though they were priceless gems. Plain old manure was too plebian for Pollard, who aspired to the high ground of science. In an accent as flat as Kansas, he told us this was Sasquatch feces.

"Fecal evidence," he said with such solemnity that I almost burst out laughing.

"Your camp, Willie," I said.

Pollard showed us scraps of fur he said were torn from the bodies of Bigfoots fleeing through dense underbrush, and, finally, plaster casts of the large footprints that had impressed Bondurant.

Elford Pollard was followed by a tall, good-looking Roger Whitcomb; he was almost, but not quite, a double for the British movie actor Roger Moore. Whitcomb, identified as the producer of television documentaries on Sasquatch, had led an Explorer's Club expedition into the mountains of British Columbia looking for the beast. There was no question in his mind: the time had at last arrived to prove conclusively the existence of Sasquatch.

Whitcomb said, "Three sightings of Sasquatch in a four-day period, plus a videotape of him at Ape Cave—what more can you ask?"

Lots, I thought to myself.

Finally, the Canadian Sasquatch hunter Emile Thibodeaux, born in Quebec, but reared in Vancouver, British Columbia, was asked his opinion. Thibodeaux, a tall, lean man with pale blue eyes— given to a pipe that he cleaned and refilled as he talked—was less enthusiastic than Pollard and Whitcomb.

He puffed his pipe thoughtfully. "I've been on the trail of Sasquatch for thirty-five years now. I started out as a believer, and over the years I've interviewed hundreds of people who claimed to have seen Sasquatch. They were dead certain they had seen him. I've examined innumerable casts of his alleged footprints. I've traveled to Europe and Russia enlisting the help of scholars there. But to be honest, and it pains me to admit it, in the end, I just don't know what to believe. I really don't."

Thibodeaux paused to scrape out the inside of the bowl of his pipe, which he tapped on the edge of his foot. He set about the task of refilling the bowl.

The interviewer asked him if he would be part of any search for Sasquatch on Mount St. Helens.

Thibodeaux grinned. He relit his pipe. "I've devoted the better part of my youth and middle years to this mystery. I'm not going to quit now. What if he's there?"

Willie Prettybird and I hitched Willie's aluminum fishing boat to his pickup and threw his crab pots and our fishing gear into the back. I hustled down to the local Thriftway and bought us a couple of loaves of French bread and half a case of Blitz to go with Willie's venison jerky.

Willie tuned his radio to some country and western music, and we lit out for the coast and some fun. On the way we razzed one another about Sasquatch. Mr. Logic and his pal Coyote or whatever Willie was supposed to be.

Willie had gotten me hooked on the gathering and preserving of wild food. In the springtime, we scouted farm ponds together for succulent cattail shoots, and even better, the cattails themselves when they were yet dark green and encased in sheaths. These, when boiled and slathered with corn oil margarine and given a hit of salt and pepper, were superior to corn on the cob, tasting roughly like artichoke hearts. This root or that seed; when we didn't have a case to work on, Willie had me out there scrounging.

There were panfish to be filleted and pickled in the late spring, sturgeon to be hauled in and smoked in the summer, and in the fall, salmon, deer, and elk. Willie had two homemade food driers and two pressure cookers and he kept them busy.

Come the third week of October, the mushrooms arrived, and Willie knew them all, from French ceps to chanterelles, shaggy manes, and meadow mushrooms. These he chopped and dried and stored in jars along with dried onions for his own soup mix.

This food was, well, soulful; there is no other word to describe it.

We spent three days on the Oregon coast, crabbing, fishing, and gathering elderberries for our supply of wine. The man who threw away his money on improbably expensive French wine did not exist who could match Willie Prettybird's fermented elderberry juice. It couldn't be done.

By the time we returned to Portland to render and strain and jug the juice, the Bigfoot story was off to a mixed start.

The good news for Sasquatch followers was that someone named David Addison, of Vancouver, Washington—across the river from Portland and not to be confused with Vancouver, British Columbia—a real estate developer, had offered a $100,000 reward to whoever could find Sasquatch on Mount St. Helens.

The bad news was that Elford Pollard, thirty-seven, whom Willie and I had seen on television showing us his "fecal evidence," had been found murdered, shot to death with a .22 caliber pistol on the shoulder of a lonely stretch of highway. His brother Alford, thirty-five, swore he was going to find Sasquatch in the name of his brother.

Chapter Three

Blessings of Boogie Dewlapp

It was our tradition, much anticipated. No session of winemaking was complete until Willie Prettybird and I had opened and sampled a jug of vintage stuff; vintage, by our definition, was anything more than six months old or that contained a hint of alcohol, whichever came first.

We had to work now and then to support ourselves, but in the main, we considered ourselves fancy dudes, gentlemen of leisure. Such high civility, it was, to kick back, our juice jugged and already settling out, and consider the effects of the remarkable yeast, surely one of the bounties of evolution, and the consequence of soil and sun and sugar on nature's own.

The five-liter jugs were so grand: four purple, fat-bodied soldiers, all lined up. We had no sooner gotten the jugs filled with elderberry juice, the plastic fermentation locks screwed firmly in place, than Willie got a telephone call.

While Willie talked, I cleaned the exteriors of the jugs with a sponge, spiffing them up for final inspection. Willie and I had gone into the woods to pick the berries, and we had rendered the juice. When the wine was ready, it would be individual and unique, soulful because it was ours.

I heard Willie tell his caller: "Oh, sure, he's here. Wiping wine jugs with a sponge. Uh-huh. Well, he can handle a sponge, so he's all enthusiastic."

"Who's that?" I mouthed.

"Boogie," he mouthed back.

I looked surprised. Boogie Dewlapp was the older, Seattle brother of Dewlapp & Dewlapp—a sleaze with a heart of gold in the firm's television ads, targeted for clients who were rural or poor or both.

If the case was in Washington, northern Idaho, or western Montana, Boogie, the elder of the Dewlapps, called me at my apartment in Seattle. If the work was in Oregon, southern Idaho or northern California, Willie got the word from Olden down in Portland.

We were freelancers, not wage slaves. We had our ad in the Yellow Pages like the big guys, with Denson and Prettybird in boldface, both in Seattle and Portland. But lately, it was true, the Dewlapps had become our principle tit. The reason was simple; we were willing to go where fancier—and no doubt costlier—investigators turned up their noses: to the sticks.

I mouthed: "Boogie?" Boogie always went through me. Portland was Olden country.

Willie shushed me with his finger. "Just a second, Boog. Let me get a paper and pen. Got Denson standing here with his mouth open and flies buzzing around. Jesus!"

I watched over Willie's shoulder as he wrote. *Russ. Amb.* "How do you spell that? Slowly, Boog." He wrote *S-o-n-j-a P-o-p-o-l-e-y-e-v* on his pad. He wrote *St. Petersburg Inst. of Pri. Stud.* "St. Petersburg Institute of Primate Study, got it."

Willie listened some more, then wrote: *Boris N. Porchnev.* He spelled for Boogie's confirmation. He also had to confirm the spelling of *troglodytidae.*

Willie ripped off the top page of the pad and gave it to me. "And then what happened?" Willie waited, listening. "Called you from St. Petersburg? She did? Really? And what did you tell her?"

Willie listened, then burst out laughing. "You did? You did? Good for you. Oh, sure. Denson can handle that. No problem. He can brush his teeth and shift the gears of his Volkswagen. But you'll have to sweet-talk Olden out of his camera.

"It's like I tell Denson, everybody is always saying how the Dewlapps are scumbag crooks and everything, but it's just not true, you know."

Willie laughed at the Boog's reply. "You did? And what did she say? All right! When you talk to her, tell her not to worry about the provisions. Denson and I will take care of that too. And my friends Bobby and Whitefeather Minthorn and their packmules and dog. Sure. That's M-i-n-t-h-o-r-n, one word, Bobby and Whitefeather, one word. Say again the names of the so-called professionals."

He noted *A. Pollard, Whitcomb, Thibodeaux.* "Oh, yeah. Denson and I saw the one who was murdered. On the tube. He showed us their RV." Willie wrote: *Bondurant.*

I looked puzzled.

To me, Willie mouthed, "The guy with the broken foot." To Boogie, he said, "All right, we'll keep in touch. You gave her our number; she can call anytime. Sure, here he is." He handed me the receiver.

Boogie was laughing. "Denson?"

"What's going on, Boog?"

"Now I don't want you saying I never did anything for you, Denson. I want you to be careful out there. Pay attention to your pal Geronimo. I don't want to be reading about you in the obits." Laughing, he hung up.

Willie, grinning, slapped his thigh.

I grabbed his pad, reading the notes. "St. Petersburg Institute of Primate Study. What the hell's this all about?"

"Well, see, the Boog was at this here hot damn cocktail party in Seattle. He says there he was with a shine on his shoes, eavesdropping on a conversation between the Soviet consul and His Honor the mayor. The Russian was telling the mayor about how this Dr. Sonja Popoleyev of the, what's that place . . . ?

"The St. Petersburg Institute of Primate Study," I said.

"Right. A primatologist. She's been reading about how they're organizing a search for Sasquatch on Mount St. Helens. There was a

famous Russian scholar who had this theory about something called
a—"

"*Troglodytidae*," I read from the paper. "Cave dwellers. I think
that would be troglodyte in the singular."

"That's it. She wanted to participate, so she sent an inquiry
through the Russian foreign ministry. The Russians were told, politely, that the search was being restricted to professionals."

"Pollard, Whitcomb, and Thibodeaux. That'd be the younger of
the Pollards."

"Alford. The Russian consul in Seattle was irked, and sent a
pissed-off note to the U.S. State Department saying how come? Professionals? What were they talking about? This woman was on a joint
project with professors from—"

I checked his notes. "From MIT, Stanford, and Carnegie Mellon
University."

"Wherever that is. She apparently spends more time in the U.S.
than in Russia, and so speaks nearly flawless English."

"Carnegie Mellon University is in Pittsburgh."

"So how come she couldn't participate, the State Department
asked? The State Department said if there really is a Sasquatch, and
it is an unknown primate, then she's right, it falls under the province
of science; it belongs to the world community."

"Good point."

"The south slope of Mount St. Helens is part of the National
Volcanic Monument, which is administered by the Interior Department, so the State Department bitched to the Secretary of the Interior."

"And the Interior Department said no Russian primatologist, no
Sasquatch search."

"The other climbers had to accept her. The only problem was
that the others were mounting expeditions with veteran alpinists and
expensive communications equipment, the works. Popoleyev didn't
have the rubles for that kind of thing."

"Moolah, moolah, moolah. That's what it always comes down to,
Prettybird."

"But the academics she works with in the United States dug into
their grant money for the airfare. She had this notion that if she could
just come up with some Indians who knew the territory, she could

field a small party. Her American professor friends called all over the country, but no luck."

"Indians?"

"At this point, Boogie stepped forward and allowed as how he knew an Indian detective who worked for his brother Olden down in Portland, the detective allegedly being a shaman, Coyote in human form. What better candidate for the job?"

"The Boog is always on his toes. You ever notice that? Always thinking."

"The Russian consul called Dr. Popoleyev, and Popoleyev called Boogie."

"Called Boogie in Seattle? She did?"

"Yes. Boogie said she was thrilled. He must have been at the top of his form. He even talked her into dealing you in as a photographer if you can run a videocamera. He said you were a jerk of all trades, but the master of none as far as anyone can tell. But you can run a videocamera."

"And have run a videocamera many times on behalf of Boogie's clients."

"He even volunteered Olden's new Sony for the job."

"I see. Are we to be paid for this adventure, or is it a freebie?"

Willie grinned. "I'm pleased to tell you, yes, we are to be paid. The Boog was in a generous mood. He said Popoleyev's American colleagues now believe they can come up with enough money from their universities, and he and Olden will make up the difference, provided it isn't outrageous."

"And provided we give them a nick of any rewards forthcoming."

"That goes without saying." Willie punched up a number on his telephone.

"What now?"

"I have to see if the Minthorns can come. Gotta have Bobby's good eyes for something like this. Plus there's Harold and Opal. And then Earl."

Harold and Opal were the Minthorns' packmules, veterans at lugging the carcasses of Roosevelt elk out of remote canyons.

Earl was difficult to classify. He was a dog, but of which breed was a matter of conjecture. He was a cur of a yellowish-brown color

Bobby called "high crap." He could flush pheasants and retrieve a splashed duck. When Bobby followed sign, it was with Earl running before him, nose bumping the ground. Although I had never seen him demonstrate his ability to protect Whitefeather, I had seen the throat of the training dummy in the Minthorns' backyard.

Willie said, "Come on, Denson. It'll be fun. Whitefeather Minthorn'll be doing the cooking, remember. You groove on her food, I know you do."

"Sure, sure. Fun." I loved it when Bobby and Whitefeather had us over for Sunday dinner and pinochle. But I didn't think Whitefeather was such a good cook that I wanted to spend my nights at the edge of timberline in order to eat her meals.

It was times like this that I began to believe the hoo-hoo about Willie's being more animal than human. He didn't care if it was raining, snowing, or hotter than the sheriff's pistol. He just plain liked outdoors better than indoors. He claimed he was just as comfortable sleeping on the ground as on a bed. I'd never seen anything that would dispute this claim.

Later, as I lay on Willie Prettybird's comfy couch to rack out for the night, I wondered what kind of scientist Dr. Sonja Popoleyev would turn out to be.

The chap from the British Museum had given the gullible a high-minded phrase to cling to, "consensus opinion," thus conferring the mantle of "science" on the search for Sasquatch.

If Bondurant'd had a South Dakota accent, he could be kissed off as a pretentious nerd.

As a longtime, avid reader of science articles in other people's magazines—famous for heading straight for my friends' coffee tables, first chance—I had long since learned that a piece in the *National Gleaner* was not the same as one in the *New England Journal of Medicine.* It was, in fact, possible to rank science in descending order of reliability:

As I saw it, plain old, *yawn*, science was based on the search for truth.

Grant-application science—in which an investigator pursued the suggestive, but elusive, maybes, might bes, and could bes—was aimed at prying research grants from my wallet, that is, from the taxpayer's wallet.

Media science, the zone of no-brainers, was fueled by hysteria and a craving for attention.

The proles knew the British Museum was big potatoes in the intellectual world. It was right up there with the Museum of Natural History, the Smithsonian, and other big-spuds museums, whose various experts and scholars, everybody knew—or wanted to believe— were interested in just plain science.

Bondurant had said Sasquatch "might be" there. When a Big Potatoes expert made an assertion that appeared to agree with the prejudices of the popular imagination—especially when supersitition was at stake—desire nearly always prevailed over common sense.

In this case "might be there," or "could be there" meant "is there." "Can't rule it out" translated as "is true."

Bondurant had said "if" just one footprint turned out to be genuine, then the geneaology of the human family would have to be altered. If . . .

If, if, if . . .

If only I had a pig that could sing and a horse that could fly . . .

Chapter Four

Her Fame
Precedes Her

Willie Prettybird and I and Bobby and Whitefeather Minthorn weren't the only ones awaiting Sonja Popoleyev's arrival at the Portland Airport. The participation in a Sasquatch search by a female Russian primatologist wasn't bad theater.

As Popoleyev's band of redskins, plus one, we were ushered up front to greet her.

Raisa Gorbachev should have forever retired the stereotype of Russian women looking like bags of potatoes. But I was John Denson, not Comrade Gorby. I braced myself for a clone of Irina or Tamara Press, the Soviet shot-putters who had retired after chromosome checks became mandatory. Wrong.

It took a few seconds for me to comprehend the possibility that the slender, mid-thirties blonde with the elegant stride and lapel pin of the Russian flag on her tailored jacket was Sonja Popoleyev. Then she smiled, partly amused, partly curious, and maybe a little embarrassed.

She had intelligent green eyes. Her rich blond hair, which she wore in a ponytail, fell to the small of her back. She wore form-hugging black slacks, and a simple white blouse, the top two buttons of which, teasingly, were undone. Although she was obviously wearing a bra, it didn't take X-ray vision to know that her breasts rode high on her ribs entirely as a gift of nature. As a girl, she possibly had been downright skinny. Not now. She had one of those rare, naturally long, slender bodies, that would—in the right circumstances—bend like a willow.

This was a woman who could turn a man's mouth dry. I inadvertently groaned and licked my lips. Couldn't help it.

She spotted Willie, who was holding one of his smoked salmon as a gift, and strode directly to us, hand outstretched. We introduced ourselves. "Pleased to meet you, Mr. Prettybird. And you, Mr. Denson. And you must be Bobby and Whitefeather Minthorn." She gave us all firm handshakes.

Willie, who had had the presence of mind to arrange delivery of Popoleyev's luggage to her hotel, took her by the elbow and led her through the phalanx of reporters and photographers.

"Later, later. She'll give interviews later," he said. Willie, in a cosmopolitan, man-of-action mode, looked as though he'd been escorting VIPs for years, and would brook no nonsense from pointy-headed reporters.

Popoleyev said, "I'm extremely pleased to be here, but I think Mr. Prettybird is right. The time for interviews is later. I'm flattered by your interest, but I'm very tired."

"Well done," Willie muttered.

"Good woman," I said.

"A team already, eh, Mr. Denson." She smiled. What a smile! And she had perfect white teeth. She was downright sensational.

But then, as we headed down the carpeted airport hallway, I dropped back momentarily, pretending to tie my shoe, but really to scope her high, tight, exquisitely formed rump. I thought it was neatly done. Peripheral vision.

Who could have known?

Sonja Popoleyev suddenly turned, amused, and looked back at me.

I felt like a dog caught eating garbage.

"Well, what did you think, Mr. Denson?"

I popped to my feet, momentarily nonplussed. Caught. What did I think? "About what?" I said. Later, I knew, I'd think of something clever I *should* have said.

"In good form, is it?" She twisted, checking out her rump.

I blushed. A grown man. Of all the silly-assed reactions. *About what?* God, how embarrassing.

Willie, Bobby, and Whitefeather whooped with laughter.

Willie said, "Way to go, Chief Dumbshit." He said this quickly, *Dumsht.*

"Is that your nickname, Mr. Denson?"

"It's his Indian name," Willie said quickly.

"Like *Dancing with Wolves*," Bobby added.

"A term of affection then," she said. "Chief Dumsht. Do I have that right?"

"Right on the money," Willie said.

Popoleyev said, "I'm sorry if I embarrassed you, Mr. Denson. I love observing fauna in the field."

"Ah, I see. Then you'll want accurate data so as not to skew your results."

"Oh, absolutely."

"Then you should note in your journal that what Willie really called me was Chief Dumbshit, as in retarded excrement."

Willie said, "Denson says I stole the expression from the Irish, but I say it's Redskin through and through."

Popoleyev laughed. "A tease then, eh, Mr. Prettybird?"

"It equals out," I said. "I call him Tonto."

"Which means?"

"'Fool,' in Spanish," Willie said.

"It looks like we're going to have a good time at least. By the way, Mr. Denson, what you did was species typical, normal for your gender. The explanation is very likely ultimate, rather than proximate. But perhaps in this case a little bit of both."

Ultimate? Proximate? "Can you tell us the difference between the two?"

We stepped off the escalator and headed down a cement floor with parked cars on both sides.

Popoleyev said, "An ultimate analysis attempts to answer the animal 'why' of our behavior. Ultimate behavior, encoded in DNA and passed from generation to generation, is everywhere the same. It is, to oversimplify, instinctive behavior. Proximate behavior, crudely put, is learned and varies from culture to culture."

"Say it again," I said. I stopped at my bus and started digging for my keys.

"Ultimate behavior, the 'why' of what we do, may be traced to the genetic urges of our brain stems. An animal behaves as it does because its ancestors promoted their success by similar behavior. You should keep in mind that we are only twenty percent more evolved than fish. In a proximate sense, an animal behaves as it does because it inherited a particular complement of genes and because it has encountered particular circumstances in the past."

I started unlocking the door. "Mmmm. Particular circumstances. I bet they're called 'stimuli' in your research lingo."

"But ultimate and proximate behavior are so intertwined in our species that it's difficult to separate them. That's the challenge to scholars."

"Long-legged blonde plus tight slacks and a splendid rump equals extraordinary stimuli."

"Thank you, Mr. Denson. But, you know, a Kalahari bushman wouldn't give me a second glance. He likes his behinds big and fat. A proximate taste, to be sure."

Everybody was aboard. I cranked up the bus and headed out of the lot.

Popoleyev said, "Both males and females of a species select their mates according to inherited evaluative mechanisms that promote the fitness of their offspring, fitness being a neutral, value-free term."

"Meaning what, exactly?"

"Meaning that if an animal survives, it's fit. If it becomes extinct, it is unfit. That's all the term means, nothing more. The only way to ascertain the ultimate causes of an animal's behavior is to study it in the natural environment in which it evolved."

"I take it in the case of humans, this is impossible to find."

"We humans are cooperative predators, which is how we feed ourselves, and a tournament species, which is how we select our mates. We spent all but a diminutive fraction of our evolutionary history as hunters and gatherers, living in small, mostly nomadic bands. In this manner we spread out from our place of origin, which is Africa probably, but maybe Asia. Everything since agriculture, permanent settlements, and organized religion is, in an evolutionary sense, an unnatural environment."

I headed up the on ramp to I-205, heading south. "Which is why you want to study Sasquatch?"

"If they're primates, that would be fun, wouldn't it? If they're up there, they should be left alone so we can study them without environmental contamination. We have cameras and parabolic microphones to gather all the data we need. We can share everything with the public."

I slowed for the exit to I-84 west to Portland.

Looking around, she said, "What a beautiful city! What are those glass spires on the right over there?"

"The convention center. That's the Willamette River up ahead. It empties into the Columbia, which you passed over before you landed."

"A city with a river and bridges. St. Petersburg, too, is a city of bridges. Why, this is a lovely place!"

"The mountain to our right there is St. Helens, where we'll be searching for Bigfoot. That's Mount Hood behind us. From some parts of Portland, it is possible to look north on a clear day and see seven such snow-capped mountains."

"They very thoughtfully gave me a window seat as we were coming down from Seattle, and I could see where the eruption blew out the north side. It must have been something."

Willie said, "Denson and I were at a dart tournament in a tavern that day. We watched the whole show from the front steps. We've got a room reserved for you in the Mallory Hotel. It is less showy than the Benson downtown, but closer to an apartment a lawyer keeps for Willie in Northwest Portland."

"I'm sure whatever you picked out will be fine by me. Did you win the dart tournament?"

Willie said, "Denson clutched at crunch time. His hands were shaking so bad everybody had to stand back when it was his turn. He was sweating like a turkey in November."

I said, "The truth was Willie couldn't hit a double-sixteen, the easiest out on the board because you practice it the most and shoot it the most."

Willie made a defeated sound with his tongue and lips.

I turned onto the Everett Street exit and slowed, alert to the possibility of a bum returning to his shelter under the freeway overpass. No bums. Good. It was lousy for visitors when untidy drunks and beggars spoiled the picturesque vista of snow-capped mountains.

Willie said, "After we get you settled in at the Mallory, we'd like to treat you to a supper if you're up to it. The Minthorns brought along a couple of pheasants to roast."

"I'm too wound up to go to sleep. I'd be delighted to have supper with you; besides, we should talk about the expedition. We're supposed to begin the search the day after tomorrow."

At the Mallory, we waited while Dr. Popoleyev checked in, then stopped at the Thriftway on Twenty-first for Willie to pick up a few things. It was there, as we waited in line at the checkout stand, that she suddenly looked horrified.

I didn't know what what was wrong for a moment, then I understood. There on the sleaze rack, the *National Gleaner* had a full-page headline that said: RUSSIAN SCIENTIST SEEKS SEX WITH BIG-FOOT! The kicker at the top said: SHE SAYS SIZE OF FEET DETERMINES SIZE OF ORGAN.

Astonished, she opened the paper. The lead paragraph of the article, printed in boldface, said:

"The *National Gleaner* has come by confidential information from reliable sources that the Russian 'sex expert' participating in the search for Bigfoot on Mount St. Helens goes to sleep every night dreaming of having sex with the elusive beast who inhabits the mountains of the Pacific Northwest."

The second paragraph, while not in boldface, was just as playful.

"In her successful bid to join the Bigfoot search on Mount St. Helens, an inebriated Dr. Sonja Popoleyev confided to American State Department officials at a diplomatic gathering that numerous academic studies have shown a 'consistent positive correlation between size of penis and size of foot.' If those footprints are anything to go by, we're talking a truly king-sized c**k."

"*Gleaner* sources in St. Petersburg say Popoleyev has had numerous sessions of psychological counseling of an undisclosed nature. She claims her international search for giant penises is a form of 'primate research.' "

She closed the paper. She held the front page at arm's length, staring open-mouthed at the headline. "What? What? What on earth is this?"

"Ahh," I said. "That, Dr. Popoleyev, is America." Sex expert? I bought a copy of the *Gleaner*, a souvenir of Sonja Popoleyev's arrival. When I looked at the top of the story again, I found a whoopsie! "This must have been one of his last stories."

"One of whose last stories?" Willie asked.

I showed Willie Prettybird the paper, which was published weekly. Elford Pollard had written the story on Sonja Popoleyev. "The Sasquatch guy who was murdered."

Chapter Five

Lineage of
Cave Dwellers

Willie Prettybird and Whitefeather Minthorn had, in Whitefeather's words, "put on the dog" for Sonja Popoleyev, raiding their larder for the best in the way of good eating.

While Dr. Popoleyev called Sasquatch Central or whatever they called search headquarters, Whitefeather, with Willie's help, laid a spread of goodies to sample before the main feed. They produced smoked salmon with Whitefeather's special dill dip; pickled morels; smoked lamprey, a Pacific eel; smoked sturgeon; caviar; blackberry jam; bread made from screwbean flour and roasted tarweed seeds; and Whitefeather's special venison sausages, the interiors of which were crunchy with chopped Oregon white truffles.

When you took a bite of Whitefeather's special sausages, you learned what good eating was all about.

After Popoleyev finished talking to the search organizers, she joined us at the smorgasbord, accepting without hesitation Willie's offering of our two-year-old Extra Special Reserve elderberry wine.

Willie said, "Everything's go, I take it."

Popoleyev said, "I talked to Ms. Donna McGwyre, who is the manager of Cascade Run where this will all be based. I take it we'll have no problem finding Cascade Run."

Cascade Run was locally famous as the ambitious resort community that never got off the ground. Willie smiled. "I think we can find it."

"She has made tentative appointments for me to talk to Tom Bondurant at nine o'clock in the morning, and to Mr. Pollard and Emile Thibodeaux in the afternoon, and I said okay. We have our first joint meeting at ten o'clock."

Bobby said, "We'll be pulling a horse trailer, so we better be moving with the birds."

"Seven at the latest," Willie said.

Popoleyev said, "Supper and a little talk will be just right before bed. I'm too keyed up to go to sleep now."

Willie said, "Okay, a little food and it's off to bed."

"Tomorrow night, I'll sleep."

Bobby said, "More wine then." He refilled our glasses.

Whitefeather said, "Maybe you can tell us something of what scientists think about Sasquatch. We're all dying to know what it is we're after, other than a large, hairy beast with big feet."

Popoleyev hesitated. "Are you sure? This kind of evolutionary lingo puts most people to sleep."

"Let's have it," Willie said.

Popoleyev took another sip of elderberry wine, thinking about her answer. "Okay, you asked for it. First, you should picture an ancestral chart of primates that looks like a tree. This tree, with its roots most likely in Africa, goes back some five million years. At its base, the trunk, are the common ancestors of all primates. This trunk eventually split into two main branches. Humans are found on one branch. Apes, gorillas, and chimpanzees are on the other."

Whitefeather said, "Bobby having strayed from the ape and gorilla branch."

Bobby said, "Hey!"

Popoleyev said, "Your husband appears to be firmly on the hominid branch, Whitefeather. Mmmmmm. This really is good wine." Popoleyev held it up to the light. "It's beautiful too."

Willie said, "Prettybird and Denson's two-year-old Extra Special Reserve elderberry wine."

"Denson and Prettybird's," I added quickly.

Willie looked disgusted. "Denson's good at cleaning the jugs, I'll give him that." He topped off her glass. "So what happened to the branches of the primate tree?"

"You're going to get me loaded, Willie."

"Do you good."

She laughed. She had dimples. Ooof! "On these primate branches, families, are limbs, species. Some of the species lived. Others died out. We ordinarily choose our candidates as progenitors of Sasquatch from the list of primates that went out of business."

"Now we're getting down to it," Bobby said. "Progenitors. This is where all the begatting stuff comes in."

Whitefeather gave her husband a look of mock reproval.

Popoleyev laughed. "One popular candidate is the unsuccessful ape *Gigantopithecus,* the remains of which have been discovered in India and China. He's a favorite of the monster enthusiasts—he's often suggested as Yeti—but there's no evidence that he was bipedal. Also, he's a vegetarian, probably not the diet for the altitudes associated with Sasquatch."

"Scratch *Gigantowhatever* from the short list," I said.

Willie said, "Throw the sucker out."

Whitefeather refilled our glasses.

Popoleyev said, "A second nominee is *Paranthropus robustus* or *Australopithecus robustus,* depending on whether one believes he is a failed ape or a failed human. The former, most likely. He was thick and heavy and not much of a biped. He was also a vegetarian like *Gigantopithecus,* and there is no reason to suggest that he was around later than a half million years ago." Popoleyev looked about, soliciting opinions.

Whitefeather said, "Too hard to pronounce his name."

"I agree," Willie said.

"A third candidate, *Homo erectus,* also called the Java man or Peking man, lived in caves, as evidenced by the sites excavated at Choukoutien, near Peking. When he was there, the vegetation in China was similar to the Pacific Northwest today—conifers, plus deciduous shrubs and trees. He hunted large animals, used fire, and made tools. Sasquatch doesn't appear to have any culture, which *Homo erectus* almost certainly would."

Willie said, "So a person would think."

"The last candidate, *Homo sapiens neanderthalensis,* an Ice Age hominid, used fire and made tools. The Neanderthals abruptly disappeared when the polar ice sheets receded. They were either eliminated by the Cro-Magnons or absorbed by them through interbreeding, in which case we all have some Neanderthal blood in us."

Whitefeather said, "Which leaves Other. Or None of the Above."

"Yes and no. Boris N. Porchnev believed that the Neanderthalers, as well as the Java and Peking man, belonged to a pre-*sapiens* branch on the primate tree. This was *Troglodytidae,* a separate family, neither ape nor *Hominidae,* a relic humanoid line that began with *Australopithecus africanus. Pithecanthropus* would be in this family, and also fossil Neanderthals. Sasquatch may be a modern survivor, *Troglodytes recens*—literally, recent cave dwellers."

Willie looked impressed. "How did he wind up in Washington State without being recruited by the Huskies?"

Popoleyev grinned her wonderful grin. "Porchnev's followers believe that *Troglodytes recens* may be a nocturnal solitary that migrated from Asia to the Americas via the one-time land bridge over the Bering Straits. Flesh-and-blood *Troglodytes recens* would need a minimum population in order to avoid extinction—say at least a thousand of them. The question is: could that many creatures avoid detection and documentation with all the hunters and outdoorsmen you have in these mountains? That stretches credibility, it truly does."

Willie said, "After we eat we can watch the tape of the Sasquatch seen at Ape Cave."

I said, "Have you seen that tape, Dr. Popoleyev?"

"Oh, yes, many times. It was on CNN, and I taped it with my VCR."

Willie and Whitefeather offered a salad of fresh watercress and chilled, spiced crawdads. Both watercress and crawdads came from the creek by Willie's cabin.

Popoleyev, munching on watercress and crawdads, said, "Have

you ever noticed that in all the reports of Sasquatch stories, he rarely causes any harm? In fact, Sasquatch runs from confrontation. There are stories in the literature of him returning lost babies and performing other exemplary deeds."

Popoleyev paused while Whitefeather brought on a tureen of soup, an elk consommé in which floated elegant, pale-green buds.

Popoleyev, sampling a bud, said, "These are good. What are they, Whitefeather?"

"Milkweed buds. We collect them every spring and freeze them."

Willie said, "You're suspicious of Sasquatch the boy scout, I take it."

"A number of years ago, a tiny tribe of nonaggressive, cave-dwelling people was allegedly found in the rain forests of Southern Mindanao in the Philippines. Their near-saintly character was unlike any that had ever been reported in the literature and contradicted everything we had learned about human nature. There was nothing like it in the anthropological literature.

"The only evidence of 'habitation' in the Tasadays' cave were some fragments of food, some splinters of bamboo, some betel-nut spit, and urine from a child—no evidence at all that anyone had actually lived there for any period of time. Although three international conferences have declared the 'discovery' a fraud, the Tasaday are routinely listed in Philippine guidebooks as though they actually existed." Popoleyev shook her head in resignation. "We see what we want to see. Desire has become reality. That could be the case with Sasquatch."

After the main course of roast pheasant, with seasoned wapatoo as the vegetable, we kicked back with huckleberry shortcake and Willie's Extra Reserve blackberry brandy, and reviewed the Ape Cave tape of Sasquatch on Willie's VCR.

"What's your opinion of the tape, Dr. Popoleyev?" Willie said.

"I really don't know. There's so little of it. If there is a troglodyte and he's found, what do you think will happen?"

Willie said, "Depends on who finds him."

"Mr. Denson?"

"There'll be no shortage of people who'll try to make money off him. Remember the paper at the grocery store."

Her face tightened. "Capture him, you mean. A *Troglodytes recens!*"

"That'd be my bet."

"Then we must find him first. We must be the first. We must."

"How about some more brandy?" Without waiting for an answer, Whitefeather gave Popoleyev a refill.

Popoleyev didn't hesitate at taking another glass. "There's something I'm curious about, Mr. Denson. Are you and Willie like the private detectives in the novels and movies? I mean, do you carry pistols and everything?"

Willie laughed. "Pistols? If Denson carried a slingshot, it'd probably backfire on him and put his eye out."

I said, "Wait a minute here!"

"It's true and you know it."

Popoleyev said, "And you, Willie?"

Willie looked shocked. "Me? Carry a stupid gun?"

Popoleyev laughed. "The answer is no, I take it." She raised her eyebrows. "Beautiful women at every turn?"

Both Willie and I laughed at that.

Catching her green eyes, I said, "What about you? We know you're a primatologist. We know your institution has to do with primates. In his silly article Elford Pollard called you a 'sex expert.' Was that just nonsense or what?"

Chapter Six

Popoleyev's Monsters

Sonja Popoleyev, looking amused, twirled the brandy in her glass. "It is nonsense, and it isn't. But I'm not a sex expert like your Virginia Masters or Dr. Ruth as the use of the term would suggest. Let me try to explain, and then I have to go to bed.

"Insects have their own strategy for survival. Birds too. Primates. All animals. Four years ago, I was invited to join some American academics in the designing of a computer program that, given the barest of clues, would predict the reproductive strategies of primates at any point along their evolutionary path."

"The primate lineage chart has apes and men as the two main branches, or families. Along those family branches are many dead limbs, or species. Some made it. Some didn't. If we analyze a bone fragment, say, and enter the data into the computer, it will give us the name of the species, the point in the animal's evolutionary history, and summaries of the reproductive strategies of both genders. These are simulated animals and animal behavior."

"Your project includes all primates then, men and apes."

"Yes, it does. The other members of the project are Dr. Kenneth Bowder, of MIT, and Dr. Edith Robbins at Stanford. The third member, Dr. Keith Inskeep at Carnegie Mellon, died last year of cancer.

"We've written behavioral profiles of scores of species of monkeys and apes, as well as the hominids who left bone fragments and footprints in Olduvai gulch. We've done Lucy. And we've produced simulated male and female Neanderthals based on fossils found in an Israeli cave. We've used the bones of Java man, and duplicates of the bones of Peking man."

"You're studying the evolution of sex?"

"Of sexuality. Yes."

"Among humans?"

"Among primates, which includes humans."

"You do this using computer simulations?"

"Well, *we* do. The three of us, now that Dr. Inskeep's gone. And I'd be lying to you if I said that human reproductive behavior doesn't attract the most attention. Our simulations are pretty clear-cut and noncontroversial with all primates until we get to Stanley and Blanche. Then the ultimate and proximate causes of behavior become a snarl and a tangle, and there are nearly as many opinions as there are scholars."

"Stanley and Blanche?"

Popoleyev grinned. "Our simulated humans, named after Blanche DuBois and Stanley Kowalski in *A Streetcar Named Desire*— chosen by Dr. Inskeep. The name of any species inevitably plunges one into a swamp of stereotypes, Mr. Denson. All primates are genetic cousins, so we like to use nicknames."

"So Blanche and Stanley follow the rules of evolutionary logic and genetic inheritance."

"As accurately as our computer is able to deduce, given the power and the reliability of our program. The question of evolved sexual strategies is central to the existence of any species: how does this beast reproduce itself so that the next generation will survive?"

"Did you succeed?"

"We think so. There are times when we almost wish we hadn't." Popoleyev grimaced. "Stanley is not what you would call 'trainable' in any meaningful sense of the word. We have to keep him in a cultural cage and on a social leash."

Whitefeather rolled her eyes. "God, I guess!"

Bobby gave his wife a pretend cuff. "Watch that stuff, woman."

"But Blanche is better," I said.

"The way I see it, yes."

Willie said, "You women. Stick together."

Popoleyev said, "She's the more malleable and adaptable of the two. More flexible."

I said, "So what's the current status of Stanley and Blanche?"

Popoleyev laughed. "Not all researchers will admit we've learned anything, to tell the truth. They claim we haven't entered the right data; garbage in, garbage out, and so on. They have this or that nitpicking complaint. Dr. Inskeep, whose idea it was originally, was widely recognized and honored for his brilliance. But for what are essentially political reasons, Stanley and Blanche are controversial and are likely to remain so." Popoleyev closed her eyes and sighed. What a beauty!

She said, "Not being able to do anything about Stanley's genes is the bad part, it's so. Stanley's sexual strategy is regarded as so barbarous and unpopular it's been almost impossible to get grant money to continue our work. You have to understand that we're the product of some five million years of evolution. Genetically, we are only one percent different from chimpanzees, which is why Jane Goodall spent the better part of her life studying them."

She took a sip of her brandy. "To be recognized as valid, Mr. Denson, the results of a scientific experiment ordinarily must be able to predict. We needed something dramatic to demonstrate the validity of our work, but we can't just pop to the past or hop to the future like Mr. Spock in your television series.

"Not long before he died, Dr. Inskeep had this idea. What if Boris N. Porchnev was right? What if there was another main branch on the evolutionary tree, another family of primates, the *Troglodytidae?* And what if the stories we'd been hearing about Sasquatch were true? And what if Inskeep gave our experimental program one of his footprints to predict the behavior of Sasquatch or *Troglodytes recens* or whatever he was?"

Popoleyev raised her eyebrows, and gave us a lopsided grin.

"And what, additionally, if the computer's simulation turned out to be accurate in both large and small measure? What then, Mr. Denson?"

"You used your system to predict the behavior of Sasquatch?"

"Dr. Inskeep did, yes. He visited a number of Bigfoot experts—including Dr. Bondurant of the British Museum and Emile Thibodeaux—and on their recommendation selected a single set of Sasquatch footprints. Our program delivered behavioral profiles of Fred and Wilma."

"Fred and Wilma of the Flintstones."

"I'd never seen the cartoon myself, but I didn't care. Dr. Inskeep was brilliant, but loved to have a good time. Fred and Wilma started as a joke with him. He used to take friends into his den and entertain them with his Sasquatches on his computer terminal."

"This was *Troglodytes recens.*"

"No, unfortunately, not *Troglodytes recens.* At least not the way Porchnev's followers saw it. The computer predicted Sasquatch would be diurnal and social as are other primates, including *Homo sapiens sapiens. Troglodytes recens* would be nocturnal isolates, which would have a profound effect on their sexual evolution.

"So Dr. Inskeep, in order to humor me, instructed the computer to calculate the likely behavior of a solitary *Troglodytes recens* with night vision who had feet like those."

"And these are named?"

"Dr. Inskeep didn't give them the usual male and female names. Instead, he dubbed them 'Popoleyev's monsters.' And that's what Ken Bowder and Edith Robbins still call them. So does everybody else who knows about them.

"Dr. Inskeep said if, when Sasquatch was discovered, we were the only researchers who had predicted their behavior in advance, well then, let people laugh if they will. He said, 'He who laughs last—' "

" 'Laughs loudest.' " Willie said.

"That's right! You Americans!"

Whitefeather said, "Are Fred and Wilma common knowledge among your critics?"

Popoleyev sighed. "Oh, sure. My nocturnal monsters, too, although not everybody takes them seriously. They're Popoleyev's monsters. The beast that stalks the night."

I said, "I take it that if we find Sasquatch and your computer is right, there'll be a furor in the academic world."

"Oh, you can bet on that. There'll be those who say, So what? We just lucked out. Almost everything will come down to the accuracy of our predictions. The closer the match, the stronger our argument for the accuracy of our work. And keep in mind, *Troglodytidae* may yet exist; *Troglodytes recens* may be diurnal and social."

"The Neanderthal man would, at long last, have a proper and secure place on the charts."

"He would no longer be considered a failed hominid. Also, here's another one we have to think about, Mr. Denson. We need both accuracy and state of nature to prove our point and shut their mouths. It won't make any difference whether Fred and Wilma are accurate if Sasquatch's environment has been dirtied. If that happens, we lose state-of-nature, and all our hard work. Dr. Inskeep's brilliant gamble will have been wasted. Our critics would taunt us!"

Willie said, "Would they go so far as to foul the environment themselves?"

She looked worried. "Good question, Willie. Inserting ourselves into their lives will kill their culture. Once exposed, Sasquatch's natural way of living will be impossible to restore."

Bobby said, "Here you go, little Eve. A shiny red apple for you to enjoy. They're delicious. They just squirt juice, they're so wonderful. Try one."

Popoleyev grinned. "Yes. One bite and that's the end of it."

I said, "How does Thomas Bondurant feel about *Troglodytes recens?*"

"Oh, he seems to be neutral on the matter, although I suspect he thinks we don't have much of an argument. If we do find a Sasquatch, it will take an analysis of its genes to settle the matter. Most Sasquatch hunters don't care one way or the other. They're interested in monsters, not questions of evolution. Incidentally, I know Tom Bondurant a little from having bumped into him at international meetings. Our library has copies of some of his photographs of Sasquatch footprints. Ms. McGwyre said she's certain he has his best photographs with him, and she'll ask him to bring them along."

"Sure, I'd like to take a look at them," Bobby said. "I'd like to be the man who tracked down a *trogol . . . trogola . . .*"

"Troglodytes recens."

"I'll need all the help I can get with whatever they're called."

"I'll ask him to include a photograph of the footprints Dr. Inskeep used to write Fred and Wilma. We'll see if you'd have picked the same ones."

She rose. "After all this delicious food and drink, time for sleep. Do you suppose you could drive me to my hotel? Tomorrow we go to St. Helens. *Troglodytes* awaits us!"

Chapter Seven

On Doing
without Estrus

The next morning—yet another day with the skies crowded with flights of ducks and geese—Bobby and Whitefeather Minthorn arrived in their pickup with Earl sitting between them in the middle of the front seat. Their camping gear was packed in the bed with a tarp tied over it.

Harold and Opal, side by side, waited patiently in their trailer.

That was it. Bobby and Whitefeather Minthorn spent half their time packing into the mountains to hunt and fish. They were veterans and knew what had to be done.

Harold and Opal didn't just stare stupidly at me when I scratched their necks.

Harold's eyes said: We're in the trailer, whoever you are; we're going for a ride, and that means we're going to have some action; let's do it.

As I scratched Opal's neck, I imagined her eyes as saying: a little lower please. Or did she mean a little higher? Opal's mulish brown eyes were not to be confused with Lauren Bacall's, but as mules go she seemed good company.

Earl fancied himself a dog of action, and he was unable to mute his enthusiasm for whatever adventure lay ahead. When I reached in to give him a comradely pat of encouragement, his tail went *whap, whap, whap* on the plastic seat cover, and he honest-to-God smiled. Ever since I'd seen his training dummy in the Minthorn's backyard, I'd made sure Earl knew I was his friend.

With Bobby and Whitefeather following my VW bus in their pickup, we drove to the Mallory to pick up Sonja Popoleyev. Popoleyev, wearing hiking boots, jeans, and a puffy green nylon windbreaker, waited on the sidewalk with her bags.

Willie retreated to the seat in the rear of my rig so Popoleyev could have the passenger's side up front. I checked my mirrors to make sure the Minthorns were still behind me, and we headed up I-5 for our rendezvous with the other Sasquatch hunters.

The owners of Cascade Run, a vacation hideaway and retreat on the north shore of Swift Reservoir on the Lewis River, had volunteered their facilities as a headquarters, and it was there that the participants would coordinate the Sasquatch search.

I told Popoleyev that this was in Skamania County, Washington, where Willie and I had one year earlier helped solve the murder of the spotted owl near Sixkiller. Prettybird had argued passionately that the animal people were counting on me to help solve the mystery.

She gave me a *really?* look.

I said, "Yes, the animal people. Got their own private dicks. Willie and me."

The day was as clear and warm and fine as that long-ago day in May 1980 when Mount St. Helens popped its top. A lateral blast of 650-degree molten lava and gas, traveling hundreds of miles an hour, ripped out the northern flank, flattening 230 square miles of forest. An awesome plume of ashes billowed fifteen miles high—spreading across Washington, Northern Idaho, and Western Montana—and circling the Earth in two weeks.

When the fury was over, St. Helens was 1,300 feet shorter.

As we drove across the Fremont Bridge, the south face of Mount St. Helens loomed large about forty miles in front of us—the snowpack melted from all but the top of the conical mountain. It was on the southern flank, facing Portland, that the gentleman from Bakersfield had taped the alleged Sasquatch fleeing the northern entrance of Ape Cave.

"There it is, dead ahead," I said, "Mount St. Helens."

Popoleyev said, "Why, it's beautiful. Just beautiful. A gorgeous mountain."

Mount Rainier, visible from the hills of west Portland, had a certain mean look about it that I liked; you admired a proper mountain from a respectful distance on a sunny day; you didn't try to climb the damn thing. A mountain worthy of the name wasn't an up-and-back day trip.

Mount Hood, directly east of Portland, while not as big as Rainier, had a classic peaked top of the sort little kids go for when they're told to draw a mountain. Hood's profile, marked by a ragged outcropping of rock on its north face, gave it a deserved reputation as a handsome, if essentially sissy, mountain.

From a distance, the southern exposure of Mount St. Helens was that of a perfect dome, only 1,300 feet shorter than before the 1980 eruption.

As I drove over the I-5 bridge across the Columbia River, I said, "Dr. Popoleyev, tell me, if we should discover a Sasquatch, who in turn leads us to more of his kind, what manner of sexual relations would you expect Sasquatch to practice? Do Fred and Wilma—or Popoleyev's monsters—form monogamous couples?"

"Aren't you the playful one, Mr. Denson?" Popoleyev gave me a charming little half-grin.

I stopped myself from groaning out loud. She had these wonderful dimples . . .

"Denson!" Willie was worried that I had stepped into an emotional swamp, but he was curious too. After all, here was a woman who could tell you what a female *Gigantopithecus* looked for in an old man.

Popoleyev said, "No, no, Mr. Prettybird. It's perfectly all right. But you should remember, the test rests entirely on Fred and Wilma, not Popoleyev's monsters. Dr. Inskeep simulated Popoleyev's monsters to humor me."

I thought: *Lady, would I ever like to undo a few buttons and humor you.*

She said, "I'm afraid we'd be quite surprised to find Sasquatch form biologically bonded couples, Mr. Denson. They'll likely be a tournament species, just like us. Males will compete for females."

Willie said, "We're not pair bonders?"

"Not as that term is used by zoologists."

Willie said, "Tell that to a woman who wants your name on a marriage license."

Popoleyev laughed, "A male and female orangutang will share the same territory, but won't have anything to do with one another until it's time to mate, but that doesn't mean they're biologically locked onto one another for life. The pair bonders are mostly birds."

"Is there any obvious distinction between pair bonders and tournament species?" I asked.

"Tournament males are both larger and stronger than the females, and more aggressive. Some of the battles for females among male mammals are quite dramatic."

Willie said, "You should see a couple of bull elk going at it."

"We're tournament species, yes, but you have to remember that proximate behavior intervenes. We can and do form lasting couples. In the matter of Sasquatch, one would expect to find a few larger, very likely older Freds commanding several compliant Wilmas."

"The younger Freds do without." As I got older, I found the sexual misfortunes and misadventures of young men increasingly amusing.

Popoleyev said, "But there's really no mystery there, Mr. Denson. You're not even close to the good stuff. We're looking at some real perplexing mysteries."

"Such as?"

"One especially critical question with regard to *Homo sapiens sapiens* is when and why did Blanche lose *estrus?* Estrus is what you speak of in English as 'being in heat,' I believe."

"Marla," Willie said. "Remember Marla, Denson?"

"Ignore him," I said.

Popoleyev laughed. "Estrus is that time of the month that the egg has matured in a female mammal, and her body tells her it's time to get it fertilized. She is programmed to provoke the male into action. She may turn her rump up or emit a special odor. Evolution has provided any number of signals."

Willie closed his eyes and inhaled deeply.

"There's no controlling him," I said.

"Blanche among all mammals does not have estrus because at some time in the past, those Blanches who learned to conceal it survived at the expense of those who did not, until eventually it disappeared."

Willie said, "Not with Marla, it didn't."

Popoleyev said, "The loss of estrus is why Blanche is the sexiest of all mammals, Willie. Blanche can have sex any time it's to her advantage. All other primate females—chimps, baboons, upland gorillas—are slaves to the dictates of their hormones."

"Does Wilma have estrus?" I asked.

"If the Sasquatches don't make tools or have any culture to speak of—and this seems to be the conclusion of the literature—then yes, Wilma will likely have estrus. If the Sasquatch cerebrum is larger and more advanced, like Blanche, she may be smart enough to observe that males will do almost anything for sex. Blanche's sexual freedom is a logical consequence of her intelligence."

"I thought the consequence of her intelligence was alimony and child support," Willie said.

Popoleyev laughed. "Of course. As Blanche's cerebrum evolved and got larger, she learned the rudiments of sexual economics: she can put a price on sex, and Stanley would pay. He couldn't help himself."

I groaned.

"Ain't that the truth," Willie said.

Popoleyev said, "You two are a pair."

Willie said, "It's either laugh or cry."

"The more Blanche was able to ignore the tyranny of estrus, the more powerful she became. When she got smart enough to figure sex was a commodity that had value, the remaining course of her sexual evolution was easily predictable. For example, Blanche, knowing that Stanleys returning from the hunt would swap an extra piece of, say liver, for sex, began to insist that she be in charge of receiving and accounting for the family's share of meat. This likely led to the cultural practice of women controlling the household budget."

I said, "It may have started with the liver, but it didn't end up that way." Jackass men we were, eternally soused on androgen. It was no wonder we were so easily had.

"As the evolving brain got larger and larger, Blanche, no longer controlled by estrus, got sexier and sexier. Sex was not just for procreation; it was for play too. That is, for maintaining the interest of her mate."

Willie said, "They say if you put a bean in a jar for every time you do it for the first two years of a marriage, and take one out for each time you do it after that, you'll never empty the jar."

Popoleyev laughed. "Blanche's strategy changed because she had no choice. The larger and more complicated Blanche's brain became, the longer it took to rear her offspring to maturity. And sexually, Mr. Denson, that was the source of a terrible evolutionary catch that determines the way female *Homo sapiens sapiens* live their lives to this very day."

Popoleyev, having lapsed from the refuge of pseudonym to the naked Latin for our species, descended into a thoughtful, if not gloomy, silence.

Some thirty miles north of Portland, we left the freeway and drove forty miles up the Lewis River past two reservoirs, Lake Merwin and Yale Lake, past Coulter and the southern edge of the National Volcanic Monument. When the mountain was clearly revealed above us, I pulled over so Sonja Popoleyev could enjoy the sight.

She was pop-eyed, and hopped out into the crisp air, binoculars in hand.

Up close, Mount St. Helens was awesome.

In the valleys, the colors went to greens, and the light was yellow. At 5,000 feet, the landscape was a startling light gray from volcanic ash, and the light was white. The mountain, thus viewed with unfamiliar clarity rather than through the urban haze that most of us never leave, was so startling as to be surreal.

As a young man fresh off the farm, I once walked by the open door of the Café Metropole in New York, and the jazz trombonist Jack Teagarden was holding forth inside. This was Dixieland. Toe-tapping hot jazz! I went in, feeling all cosmopolitan and big league, and ordered a sweating, long-necked bottle of Eastern beer. Out West it was stubbies always. There was something extra hip about those tall bottles. And who should walk in but the stylish French actress Catherine Deneuve, then in her prime, and an older woman friend.

I had seen Deneuve many times in the movies, regal and elegant, but I was unprepared to see her in the flesh. I was shocked, and I marveled at how beautiful she truly was, the most elegant of longnecks among peasant stubbies.

That was the way the spendid Mount St. Helens looked now: a zone of extraordinary beauty, made possible not by a switch from film to three-dimensional reality as in the case of the actress, but by alpine light in thin, clean air.

By sundown, the temperature at timberline would plunge.

And if the wet marine air kept pushing up from the southwest . . .

I didn't want to think about it. Besides, it was time to push on to Cascade Run.

Ten minutes later, we arrived at the base of a ridge named the Devil's Backbone. Here, developers, if not the devil, had built Cascade Run on the shore of Swift Reservoir.

Cascade Run was, I suppose, modeled after the more successful Black Butte Ranch and Sunriver in Oregon. It had everything going for it: trout fishing, boating, nature tails, horseback riding, crosscountry skiing and odious skimobiles in the winter. But ever since the northern flank of St. Helens disappeared in 1980, customers had been chary about buying expensive chalets there.

I pulled in behind a line of cars waiting at the entrance to the main parking lot, which was being attended by uniformed guards. Most of the cars in front of us were being turned away. In the lot, I could see vans and cars from KING and KOMO television in Seattle, and KGW and KATU in Portland.

In ten minutes, we were at the gate. The uniformed guard said, "I'm afraid the lot's full, sir. They're planning the Sasquatch search today, and we have media people here from all over the country."

"I see."

"But the restaurant and bar are open, and we'll have Bigfoot lectures and displays all day. You'll get to see Bigfoot Central, which will remain in constant contact with the base camps and the searchers on the mountain. We've got a heated indoor swimming pool and an exercise room with the latest equipment, plus a sauna and hot tub. Also, Mr. Pollard's display of Sasquatchiana will be open. There'll be a slide show every hour, where you can ask questions."

"That's impressive! What do you think, Willie?"

"I want to see the Sasquatchiana," Willie said. "Can't wait."

"We've established a shuttle bus from Cougar, and we've commissioned special drinks this afternoon, Bigfoot Bangers, containing four different kinds of Caribbean rum—three Jamaican and one Puerto Rican."

"We're the Popoleyev party. Also the pickup and trailer behind us."

"Yes, sir. There is parking space reserved for you in front of the main auditorium." He looked momentarily confused. "Is this all of you?" He looked at the horse trailer, his brow furrowed.

"That's it," I said. "Three Redskins, a Russian, and a damned fool. That's plus two pack mules, Harold and Opal, and a dog with high-cur fur. Plus all our gear. Enough stuff to get us to the North Pole if we wanted."

"High-cur fur?"

"That's sort of a brownish-yellow. He answers to Earl."

The guard blinked.

I put my bus in low gear and idled through the parking lot. In my rearview mirror, I could see the guard on the phone saying Dr. Popoleyev and her party had arrived. It was twenty minutes until nine, plenty of time.

Then I saw why the parking lot was so full. The reason was not solely due to Sasquatch buffs or vehicles from the mass media. I counted eight squad cars from the Washington State Patrol and four belonging to deputies of the Skamania County Sheriff, my old pal Sheriff Bert T. Starkey.

Chapter Eight

He Comforts
the Widow

We were about ready to open the carved wooden door to the Execu-Lodge when it opened for us, and we stepped aside to make way for a mixed troop of Washington State patrolmen and deputies of the Skamania County Sheriff's Department. They spilled into the bright morning sunlight, squinting and digging for sunglasses.

The officers were obviously accompanying, rather than officially escorting—as in having arrested—Alford Pollard, identifiable by his red hair and nose. Alford was lean and quick, terrierlike, smaller than Elford, who had been slightly pudgy in build. Alford was a fox terrier where Elford had been a hound.

The pack of officers, spiffy in their creased uniforms—with belts, buckles, straps, and polished shoes all squeaking different tunes— were led by my old friend Sheriff Bert T. Starkey, who was grim-faced and all business. Their guts pushed hard against their belt buckles. They had pasty complexions. They compensated by having perfected squinty-eyed, cool-mother Clint Eastwood looks.

Pollard had a comforting arm around a snappy-looking brunette in a black dress and black hat. She was petite, perky, button-nosed, with freckles and big, blinky brown eyes. Debbie Reynoldsish.

What was with the black outfit, I wondered. Was she in mourning? If she was a sister or cousin, she didn't reflect Pollard genes, I didn't think. Could she be Elford's widow? Yes, most likely.

As they passed, the thoughtful, gentlemanly Alford put his hand on her diminutive waist, comforting her with a gentle squeeze. The amount of flesh thus gripped seemed generous for squeezing a widow.

Did his hand linger a half-second too long? As he removed his hand, did his fingers trail an itsy-bit too much?

He murmured something in her ear. More support from the thoughtful brother-in-law, if that's what he was.

She bobbed her cute head, acknowledging whatever he had said.

Pollard then muttered to the officer to his left, gesturing angrily with his free hand. He was sore as hell about something.

Whatever was the source of his anger, he by-God wanted something done about it. It was impossible to tell if this emotion was genuine.

When the officers and Pollard had passed, Popoleyev, staring at their backs, said, "Who was that, Mr. Denson?"

"The younger Pollard, I believe," I said. "Willie and I saw his brother on television."

"Alford Pollard. I thought that might be him. What has happened? He's not in some kind of trouble, is he?"

I said, "I don't know, but I expect we'll be finding out in a few minutes."

"I have an appointment for a get-acquainted chat with him this afternoon, don't I? I'm sure all his problems will be resolved by then."

Judging by serious faces on the Grand High Sheriffs as they had spilled out of Execu-Lodge, to say that Alford Pollard was going to get all his problems resolved in a couple of hours was like saying the fry cook surely knew how to cook an egg over medium.

If the scumbag story Elford had written about Sonja Popoleyev in the *Gleaner* was typical of his journalism, there were probably plenty of people with motive for doing him in.

Chapter Nine

Minthorn
Checks the
Prints

Thomas Bondurant was very ta-ta British, gentlemanly, if not downright courtly, as he welcomed us into the Stag Room, He appeared indifferent to the fact that his left foot was in a cast. Stiff upper and all that.

The Stag Room, presumably named for the elk's head mounted over the fireplace, was imitation men's club, as imagined by an addict of late-night movies. If somebody fired a weapon in the Stag Room, the bullet would ricochet off varnished hardwood for hours or until it plopped into the leather couch or the elk's snout.

The hardwood walls were hung with handsomely mounted George Bellows sporting prints, and old photographs of loggers and miners. A splendid antique grandfather clock went *tick-tock, tick-tock* in one corner.

A real men's club would have smelled old; the Stag Room had the odor of the day before yesterday.

With Bondurant was Donna McGwyre, the manager of Cascade

Run. He introduced us. McGwyre, a good-looking, long-legged brunette in her late thirties, wore one of those pretend men's suits—blue skirt and jacket, white blouse, red bow tie.

A swarthy waiter with starched collar, looking like a refugee from the Italian Riviera, hovered at the polished cherry table displaying coffee and croissants. This, I assumed, was where local moguls in forty-dollar neckties gathered to connive at power breakfasts—swapping minimarts and developing mobile-home hookups. With the attentive Guido at their elbow, and with such a splendid silver coffee urn, they surely felt like Rothschilds and Krupps.

As we got ourselves coffee and croissants, Bondurant said, "I took the liberty of inviting Ms. McGwyre to join us for a few minutes. I do hope you don't mind, Dr. Popoleyev."

"Not at all."

Bondurant said, "She's in charge of our introductory meeting in the auditorium at ten, and there are still details that need her attention. I've been giving her a crash course on Sasquatch lore."

"Once word got out that a Sasquatch was spotted, we've been getting calls from all over the world," McGwyre said. "I never realized."

I said, "How's your broken foot coming, Dr. Bondurant?"

"It's coming along fine, thank you. I can walk on it. I just can't climb mountains with it."

When Popoleyev introduced Bondurant to Bobby Minthorn, Bondurant was especially gracious. "The people in the universities have their special lingo to explain the workings of this or that kind of primate foot—you should hear them prattle on at the New Scotland Yard. I read in the papers that you have extraordinary skills as a tracker of game in the Pacific Northwest, Mr. Minthorn. I'd be delighted to share my photographs with you."

"I'll do my best." This was Bobby's moment, and he wanted to flash his stuff. I don't blame him. A little pride. I'd have felt the same way.

"If you'll remember my name when you find Sasquatch."

"Sure," Bobby said.

Bondurant said, "First, Mr. Minthorn—if you don't already know—based on your experience as a tracker, can you guess the chief difference between the way humans move and other two-legged, or even four-legged animals?"

Bobby Minthorn closed his eyes in thought. Then, looking at his feet, he slowly walked the length of the room and back. He said, "We stride. We land on our heel and push off with our toes in ways other animals don't. Our foot rolls from heel to toe. The rolling motion of our foot is probably the chief difference."

Bondurant grinned.

Popoleyev said, "I told you he was good."

"There are two principal types of Sasquatch footprints found in the Pacific Northwest. Furthermore, these two types are found in specific geographic areas, and these are distinctly different footprints that would belong to different kinds of beasts. Both may be fake. One may be fake and the other real. But two distinct types of previously undiscovered hominids living cheek by jowl in so small an area? That's close to impossible. I think it's safe to assert that they are not both real.

"Mr. Minthorn, I propose to show you photographs of each kind of print, by itself, without identifying it or commenting on it further. These are pictures of both footprints and footprint casts. I'll also lay out some human footprints. I want to hear what you have to say. And I suppose I should tell you, I've done this many times before with expert trackers, including Sherpas in Nepal. I'll take a skilled indigenous tracker over Scotland Yard any day."

Willie said, "He's got you on the spot, Minthorn. Your bluff called."

Minthorn glanced coolly at Willie. "I'm game, Dr. Bondurant. Let's see your pictures."

Out of a large manila envelope, Bondurant removed a thick handful of eight-by-ten colored glossies of footprints. The glossies were mounted on thin cardboard. As he spread them out on the table, I found myself wishing I believed in something superstitious that would help Bobby Minthorn out.

As Bobby studied the pictures, eighteen in all, I browsed through them with Popoleyev, Willie, and Whitefeather. Five of the prints were human and easy to spot. They weren't as wide as the alleged Sasquatch prints, and had definite arches. The human prints weren't as big, period, but beyond that they looked more "real" for some reason. There was another difference, something to do with the toes, but I didn't know what it was.

Finally, Bobby said, "Okay, let me tell you what I think, Dr. Bondurant. First, the five human prints just jump right out. The weight of the Sasquatch prints appears to be borne by the inside of the foot, rather than the outside. You see it here where the heel strikes." Leaning over the table, he pointed to the outside of the heel of a human print, then to the inside of a Sasquatch heel.

Bondurant leaned over the table as well. "An ape makes a print like that. But apes are only part-time bipeds. Among living primates only *Homo sapiens sapiens* are full-time bipeds."

Bobby said, "Also, the toes are close to the same size. It doesn't really have a big toe. A human takes off from the inside of his foot, which I assume is why our inside toe is so big. Whatever made this print took off from the outside. Its foot rolls inside-outside instead of outside-in. It's pigeon-toed."

"Yes, it is." Bondurant studied the photographs.

Bobby said, "I assume the weight of the beast is what pushed the ridge of dirt up between his toes and the ball of his foot." He picked up a photograph and studied it.

"It appears that way."

Pointing to the front of the footprint in his hand, Bobby said, "The ridge of this print is almost as straight as a ruler, but that part of the foot is rounded in all the footprints I've ever seen."

Bondurant picked up a Sasquatch print and examined it. "It slants forward from the outside to the inside of the foot, but, as you point out, there's no curve, and biology works in curves, not straight lines."

"And the outside of the foot comes in here just a tad." Bobby Minthorn pointed at the outside middle of the photograph Bondurant was holding. Bobby said, "Because of the arch, only the inside of the human print curves in."

"They're slightly concave on the outside, yes. That's the identifying signature. These are called the 'hourglass' footprints in Sasquatch literature."

"They've got a lifeless feel about them."

Bondurant said, " 'Static' is another word I've heard used. Mr. Minthorn, my congratulations. You could keep up with the best

Sherpa I've ever met, and I've shown these same pictures to some good ones. You're correct to note the importance of the human big toe."

Bondurant retrieved the first set of photographs and spread a second round of eighteen pictures, only this time it was tougher to spot the human prints.

Upon seeing the new photographs, Minthorn smiled.

"Know these already, eh?"

"I think so."

I leaned over the photographs, deciding, finally, that the human footprints had more of an arch and were narrower than the Sasquatch prints. One set of flat-footed Sasquatch prints was unusual. The right print had a bulge on the outside of the foot just in front of the heel. The left print looked twisted; the beast obviously bore its weight on the outside of that foot. The left foot was also broader than the right, owing to a huge bulge on the outside, highlighted by two knobs or bumps that poked out just behind the little toe. Whereas the right foot had toes that were larger, and perhaps fatter, than human toes, the toes on the left foot were all messed up. The big toe went right, to the inside; the second toe poked slightly left where it competed for space with the third toe; the fourth toe was overly large; and the little toe was a shapeless mess, as though it had been squashed flat. If this was a fake print, the perpetrator had a real imagination.

Minthorn studied the prints briefly, then said, "These are pictures of the Sasquatch footprints found here in Washington State."

Bondurant said, "Mr. Minthorn, out of all these pictures of both types of footprints, can you pick out one set of prints that you think would be the most likely candidate to be that of a Sasquatch?"

"Okay, smart guy," Willie said.

"Mr. Big Talker," Whitefeather said.

Minthorn smiled. "These," he said, tapping his finger on the prints with the messed-up left foot. "A Sasquatch with a clubfoot. Toes all scrambled up like that. Gotta be these."

Popoleyev clapped her hands together. "Da! Bobby!"

Judging from Popoleyev's joy, there was little doubt Bobby Minthorn had picked the footprints Inskeep had used for *Troglodytes recens*.

Bondurant cocked his head and said to Popoleyev, "You didn't tell him?"

Popoleyev pretended to be offended, but under the circumstances, she didn't mind being teased. "I told you I did not."

I said, "But you're a Russian, after all. We have to take that into account."

"Mr. Denson!"

Bondurant said, "Mr. Minthorn, you picked what are called the Bossberg prints after the location where they were found. Bossberg is located on the eastern side of the Cascades just south of the Canadian border. They were found by a butcher in October 1969."

Popoleyev said, "These are the footprints, Mr. Denson. Fred and Wilma's feet. If the Sasquatch on this mountain has feet like these . . . think of it!" Sonja Popoleyev was buoyant.

Bondurant said, "Inskeep chose these prints after talking to me, among others. I recommended that he talk to Emile Thibodeaux. Emile followed a trail of these prints for nearly a half-mile, close to two thousand prints in all. His clubfoot would be common, incidentally, either inherited or caused by injury. The specialists in the British Museum and Scotland Yard both say injury in early childhood."

I picked up the picture and studied it. The feet were both long and wide. Big feet. No doubt about it.

Bondurant, looking at the picture over my shoulder, said, "It's seventeen-and-a-half-inches long and seven-inches wide. We've got reports of footprints from twelve to twenty-two inches, but most run from about fourteen to eighteen inches. Seven to eight feet is generally the reported height. Judging from reports of their build, an eight-footer would weigh in at eight hundred pounds or so."

"Are there low and high seasons for the reports?"

"Low is December to April. There are two highs, June and July, and October and November. The highs correspond with the presence of tourists and hunters in the woods. Isn't that how you understand it, Donna?"

Donna McGwyre said, "That sounds right." She checked the grandfather clock. "Say, I've got to get a move on. I'll be seeing you all in the auditorium in a few minutes. I was very impressed with your knowledge of footprints, Mr. Minthorn. Later, Tom." And she was off, with a brisk stride.

When she had gone, Willie said, "What time of day is Sasquatch usually spotted?"

Bondurant grinned. "At night, by a three-to-one margin. Chalk one up for *Troglodytes recens*. But in all honesty, that's a hard one for me to take. Except for a single species of monkey in South America, all primates are diurnal."

"Meaning we are active during the day."

"Yes," Bondurant said.

Minthorn said, "Do his eyes reflect light at night?"

"The reports range from green to yellow, red, and white. Most are red or white."

Popoleyev said, "Bobby, the eyes of nocturnal animals reflect light off a layer of the cornea called tapetum, which ordinarily gives a green eye shine. Diurnal animals, including humans, don't have tapetum in their cornea, although their eyes sometimes give off a red or pinkish color."

Willie said, "Like when I try to use the flash attachment of my camera. What sex of Sasquatch do people think they see?"

Bondurant said, "The reports are of males over females by a five-to-one ratio. The usual sighting is of a single male Sasquatch at night. For what it's worth, most sightings of Sasquatches are reported in British Columbia, but the most footprints are found in northern California.

"The hourglass prints are associated with Blue Creek and Bluff Creek in northern California. Many of these hourglass prints have been found. And they are uniformly, consistently the same. Unless you admit the possibility of uniform, consistent fraud, I have to admit this poses logical problems."

I said, "Tell me, Dr. Bondurant, what is it Sasquatches are supposed to eat? Don't we need to know that if we're going to plan any kind of systematic search?"

Bondurant said, "Some years ago two Canadians from the Provincial Museum in Victoria came up with an ingenious notion that I still find fascinating. They suggest that Sasquatch might well survive on a strategy similar to that of the wolverine, a rapacious meateater more than a yard long, including its tail.

"A wolverine's home range is about two hundred miles, and it occupies the same high-elevation habitat attributed to Sasquatch. Wolverines freeze food in holes they dig above the snowline. When food is scarce in the winter, they dig food out of these natural freezers and take it down the mountain to thaw out."

Willie said, "Smart wolverines!"

Minthorn said, "You don't often run into wolverines."

Popoleyev said, "You shouldn't run into wolverines or *Troglodytes recens* very often. They're both isolates."

Bondurant said, "I do sincerely wish you luck with *Troglodytes recens*, Dr. Popoleyev. It would be fun, wouldn't it? A new family of primates, right under our noses? Can you imagine the whimpering and whining and denial?"

I said, "So what's the catch with the prints of the Bossberg clubfoot?"

"The catch?" Bondurant smiled. "Well, for one thing, two of the figures associated with the prints, one being Emile Thibodeaux, have long been associated with the search for Sasquatch. My friends in the British Museum consider that a no-no.

"In fact, a butcher found the prints, but a second man, locally held to be full of horsefeathers, brought them to the attention of Thibodeaux. The two of them returned to follow the trail as far as they could."

"Lot of people full of horsefeathers in some of these little towns."

"If you categorically deny the possibility of Sasquatch, then all believers have to be held suspect. But what if you're wrong?"

"Let me put it to you this way, Mr. Denson. Suppose you, I take it a thorough-going skeptic, are backpacking at a lake up in the high country, and you happen onto some incredible footprints. You're isolated, as far as you know—miles from all other known humans. The next time you heard a Sasquatch story, wouldn't you listen a little closer?"

"I would. Yes."

"Of course you would. What if the Sasquatch believers aren't all crazy? What if some of them are obsessed for the reason that they actually saw one or followed one?"

I wasn't convinced, and he could see it.

He smiled. "Or think they saw or followed one. Would that be better, Mr. Denson? You're like one of those chaps at Scotland Yard. They say it's extraordinary what a skilled barrister can do with eyewitness testimony." He eyed the grandfather clock. "Say, you know, it's getting that time. I think we'd better push off for the meeting ourselves."

Chapter Ten

Man with Bad
Manners

Our group strung out down the hallway as we left the Stag Room and headed for the auditorium, where Donna McGwyre had things ready to go for the general meeting that would begin the launching of our coordinated Sasquatch search. Popoleyev and I went first, followed by Whitefeather Minthorn and Willie Prettybird, and then Thomas Bondurant, slowed by the cast on his foot, and Bobby Minthorn, still talking about footprints.

Hey, I'm a laid-back kind of guy. Or try to be. I always thought "live and let live" made a lot of sense. I just stepped around the corner, talking with Sonja Popoleyev, certainly not doing anything outrageously Stanley or otherwise provocative, when . . .

. . . a man pulled by a large, expensive-looking, fluffy dog and trailed by a succulent blonde with an explosively wrapped butt ran *bang!* flat over me, and rebounded, slamming into Sonja Popoleyev.

All three of us tumbled to the floor.

On the way down, I banged my elbow against the wall. My crazy bone. *Ay!*

The woman with the sublime butt, who'd escaped the action unharmed, hopped to one side. "Oopsie doops! Oopsie doops!"

My elbow! My elbow!

Popoleyev had not only been unceremoniously bashed into an undignified landing, but in the process had lost one of her contact lenses. She held both hands wide, trying to protect the territory beneath her feet.

The man scrambled to his feet and felt his face with his fingertips. He was in his late fifties and wore freshly pressed khaki chinos and a herringbone jacket over a just-folks sweater and blue cotton broadcloth shirt. Cuff links. He was wearing cuff links.

"My contact!" Popoleyev, on her knees, holding both sides of her head with outstretched palms, squinted at the floor.

I got to my knee, staring at his crispy creased trousers. My elbow was paralyzed with pain. *Aaayyy!*

Above me, the owner of the chinos said, "Jerk!"

I was frozen by bolts of pain that shot up and down my arm. My elbow hurt so bad, I literally couldn't speak.

Chinos seemed surprised that he still had the leash. The dog was bouncing happily about, drool streaming from its mouth. He yanked at the dog's neck. "Fuckin' thing!" he muttered. "Rudy!"

Rudy, who must have been following the couple, accepted the leash. He wore what I took to be a chauffeur's outfit. Rudy said, "Sit!"

The pedigreed dog sat, tongue out, drool flowing.

The blonde, in her middle twenties, said "Oooo, baby! Oooo!" and scratched the dog behind the ears in an attempt to calm it.

Ms. Oopsie doops. I thought, *I'd like to oopsie those doops of yours, lady.*

"Are you okay?" she asked me, a horrified look on her face.

I moved my mouth, but my elbow hurt so bad I couldn't talk.

The dog started to get up.

Rudy gave him a yank. "Sit!"

Chinos was so joyful at ridding himself of the dog that he stepped in the middle of the no-no zone that contained Popoleyev's contact lens.

"Ahhh!" Popoleyev was horrified.

"What?" He glanced down at her, scowling.

He grabbed the succulent blonde by the hand and continued on his way. He did not look back. The blonde did. She looked embarrassed and concerned, as if she wanted to return and help Popoleyev find her lens.

However, Chinos pulled her into the auditorium where we were headed.

"Ahh, here it is. It's okay." Popoleyev held her contact lens between thumb and forefinger. She squinted after the disappearing couple. "I was lucky that man didn't step on it. Did you see where he stepped?"

"Bigfoot," I said.

The rest of our group, having witnessed the incident, joined us now that the lens was found.

Bondurant was concerned—and annoyed at whoever it was who had run over us. "Are you all right, Dr. Popoleyev?"

"No permanent damage. I'll survive," she said.

"And you, Mr. Denson?"

"Wounded pride," I said. "Hit my crazy bone." I flexed my arm.

I'm a private detective who doesn't carry a weapon. I'm known for it. All Denson carries in his pocket is spare change and a cue stick for pocket pool. Everybody knows that. Better to find the smart way out than to fight. Now, the aggressive, combative, nearly irrational Stanley in me had welled up. I was awash with adrenaline.

It was like I had walked into a saloon in Missoula, Montana, with old boys with spurs on their boots playing poker in the back room. I'm looking for this total black hat in a fifty-dollar suit and a Latin Lover moustache. And I have the sudden, irresistible urge to blow his motherfucking brains clear through the wall and out into the parking lot.

The auditorium was packed to capacity with two hundred-odd reporters, photographers, and followers of Sasquatchiana, whose appetite for excitement must have been whetted by the earlier appearance in the building of Sheriff Starkey and his deputies.

A long table covered with a white tablecloth had been set up on the stage at the front of the auditorium. A podium and microphone dominated the center. The Sasquatch searchers, identified by table placards, sat on folding metal chairs on either upstage side. Each had his own microphone.

To the audience's left: Emile Thibodeaux, Roger Whitcomb, and Donna McGwyre, the Cascade Run manager. To the right, Alford Pollard's assigned seat was empty. Popoleyev's and Bondurant's seats waited there.

The lean and fit Emile Thibodeaux, with a long, deeply tanned face, was a leathery sixty or so. He wore old blue jeans and a red-and-black-checked flannel shirt. Roger Whitcomb, with a square jaw, even nose, and sparkling white teeth, was in his late thirties. He wore designer jeans and an aqua shirt. His nylon windbreaker, in an off-blue that complemented his shirt, was hung over the back of his chair.

"You're on your own," I muttered to Popoleyev.

"Go for it," Willie said.

Popoleyev took a quick deep breath to steady her nerves. Then, long legs scissoring, accompanied by the audience's spirited applause, she strode up the aisle to the stage, followed by Bondurant. Willie and I and the Minthorns threw in a few shrill whistles for good measure. Bobby's contribution, made with forefingers at his front teeth, was so piercing as to nearly make me wince.

Popoleyev, acknowledging the applause with a gracious smile, stode down the rear of the table, in turn shaking the hands of Thibodeaux, Whitcomb, and Donna McGwyre. Bondurant did the same, and they took their seats.

McGwyre stood and stepped to the microphone at the podium in the center. She used a ballpoint pen to deliver a basic Rotarian opener, rapping on a pitcher of water: *ting, ting, ting! Ting, ting, ting!*

"Now that we're all here, we can begin."

I scanned the room, trying to spot the jerk who had run over me. Was Popoleyev looking for him too? I bet she was.

McGwyre said, "Alford Pollard has been delayed, but will be joining us shortly. In the meantime, I'd like to introduce the other participants in our coordinated search. If you could please hold your applause until I've introduced everybody, the sooner we can answer your questions."

"On my far right, said to be the bloodhound of Sasquatch, a man who has devoted thirty years of his life to the pursuit of Bigfoot, Emile Thibodeaux, of Cle Elum, Washington. Next to Mr. Thibodeaux is Roger Whitcomb, of Los Angeles, whose documentaries on Sasquatch you may have seen on television.

"To my left are Dr. Sonja Popoleyev, primatologist at the St. Petersburg Institute of Primate Study, and Dr. Thomas Bondurant, director of primate studies at the British Museum."

The audience applauded vigorously. Except for the murder five days previously of Elford Pollard, the coordinated Bigfoot search was off to a civilized beginning.

McGwyre said, "I'd also like to introduce David Addison, who, you all must know by now, has offered a one-hundred-thousand-dollar reward to anybody who is able to capture a Sasquatch on Mount St. Helens."

That brought the applause.

Capture? Popoleyev wasn't going to like that.

"Mr. Addison, why don't you and your lovely wife Laraine stand up so we can see who you are?"

The Addisons, who were seated out front with the proletarians, rose to accept the applause. Addison, holding his herringbone casually in one hand, smiled appreciatively at the applause.

Hey, this was the moron who had run over us in the hallway. Mr. Pressed Chinos. I glanced at Willie.

"Easy, Chief."

"My behind too."

Laraine Addison wore one of those clinging body-stocking dresses over a body that was a genuine groaner. Succulent was the only word that did her justice. She was sleek with body fat; perhaps too sleek for the long run, but currently sexier than hell. Her rump was a form of centerpiece.

Mr. Big Man, Mrs. Splendid Butt.

If Addison was such a Sasquatch enthusiast, I wondered why he hadn't extended the reward to a Bigfoot found anywhere in the Cascades. Why just St. Helens? One had allegedly been spotted on Mount Baker, hadn't it? And one on Mount Rainier.

Popoleyev's hand shot up.

"Dr. Popoleyev?"

"Perhaps, Mr. Addison, you mean to offer the reward to anybody who is able to conclusively locate Sasquatch. To capture one would be criminal. This point is critical to us in the scientific community."

Bondurant said, "I heartily concur with my colleague. If he exists, Sasquatch is not some beast to be exhibited in a zoo. That would be barbarous in the extreme. He is a form of hominid, our evolutionary cousin."

Popoleyev said, "Capture is not only unnecessary, but an impediment to learning. Skilled wildlife photographers with proper lenses can satisfy the public curiosity. Furthermore, anybody who should go so far as to shoot one, should be prosecuted for murder. As I understand, Skamania County, Washington, is the only county in the United States where there is a law on the books prohibiting the killing of a Sasquatch.

Bondurant said, "There is, indeed. It carries a ten-thousand-dollar fine."

Addison cleared his throat. "If anybody kills a Sasquatch, he'll answer to Sheriff Starkey."

Unleashing Bert Starkey on a Sasquatch murderer didn't strike me as the most menacing of all threats.

Popoleyev said, "I think we need to remind ourselves of this just and sensible law in Skamania County. To shoot a Sasquatch is no less an offense than to shoot a human being. It's murder."

Addison, who hadn't bothered to look at us in the hallway, had no idea why Popoleyev might have cause to press him with such ardor. She had Bondurant agreeing with her, and Bondurant was not only British Museum, but sounded as if he were doing James Mason imitations.

Addison didn't want to come off as provincial and encouraging murder. He nodded to McGwyre.

McGwyre said, "Mr. Addison offers a one-hundred-thousand-dollar reward to anybody who is able to conclusively locate a Sasquatch on Mount St. Helens."

Popoleyev said, "No money to anybody doing violence to Sasquatch. No weapons are necessary, please."

"No reward for violence," Addison said.

Dr. Popoleyev said, "Thank you, Mr. Addison, on behalf of all my colleagues at the St. Petersburg Institute."

A thank-you on behalf of her colleagues in St. Petersburg? An internationalist! Addison liked the sound of that. He glowed as though he had a vacuum tube for a head.

Laraine Addison swelled with pneumatic pride as she applauded her husband; some parts of her were more swell than others.

I reached for the sky, waggling my damn-fool arm with all the vigor I could muster.

Donna McGwyre blinked, instinctively wary. Common sense told her so insistent an arm could signal trouble. "Yes, sir. If you could identify yourself, it might help the rest of us."

"Certainly. My name is John Denson, and I'm a photographer with Dr. Popoleyev's party. However, this question is mine, not hers, and should not be identified with her team. I assume Mr. Addison's generosity is aimed at the truth, which is our larger goal on this expedition, is it not?"

McGwyre looked puzzled. "I'm afraid I don't understand, Mr. Denson."

I said, "Well, what if some kind of fraud is being perpetrated on the community?"

Heads turned. This was Sasquatch turf. There *was* a Bigfoot. There *was*. Nobody liked hearing talk of fraud. This was their space, not mine. Couldn't they be left alone by wiseacres?

I was glared at and stared at. Not liked at all.

An elderly man shouted, to passionate murmurs of agreement, that I should go on back to California where I came from.

McGwyre blinked. "Sir? I'm afraid I don't understand."

"Will Mr. Addison agree to pay the one-hundred-thousand-dollar reward to anyone who is able to prove that this whole business of an alleged Sasquatch sighting is a fraud? I'm not saying it is, mind you, but it could be, couldn't it? It's difficult to believe it's outside the realm of possibility."

The silence that followed was cancerous.

Willie muttered, "Kemosabe! You're gonna get us killed."

I said to Willie, "You know, like I always tell you, Prettybird, little man whip a big man every time . . ."

"If the little man's in the right and just keeps coming. Horsepucky."

"You just won't listen."

Through the crowd, Addison looked at me blandly, hating me, but trying not to show it. He had no idea who I was, other than a member of Popoleyev's team. He was determined to remain casual and in-control in front of his young wife.

His wife was trying to whisper something in his ear, no doubt trying to tell him about the hallway, but he ignored her.

McGwyre glanced at Addison.

Addison's mouth tightened. It was hard to tell whether he recognized me or not.

Rubbing my elbow, I said, "It's the easiest thing in the world to offer a reward knowing it will never have to be paid."

Under his breath, Willie said, "Chief! Chief! Hey!"

Laraine Addison again tried to tell her husband something.

But he was engaged in a form of combat and couldn't be bothered.

I said, "Shucks, I tell you what, Mr. Addison, I hereby offer to give the pink slip to my Volkswagen minibus to anybody, including especially you, who can conclusively locate a Sasquatch. Locate, not capture. And not harm in any way."

"Chief!"

"You're on," Addison said, speaking directly to me for the first time. Then, he said, "Make the announcement, Don."

McGwyre said, "Yes, sir, Mr. Addison. A one-hundred-thousand-dollar reward to anybody who can prove fraud. Correct?"

Addison looked sour.

"And my bus for a Sasquatch," I said. "A deal's a deal. Right, dude? The bus has recaps, but with plenty of rubber. It's got a rebuilt engine, and the carburetors are both tuned. It's ready for Mexico, if you want to go. Or Brazil."

I looked straight at Addison and stopped rubbing my elbow long enough to give him a wink and a triumphant thumbs up. The bastard!

Willie, giggling, muttered, "Chief!"

Addison's wife finally got her husband's attention, glancing toward Popoleyev then me as she talked. Once, she gestured to the hallway with her hand.

He listened to what she had to say. Watching me, realizing the consequences of a stupid unacknowledged oopsie doopsie, his face tightened.

Using my finger as the barrel of an imaginary six-shooter, I tapped it twice in his direction, *bang, bang,* then coolly blew the smoke away. I said to Willie, "That man just doesn't have any manners, Willie."

Willie giggled. "You and Dr. Popoleyev drew on him one right after the other, poor bastard."

Heads turned as Alford Pollard and Elford Pollard's widow entered the room. Pollard, looking grim and determined, strode to the front of the room and took his seat alongside Sonja Popoleyev and Thomas Bondurant.

Chapter Eleven

I Accuse!

Alford Pollard leaned toward his microphone and bit his lip. He started to speak, but stopped, overcome with emotion. He took a drink of water. "I apologize for being late, but I've had a setback that's difficult to accept. I . . ."

He took another drink. "By now you all know my brother Elford was murdered last week. Elford and I were like this." He crossed the forefinger and middle finger of his left hand and held it high. "Like this. I loved him. How I dearly loved him. Dear God!" Alford choked back a sob, then rested his forehead on the heel of his hand while he recovered.

"Some of you may have seen me with the police officers this morning. But before I tell you what's happened, I would like you all to meet and give a hand of support to little Judy Pollard, Elford's bride of two months when he was killed."

The petite brunette in the black outfit rose to acknowledge the applause.

Alford said, "To know Elford was to love him, Judy."

When the applause for the widow Pollard had died, Alford said, "It now is my unpleasant duty to tell you that the exhibit of Sasquatchiana that Elford and I spent eight years assembling has been stolen."

This was met by groans from the audience. Pollard's Sasquatchiana was obviously a principal attraction for the folks whose automobiles filled the parking lot. Few of them had known Elford Pollard well enough to mourn his absence, but they all wanted to see the Sasquatch footprints.

Donna McGwyre said, "This is of course a disappointment to us all. However, we are assured by Sheriff Bert Starkey and the Washington State Patrol that an RV won't make it far without being spotted."

Alford said, "My brother, now this." He narrowed his eyes, suddenly looking sore as hell. "Well!" he shouted.

Silence.

It was unclear if Pollard expected any kind of reply. He narrowed his eyes, and in a low, menacing voice, said, "So much for the so-called seekers of truth. They murder. They steal."

Pollard looked to his left at Bondurant and Sonja Popoleyev, then to his right at Thibodeaux and Whitcomb. Was he blaming them for Elford's murder?

"So much for science," he said. "Now we know. But what in heaven's name can the murdering thief be thinking of? Does he seriously think the truth is to be denied? Why? Can anybody in this auditorium answer that question? If they can, speak now!"

Pollard gestured to the right side of the auditorium, as though waiting for an answer. He got none, of course. He addressed the center. "Well?" No reply. "How about you folks?" He glared to his left, where Willie and I stood leaning against the wall.

I had survived lynching so far, and was doing my best to keep a low profile.

Willie whispered in my ear. "He's definitely one of yours, paleface."

"Bull too," I whispered back.

"Would you, madam, care to speculate?" he asked McGwyre.

Speculate about murder? In public? McGwyre cleared her throat.

Pollard shouted into his mike, "That vehicle contained two hundred and seventeen casts of Sasquatch footprints! Dr. Bondurant here has said publicly that footprints are the most persuasive evidence we have. But now, stolen. Gone! Plus more than a hundred examples of Bigfoot droppings. Priceless scientific evidence. Priceless. Also gone!"

Since Thibodeaux, Bondurant, and numerous others had casts of the same footprints, I thought the seriousness of the loss was overstated. Still, I could understand why he was pissed.

Pollard said, "Elford and I brought our exhibit here openly and honestly, without reservation or hesitation. We offered the entire contents, with nothing withheld, for examination by any reputable scientist in the world using whatever technical apparatus might be at his disposal. Isn't that right, Ms. McGwyre? Correct me if I'm wrong."

McGwyre nodded her head. Yes, that was right.

"Somebody murdered Elford. What do you want to bet it was the same bastard who stole our exhibit?"

Sonja Popoleyev looked at Willie and me, asking us with her eyes for help.

I put a finger to my lips, advising her to say nothing.

Willie did the same.

Pollard said, "Well, let me tell you all something. My brother Elford would turn in his grave if I backed down one inch from the pursuit of the truth. In Elford's name, and in the name of science and the truth, I demand that my RV be returned with all its contents intact."

Willie whispered, "What do you think, Chief?"

I whispered back. "I think his concern for science and the truth is maybe stretching credibility too far."

"Mmmmmmm."

"A plea to Elford's memory would have done the job."

Pollard said, "I challenge the thief: let truth and falsehood be put to the test and truth shall prevail."

"With apologies to John Milton," I muttered.

"Who's that?"

"The man whose line that was."

"Ahh," Willie said. "College man."

Pollard wheeled, pointing his finger at Emile Thibodeaux. "You!"

Thibodeaux blinked. "What?"

"You!"

Thibodeaux was pop-eyed. "Are you, sir, accusing me of murdering your brother?"

Pollard didn't answer. Instead, he pointed at Whitcomb. "Or you!"

Willie whispered, "This is getting good."

Whitcomb glared at Pollard. "Why, you dumb bastard! Who the hell do you think you are?"

Popoleyev paled. Was she to be accused by this pipsqueak Robespierre?

Willie tensed. If Pollard said anything to Sonja Popoleyev, he was going to have a pissed-off Redskin on his hands.

"Easy, Willie," I said.

"Gentlemen, please," McGwyre said.

Thibodeaux tilted his head to one side. He tapped the bowl of his pipe on the heel of his hand. In as gentlemanly a manner as he could muster, he said to McGwyre, "You ignored my question, sir, but if I'm to be accused of being a murderer or thief at a public forum, I surely have the right to defend myself."

"Be my guest," Pollard said. "We might as well get it out in the open."

Thibodeaux paused for a moment, considering his reply. He give his pipe a preemptory puff, then said, "I certainly agree with Alford that it is an outrage that somebody has stolen his exhibit. I do hope that it is returned. Alford, in my opinion, is to be commended for his ingenuity. It is not everybody who can crap in pint jars and charge people admission to view it."

Pollard started to speak. "I—"

But Thibodeaux, locked into a cold fury, was not yet finished. "The source of this capitalist inspiration is clearly no mystery. As near as can be deduced by anybody who has known him for any length of time, the excitable gentleman only has two moving parts: his mouth and his asshole, and they both work the same." Thibodeaux peered at the bowl of his pipe and sat down. He dug a tool from his pocket, and started cleaning his pipe.

I thought it was a splendid reply, blood imaginatively and boldly drawn.

Pollard, livid with self-righteous fury and the warming glow of martyrdom, closed his mouth. Thibodeaux had shown he bit back.

Pollard, looking right, addressed Whitcomb. "And you? What about you?"

Whitcomb leaned toward his microphone. "I agree with Emile Thibodeaux, both on the nature of Mr. Pollard's anatomy and on his exemplary showmanship. In addition, let me say I would dearly love for him to have fulfilled his dream of a scientific examination of the entire contents of his exhibit. I hope the police arrest Elford's murderer forthwith."

Bondurant rose to leave the stage. No more scatalogical nonsense for him. He was an internationally recognized scholar of the British Museum, not a member of the faculty of Boise State. There were limits to dealing with Bigfoot crazies. He wanted nothing more to do with public jousting.

Popoleyev again looked at Willie and me, seeking our help.

We both motioned with our hands for her, yes, yes, to follow Bondurant, get the hell off the stage, which she did.

McGwyre, watching Bondurant and Popoleyev depart, licked her lips. She glanced at David Addison.

Addison was obviously dismayed at the untoward turn of events. On the other hand, his good-natured and coltish young wife seemed to thoroughly enjoy the debacle. Exuberantly, she whistled and hooted along with everybody else.

Laughing, she turned to the unamused Addison. It didn't take much of a lip reader to get what she said: "Only two moving parts. Did you hear that? Wasn't that good?" *Ha, ha, ha.*

Addison was doing his best to be hip and carefree, but he was congenitally unable to loosen up—and probably ill at ease without a necktie. He nodded yes, he had heard.

Pollard said, "I will go up on that mountain tomorrow and find Sasquatch in the name of Elford Pollard and his sweet widow, Judy. I will not fail in this. Hear it now, I swear on Elford's grave."

Donna McGwyre cleared her throat. She checked her notes as

though help was to be found there. But this was not a gathering of Rotarians, so she exercised good sense; she adjourned the meeting, saying, "Our participants should remember we have a meeting at nine o'clock tomorrow morning, followed by a press conference, after which we'll drive partway up the mountain to launch our search."

Chapter Twelve

Contents of
Bigfoot Bangers

Because of more cop business, Alford Pollard couldn't make his afternoon appointment with Sonja Popoleyev. But Emile Thibodeaux and Roger Whitcomb—both no doubt wanting to ensure her neutrality in the politics of Sasquatch—took a break from team meetings to spend a few minutes with her.

Willy and I went with her, first to Thibodeaux's room. After shaking our hands, Thibodeaux introduced us to his energetic wife, Sally, a plump, likable woman.

Sally Thibodeaux served us coffee and did most of the talking. It was apparently Sally's duty to explain her unusual husband to reporters and visitors, so that he wouldn't have to talk about himself. She seemed not to mind this small chore. She was proud of him.

"Been married for thirty-eight years now," Thibodeaux said, by way of simultaneously explaining their relationship and launching her monologue. He cleaned and smoked his pipe while his wife held forth.

Sally said, "Thirty-three years of that on the trail of Sasquatch."

"Had to have something to do after I got used to the sex," Thibodeaux said.

Sally pretended to give him a reproving look "Do you want to know about my husband, Dr. Popoleyev? Well, I'll tell you the truth; he's a good and faithful man. But he's just a little crazy, mind. Nobody who knows him ever suggested otherwise. This is an old-fashioned quest, Dr. Popoleyev. My husband won't give up. Ever. He's like Sherlock Holmes. I guess you could say Sasquatch is his Moriarty.

"By the way, Emile's far more demanding of high standards than most pedigreed scientists. I won't tell you what Emile calls them." She beamed at her husband. "And then there's that man out there with his accent, from the British Museum, no less, telling those poor, gullible . . ."

Thibodeaux gave her a mild look.

She hardly dropped a beat. "Believe me, it's a fact that whenever there is a reported sighting of a Bigfoot, well, Emile and I drop everything. Off we go. Emile is there asking the hardest of hard questions. A lot of people don't like hard questions asked about Sasquatch. You know, really, it's kind of pathetic in a way. Whitman and the Pollard brothers are just plain fools. Emile won't say it, but I can."

Thibodeaux puffed on his pipe. "Just brother Alford now, Sally."

"It's difficult to imagine anybody mourning the loss of Elford, not that Alford's any better."

"Sally!"

"Emile is open-minded on the question of Sasquatch. He was open-minded thirty-five years ago when he was convinced Bigfoot was out there, and he still is. He's one of the few passionate Bigfoot believers ever to publicly change his mind. You tell 'em, hon."

Thibodeaux said, "It's true. I grew up in Cle Elum, and when I was a kid I heard hundreds of stories. Some of 'em were intended to scare the pants off me. Others made you sit up and pay attention."

"He heard 'em from people all up and down the Cascades."

Thibodeaux said, "These weren't liars, Dr. Popoleyev. They were honest people who had seen something, or thought they had."

Sally Thibodeaux said, "Emile believes what Bondurant calls 'consensus opinion' begins to work on your mind. If you interview enough apparently honest, allegedly disinterested witnesses describing the same beast, you begin to wonder."

He looked at me. "You're a detective, Mr. Denson. We're working from induction here, from the reports. The Pollards of the world accept these reports as 'facts' and proceed to the conclusion that Sasquatch exists."

Mrs. Thibodeaux said, "So did Emile for years. If you had only heard half the stories he has."

Thibodeaux bit his lip and shook his head. "You look them straight in the eye, and you just know they're not lying. Why then . . . I'm very sorry if I disappoint you, Dr. Popoleyev."

Popoleyev said, "Oh, no, not at all, Mr. Thibodeaux. Is there anything more to the footprints of the Bossberg clubfoot that might interest us?"

"To this day I have no explanation for those footprints. They were real. They were. When I was following that trail I knew I was following Sasquatch. That's why I recommended them to Inskeep for your project." Thibodeaux shook his head. "Those footprints kept me a believer for twenty years. Tell me, Dr. Popoleyev, if Sasquatch doesn't exist, what, in your opinion, is the strongest explanation of the extraordinary number of eyewitness reports that jibe in key details?"

"You're asking what have the witnesses seen, if not Sasquatch?"

"Surely you must have thought about it. At a minimum, in order to strengthen your own case."

"The argument that I find most attractive flies under several flags. I admit I sometimes find it as convincing as Dr. Porchnev's."

"If you don't mind, let's hear it, please."

"Okay, then, for the sake of argument, I'll assert that, yes, Sasquatch exists, but Mr. Denson here is in no danger of losing his Volkswagen. Consider your reaction to the sudden appearance of a snake, Mr. Thibodeaux. You're out for a walk. A snake races by your foot. What do you do?"

"I jump."

"Me too. Children from all cultures jump when they see a snake. They don't have to be taught to fear snakes. It's instinctive. This fear is not limited to a specific kind of snake. It is generalized: 'snake' or 'things snakelike.' All snakes. Snakes may be described as being long and skinny. They slither, and their tongues are quick."

"And some of them are poisonous."

"Yes, they are. We most likely fear snakes now because our ancestors got hurt by snakes. Being afraid of snakes helped our species to survive. It's a logical and reasonable fear. It has a function: to preserve our health.

"All animals have a limited form of intelligence that enables them to stay in business as a species. At a minimum, this includes what they need to know to eat, to successfully reproduce, and to avoid danger.

"A duck sees a plummeting hawk and flies. A gazelle sees a crouching cheetah and runs. We see a slithering snake and jump back. Literature is filled with stories of snakes, dragons, and their many slithering, quick-tongued brothers and sisters. There are far more monsters of the mind than just snakes, rats, and bugs. Judging from the repeated appearance of large, hairy monsters in myths all over the world, Sasquatch may be one of them.

"There are hundreds of thousands or even millions of people prowling around in the Cascade Mountains each year. Am I right, Mr. Thibodeaux?"

"Yes, you are."

"There's no calculating how many of those campers and hikers will see a sudden, dark movement at dusk. Or the brief silhouette of a large man in the dark. Or they will glimpse a fleeing bear. Perhaps the wonder is that not more people have reported seeing one of these shaggy beasts of the subconscious."

Thibodeaux said, "You may be right there, Dr. Popoleyev."

"When those eyewitnesses look you in the eye, Mr. Thibodeaux, they're not lying. They're telling the truth. They *did* see Sasquatch. We all possess the same beast, lurking, in varying degrees of repression, in our shared imagination. It stands to reason that under the right circumstances some of us will think we actually saw him."

Thibodeaux said, "More logically put than the usual Jungian stuff. Too much pot there, sounds like. There has to be something that can rationally account for all those earnest people saying they saw the same damn thing."

"If Sasquatch doesn't exist, I think that's the most likely explanation."

I said, "Anything more you want to add about Alford Pollard?"

Thibodeaux puffed his pipe.

Sally Thibodeaux said, "Emile won't say what he thinks about the Pollards, but I will. Writing those odious, sleazy articles. And that so-called Sasquatchiana exhibit?" She rolled her eyes in total disgust. "Wasn't that a scene this morning? Wasn't it? That little twit. Pompous, self-righteous little windbag."

Thibodeaux smiled. "I think they get the point, Sally." To us, he said, "The mere mention of Alford Pollard makes Sally burn. He once called me an idiot in the *National Gleaner*."

"No, Emile. *Obvious* idiot. He called you an obvious idiot. And he hasn't apologized yet. I don't care what happened to his brother or his stupid RV."

Thibodeaux obviously liked it that his wife defended him so passionately. "Obvious idiot wasn't all he called me in that piece."

"Asinine. He called you asinine. Just because you dared to question the existence of Sasquatch. Hey, it's a free country."

"Sally's never forgotten. Of course, she's Irish. She can't help herself. Got a little Maureen O'Hara in her, don't you think?"

Sally Thibodeaux had heard it before, but she was still flattered. She said, "Oh, you!"

Cascade Run's Cascadia Bar was a hubbub of activity, judging from the people coming and going. Cascade I understood. But "Cascadia"? What the hell did that mean? Beside the front door, a bulletin board had photographs of the resort's many "prestigious mountain chalets" that remained for sale.

Why did it not occur to people that if they had to be told something was "prestigious" then it wasn't?

The prices of these chalets, with their "cathedral ceilings" and "natural-grained" cedar beams looked right for physicians, Californians, or drug dealers, but I wondered how many ordinary Oregonians and Washingtonians had that kind of money.

The glass-enclosed watering hole had an indoor swimming pool beyond one wall and an idyllic-looking pond beyond another. The swimming pool had been commandeered by squealing children with inner tubes. The pond had lily pads around the edges. A couple of carefree mallards enjoyed the open water in the middle. Snub-nosed dinghies could be rented from a quaint dock at one end.

This division of pool and pond outside the Cascadia resulted in a natural partition of guests on the inside. On one side, parents and grandparents drank coffee and watched kids and grandkids splashing in the pool. On the other, guests drank white wine or cocktails while they contemplated ducks and lily pads.

Roger Whitcomb, as one of the Sasquatch team leaders, had scored a tranquil table overlooking the pond.

He seemed preoccupied with the ducks and lily pads when we arrived, but I think he was studying the reflection of his face in the window. He had a good smile, great teeth.

With hardly any concern at having been discovered admiring himself—or perhaps he thought nobody saw—he welcomed us to his table. He eyed his image out of the corner of his eyes, and, exuding confidence, waved for a waitress at the same time.

A decal on the corner of the window said the pond contained crappie and bluegill, and children under fifteen could rent fishing poles and buy worms from the swimming pool office.

A card on the table told us about Cascadia's Bigfoot Banger, a deal at $3.95. A block of elegant script said: "This exquisite drink, invented by Cascadia's head bartender, most recently of the cruise ship HMW *Norway*, contains three prestigious Jamaican dark rums— Myers's, Appleton, and Overton—plus a touch of Puerto Rico's internationally renowned Bacardi light. If you want to see Sasquatch, you can climb a mountain or bang back one of these."

"Well, shall we order drinks?" he said. "Have what you want, my sponsors are paying. They've gotta be good for something." He liked the sound of the word "sponsors." He was pleased with himself.

When the waitress came, I said, "I want one of your Bigfoot Bangers. Mr. Whitman's sponsors are springing."

Eyeing me, Willie said, "Me too." As partners in the private investigation business, Willie and I had played a form of intellectual basketball for years; we knew how to pick-and-roll and give-and-go. On a first meeting, I usually hung back, and let other people reveal their drink orders, thus themselves, first. But this time I had spoken right up and ordered a ridiculous Bigfoot Banger. Yuch!

In short, I had stolen the ball and driven straight to the hoop. My partner knew there was a reason. I had seen something he hadn't as yet.

Whitcomb gave us a look. If I hadn't spoken up, he would have ordered the most expensive Scotch in the house. Rich and with-it men drank overpriced Scotch. Ordering the house special was gauche. And a sweet rum concoction was stupid all the way. Obvious low prole.

Now, eyeing Popoleyev, Whitcomb hesitated . . .

Popoleyev said, "Four kinds of rum. That sounds wonderful! It's always vodka, vodka, vodka in Russia. A flavor and a color for every occasion."

"What the hell," said the gallant Whitcomb, checking out the pond. "Make it four Bigfoot Bangers."

Judging from the activity behind the bar, Cascadia was moving a lot of Bangers. Two full-time Banger makers buzzed ice cubes in a frenzy, pouring long dollops of rum and colorful syrups into the mixers.

When the waitress came, I said, "You people must be moving an awful lot of rum today."

She said, "Boy, are we ever. We've got cases of the stuff stacked up in the kitchen. You should see it."

After we'd introduced ourselves and settled in with our Bangers, Whitcomb said, "I do hope you're not running into any difficulty putting your team together, Dr. Popoleyev. So much to do and so little time."

"Tell you the truth, I haven't done much of anything. Mr. Prettybird and Mr. Denson have been putting my team together."

Willie said, "The Minthorns have been collecting gear for years. They've got everything we need and then some."

"Am I right in my understanding that there are only five of you? There's a lot of mountain up there." He gestured to Mount St. Helens with his elegant chin.

"I can only put myself in Willie's hands and hope for the best. I must say, it seems like he has everything we could possibly need. And how about your own team?"

"There are twelve of us. Eight of us are members of the Explorers Club, and we're all veteran climbers. We're fit, well equipped, and determined." Whitcomb obviously thought Popoleyev was small potatoes as a competitor in the hunt for Sasquatch, but she was fuckable in the extreme. So, concentrating on his smile—which he occasionally double-checked in the window—Whitcomb hung on her every word. So interested, he was! So fascinated by her! I bet if someone gave him a test on what she'd said, he wouldn't be able to answer one question.

In his turn—his mind off his reflection—he allowed as how his team would be shooting a network television documentary of their participation. He had purchased blown-up satellite photographs of the area to help his team in their search.

As they talked, I noticed a fancy, glass-enclosed gymnasium and exercise room beyond the fishing pond that was loaded with all manner of high-tech machines. The phrase "no pain, no gain" must apply to the wallet as well as the abdominals. I wondered if an expensive facility like that could possibly be making money with so many overpriced "chalets" still on the market.

Suddenly, for the first time since we had ordered our drinks, Whitcomb acknowledged my presence. He said, "Say, you're the guy who challenged Addison to pay the reward if fraud was proved, aren't you?"

"That was me," I said.

"You know, I'm going to have a good time with that Volkswagen minibus of yours. That's what you bet, wasn't it? Your Volkswagen?"

"I'll sign it over."

"You know something, Mr. . . . ." He'd forgotten my name.

"John Denson."

"You know something, John, we may not find Sasquatch this time out, but I know he's out there, because I saw him myself two years ago on an Explorers Club trek into Western Canada. It was at dusk, and I saw him on the trail ahead of me. I was not drunk or on any kind of drug. I know I'm not a neutral, and I didn't have time to get a camera on him, but there was no mistaking: I saw Sasquatch. I did."

"For how long?"

"Oh, four or five seconds. But that's longer than you think, count 'em out."

I counted out loud: "One thousand one. One thousand two. One thousand three. One thousand four. One thousand five." He was right; that was quite a while.

"That's a lot of Sasquatch. I saw him. He was there."

Chapter Thirteen

Fate of
Precious Babies

On the way out of Cascadia, Willie said, "So tell me, Chief. What was it with the Bigfoot Bangers?"

Popoleyev said, "Huh?"

Willie said, "The wine in that place is too damn good for my partner. If they don't have screwtop, he orders draft beer. He'd certainly never order some foo-foo concoction with four kinds of rum. You want to tell us now, Denson?"

"I'm thinking, I'm thinking," I said. "You can make foo-foo drinks just as good as those with cheapie rum you can buy in Hood River. Just send a truck over and load up. You ever think of that?" Hood River distilleries in Oregon made perfectly serviceable bar whiskey, vodka, gin, and rum. It wasn't like the Cascadia bartender was competing for a gold medal in Paris.

"I still think it was a splendid treat. All that rum!" She laughed heartily. "You know, Mr. Denson. Roger Whitcomb seemed so very intent on hearing everything I said, but do you know he wasn't listening to me? Didn't hear one word."

"Looked straight into your green eyes."

Popoleyev looked annoyed. "Did you notice that? Did you?"

We told the Cascade Run switchboard that Dr. Popoleyev wouldn't be taking calls or messages until morning. Then Willie and I and the Minthorns, forgoing the overpriced food in Cascade Run's St. Helens Restaurant, took Sonja Popoleyev for proletarian cheeseburgers in Wendy's Tavern in Cougar.

Wendy's, while not offering food that was high on the hog, promised honest grease at a price people could afford. And Wendy's was where the action was in Skamania County that night, what with Alford Pollard's intemperate outburst being featured on the television news. The suggestion was that if the exhibit was not real, why would anybody bother to steal it, thus encouraging the total abandonment of logic.

Sonja Popoleyev, munching on her oversized cheeseburger, said, "You Americans are incredible. Do you want to tell me what that scene was all about today? I know he was angry, but surely there was no need for Mr. Pollard to accuse his colleagues of stealing his exhibit. He came close to suggesting one of them had murdered his brother."

"Colleagues?" I was amused.

"Aren't we all? Isn't this supposed to be a joint search for Sasquatch?"

"You and Dr. Bondurant might be colleagues. The others are competing for Bigfoot money. In the United States, any time you get enough true believers grouped around a given controversy, there's money to be made. Thibodeaux writes magazine articles. Whitcomb shoots television documentaries. Pollard is the remaining king of the checkout-stand rags."

"Like the paper accusing me of wanting sex with Sasquatch."

"The *National Gleaner*. Right."

"You all gave a splendid demonstration of male competition today."

"Huh?"

"Blanche is attuned to demonstrations of male prowess, Mr. Denson. In a state of nature, she looked for brute strength or hunting skills. With the exception of a few body builders, modern males compete in other ways. It is a much more complicated tournament."

"Ahh, a little proximate creeps in after all."

"You agressively challenged Addison and forced him to accept your bet, Mr. Denson."

"The bastard ran over me without so much as a 'hello there.'"

Willie laughed. "Naw, she's right, Chief. He was playing the Big Man, and you deliberately knocked him down a peg."

"Demonstrating my prowess to whom in this case?"

Popoleyev, grinning, teasing me with her green eyes, and munching on her cheeseburger at the same time. "To me. To every Blanche in the room. It was elementary Stanley on your part!"

Willie and the Minthorns whooped with laughter and gave me a little applause.

Willie said, "Smooth work, Chief."

"By the way, Mr. Denson, what do you think actually did happen to Pollard's exhibit?"

"I think Thibodeaux and Whitcomb are probably right about him exhibiting his own manure. My bet is that he stashed his RV somewhere so his evidence wouldn't have to undergo examination."

"And what do you think, Willie?"

"I have to agree with Denson on that one, as much as it pains me."

Popoleyev, finished teasing me, picked up a french fry and started eating it. "These are really good." She stopped chewing as a huge, jovial black man stepped through the front door.

A bearded customer in a suspendered logger's getup saw him and grinned. "Aloysius Daroun! Give 'em!"

"You bet, partner." Daroun gave the logger a high five, and within seconds was surrounded by admirers.

Popoleyev, grinning, her eyes wide, said, "Who on earth is that?"

Willie laughed. "Aloysius Daroun, a four-time all-pro defensive end for the Seattle Seahawks."

"The football team."

"Correct," Willie said. "The Seahawks've never been very good, I'm afraid. Daroun's on a one-year suspension because his urine tested positive for cocaine a second time, and he didn't show up to have it checked when the season started this year."

"Six-ten and three hundred and fifteen pounds," I said.

"Amazing."

Bobby said, "That's what his opponents say."

Daroun, his deep laugh booming above the hubbub in the tavern, obviously enjoyed the attention of all the Seahawks fans in Wendy's. He took a huge drink of beer directly from a glass pitcher, *gulp, gulp, gulp,* wiping the foam from his mouth with the back of his arm. "Thought I'd come down here and show you folks what real big feet look like." *Har, har, har!*

He put an enormous Nike running shoe against the edge of the bar. "These feet are made for walking up the backs of fancy little farts like Dan Marino and Joe Montana. Standing back there posing like faggot actors. Precious babies. Peewees!"

Grinning malevolently, Daroun pretended to wring a quarterback's neck with his enormous right hand. He flipped his imaginary precious baby round and round like a hapless chicken.

His fans all laughed.

Popoleyev said, "Who are Dan Marino and Joe Montana?"

"Quarterbacks," Willie said. "The people who pass the football and make all the money. It's his job to tackle them."

"I see."

Daroun, turning his foot this way and that, said, "You ask John Elway what a big foot is all about." *Har, har, har!* "These feet are made for walkin'." *Har, har, har!*

"He could ski on those suckers," Minthorn said.

Popoleyev said, "John Elway? Is he a quarterback too?"

"Yes, he is. Handsome blond kid. Teeth like a beaver. Daroun ran over him and knocked him cold in a playoff game a couple of years ago. A real all-star hit. Gave Elway a concussion and led to a Seahawk win."

"A concussion?"

"Elway later said that's the hardest he'd ever been hit, and he's taken some real slams."

Daroun, lover of a good time, put his foot down and gestured for a refill. He leaned over the heads of companions and fans and handed the empty pitcher to the waitress.

"A man with feet like mine gets real, real thirsty. Need to water all them big brown taters." *Har, har, har!*

Chapter Fourteen

No Farther
than the Mirror

Bobby Minthorn said, "We're all going tepee creepin' tonight, right, Willie? Denson? After we finish tepee creepin' we will gather together and swoop down on the white man's camp and drive the blue-eyed devils back where they came from after we have our way with their women." He giggled.

Whitefeather said, "You'll sleep all the way back. Lucky one of us has got the brains to drink coffee."

Minthorn said, "We'll adopt Denson for the war party. Make him a blue-eyed savage. No blood-brother shit, though. Can't do that on account of AIDS."

I wondered if I had remembered to bring any aspirin. If I didn't take a megahit of aspirin when I got back to my room, I risked a megaheadache in a couple of hours.

Popoleyev looked pale, and, for a moment, concerned. She blinked. "I think it's probably better if we go. Tomorrow . . . tomorrow, we have to . . . ." She put her hand over her mouth.

Whitefeather popped out of her side of the booth. "Let me help you, Sonja."

Quick as crabs, the two of them scuttled off to the women's john.

When they got back, we adjourned to my bus for the drive over curving mountain highway to Cascade Run. The sober Whitefeather drove. Bobby took the passenger's seat, and immediately fell asleep.

Popoleyev paused for a moment, hand at her mouth. She took a deep breath and removed her hand. "I must talk. If I don't my head will spin . . ."

"Tell us about Stanley."

Popoleyev, trying to stop the vertigo, put her arms around Willie and me.

Whitefeather, watching us through the rearview mirror said, "You want me to drive slower? Would that help?"

"No, no. That won't help. I'll be okay. The request was for me to tell you about Stanley."

"Stanley's strategy," I said.

"Stanley's strategy is simple: he seeks to duplicate his genes as many times as possible. He will have sex whenever and with whomever he can to produce offspring in his image. He competes with other males to see who can do this most often. This urge to reproduce dominates his sexual imagination."

Whitefeather braked for a tight curve.

Seeking support, Popoleyev tightened her arms around our shoulders. "Blanche's strategy is the exact reverse of Stanley's, so much so that it's difficult for her to comprehend the logic of his behavior."

"You want to understand men?" Whitefeather said, slowing the bus for yet another curve. "Good luck, is all I gotta say! Mine claims he's a Umatilla born outside of Pendleton, but I think Jupiter or Mars is as good a guess as any."

Popoleyev said, "I once h-had, oh dear, had a boyfriend in St. Petersburg named D-Dimitri. Dumb Dimitri."

"Oh?" I said.

"He was too polite by half. Dumb Dimitri." Popoleyev giggled. "As a student, I became interested in sexual strategy. I thought males and females of all species were by nature complementary. I thought that. Came from reading all those romances, I guess." She giggled. "Really!" She giggled again.

Whitefeather said, "We're complementary all right. Look at this Stanley of mine. I drive while he sits there passed out. Hot damned tracker. Lucky he's got Earl to save his bacon."

"Tell us in what way Dimitri was too polite." I snuggled closer.

"Mr. Denson!"

Popoleyev looked at Willie, then me. "You want the rest of it?"

"I'm curious about Dimitri."

"In his lifetime, one Stanley may impregnate hundreds of Blanches. But each of these Blanches, in her lifetime, produces a limited number of eggs that can be made fertile, and can bear just a few offspring to maturity . . .

"And she needs help," Whitefeather called from the driver's seat.

"Blanche needs help raising those, right, Whitefeather. It behooves Blanche—that is, it promotes the fitness of her species—to be as picky as possible about whom she lets fertilize her eggs. This is her biological burden and responsibility. The key thing to remember here is that a rrraaa-bbit, say, or sq-uuiirrel, oh dear. . . ."

Popoleyev, suddenly pale, took a deep breath and held it.

"Concentrate," I said.

She exhaled and opened her eyes. "A rabbit or squirrel is out of the burrow or nest and on its own in dayzhs or weezks." She stopped, again looking distraught.

In a moment, she had regained her composure. "Female rabbits and squirrels can have offspring until they die. Because they're never barren, they're sexually attractive for life." Popoleyev slumped in disappointment.

"Well?"

Popoleyev sighed. "By the time Blanche got crafty enough to ignore estrus, her offspring had such huge cerebrums it took forever to get them out of the nest."

"This is the evolutionary catch you spoke of on the way up, yesterday."

"It's to weep, it truly is. Blanche's babies are helpless for several years. Since it takes twenty years for her offspring to grow up, it's not functional for her to be fertile after middle age. If she bore a child when she was fifty, she wouldn't live long enough to rear it to maturity.

"At first, I thought there could be a way around this problem. I tried every theory you can imagine, but the computer kept saying, 'No, no, no, that's impossible; evolution sees to the needs of species, not individuals.' We evolved to ensure the survival of our species, not to be happy. Fitness, fitness, fitness. That is always the goal. When you are able to understand and accept that truth, both Blanche and Stanley are easier to understand."

"Stanley by necessity being a form of monster."

"In my opinion. But objectively, he's no different than other male primates. Stanley's frustration and roaming eye are entirely logical. In a state of nature, competition among sex-driven Stanleys contributed to the fitness of the species."

"Satisfaction would result in stagnation."

"Not just stagnation. *Hic! Hic!* Oh, dear. I just hate the hiccups."

Whitefeather slowed for a curve. "If not just stagnation, why?"

"Why? Extinction of the species. *Hic!* When you get right down to it, both biological and intellectual creativity are based on disatisfaction."

I said, "We search for a monster, and we need only look in the mirror. He is us."

Popoleyev said, "Look no further, Mr. Denson."

Whitefeather downshifted the VW, slowing for the Cascade Run parking lot.

I said, "I bet Stanley is responsible for the mystery we're in."

"Responsible for what mystery?"

"The mystery of Elford Pollard's murder. The mystery of why we're going to hike up to timberline on St. Helens tomorrow."

Popoleyev looked amused. "Why, I'm surprised at you, Mr. Denson! *Hic!* I wouldn't think you'd have to be much of a detective to figure that one out. Owing to his competitive and acquisitive nature, Stanley commits most of the crimes and does most of the violence."

At Cascade Run, the guard turned down his radio long enough to let us through, and Whitefeather parked the bus in our assigned slot. We crawled out into the cold mountain air, our breath coming in frosty puffs.

Whitefeather and Popoleyev went first, Whitefeather guiding the disheveled and giggling Popoleyev, who listed from side to side like a rudderless boat. Willie and I followed, guiding the benumbed and mumbling Bobby Minthorn.

Without turning around, Popoleyev said, "It took him forever to figure out that women weren't born wearing a bra. It was possible for him to remove it. *Hic!*"

"Who was that?"

"Dumb Dimitri. *Hic!*"

"I see."

"And when he finally did make his move, he didn't know how the snap worked. *Hic!* You'd have thought it was a bank vault." Popoleyev pitched sideways, but was saved by Whitefeather, who grabbed her by the collar.

"There's nothing more complicated than a bra snap when you're in a hurry."

"He fumbled and struggled until finally I had to unfasten it for him. *Hic!* Mr. Denson, do you think we women really want a slope-chested, androgynous househusband who yells 'How high?' when we say 'Jump'?" Popoleyev giggled. *"Hic!"*

"Dumb Dmitri," I said.

Following Whitefeather and Popoleyev, Willie and I wrestled Bobby through the aluminum-framed glass door. We were well down the hallway, halfway to our rooms, when we all heard it:

Two sounds somewhere between a snap and a crack that smacked of a .22. It could have been fireworks, but most likely a .22.

"Who's shootin'?" Bobby mumbled.

I checked my watch. It was 12:30 A.M. I walked back to the parking lot. It was full of cars, but I didn't see any people.

In the distance, on the guard's radio, the old hawg's delight, Arkansas Donny Mack, was singing the tune that was currently number one on the country and western charts.

> *I ripp'd off my shee-heets.*
> *Ain't cleaned 'em since May*
> *Yes, Dear God, I'm confessin'*
> *Yes, confessin'*

I need you, Cory
This ain't no story

I went back inside. Had the shot been somewhere inside the building? No, it had not. It had come from the parking lot. Maybe it was a drunk shooting the moon. I went to bed.

Chapter Fifteen

He Rattles
Denson's Chain

I awoke to a knocking at my door. No, not a knocking, more like a pounding.

I leaned over and grabbed my cheapie wristwatch from the nightstand. Seven A.M. I hadn't asked for any seven-o'clock wakeup, besides which they should use the phone. No need for banging on somebody's door.

I ran my tongue over my teeth and shook my head, slipped on a pair of shorts and opened the door a crack, leaving the safety chain in place.

Sheriff Bert T. Starkey.

What the . . . ?

"Open the door, Denson." Starkey pushed the door against the safety chain, which I found annoying, him being a uniformed officer and me standing there in my boxer shorts. There were no Blanches to impress, but I still felt competitive as hell.

"The fuck, you say. This isn't China, pal. Just who the hell do you think you are?" If Starkey hadn't pushed against the chain, I might have let him in. As it was, not letting him in was a point of honor to anybody who appreciated the Bill of Rights.

"Just open the door, Denson." He pushed the door against the chain again. His balls were in an uproar too.

"I gotta take a leak." I turned and went to the john, leaving the frustrated Starkey to cool his heels in the hallway. I took my time as a form of editorial comment. I walked leisurely back to the door. Starkey was still there, looking sore as hell. I scratched my testicles, looking unconcerned. "You want to tell me what this is all about?"

"Put some pants on and open the door, and I'll tell you."

"I don't think so."

"Jesus H. Christ!" he said wearily.

"No, just a law-abiding citizen. This room, sir, is my castle, however temporarily." I wasn't about to volunteer anything to anybody who rattled my night chain.

"Open it." His jaw tightened.

"You either give me a proper warrant signed by a judge or tell me why."

"Or you'll do what?" He tried clenched teeth.

"Shut the door in your face and take a shower and get ready to have breakfast. We're due in a meeting at ten o'clock. We've got a Bigfoot search to plan. Say, you're not rousting me at this hour of the morning to accuse me of stealing that fool's manure, are you?"

He looked disgusted.

"Or maybe you want to explain this to the Boog?"

He smirked. "Boogie Dewlapp?"

"Hey, don't laugh at the Booger Man. People who live in the sticks got a right to have a lawyer too. Even private detectives are entitled to legal counsel."

Starkey sighed. Defeat. "Somebody murdered Alford Pollard this morning. I've got two dead Pollards on my hands. Until I talk to all the Bigfoot searchers, none of you will be going anywhere, and that's a fact. Now, do you want to open the goddam door?"

He had yielded on the point that counted, and I hadn't murdered anybody. I unlatched the chain. "Sure, why not?" I let him inside and pulled on a pair of jeans. "Sit down, Sheriff. Make yourself at home."

"I'll only be a few minutes. Two of them. I've got two dead Pollards."

"There's a Gideon Bible in the nightstand. They say everything's in the Bible. So if you want to bone up."

My room had two upholstered chairs, but Starkey wasn't about to use one. He stood, looking around the room.

I hopped up on my bed and sat squat-legged. "Somebody actually bothered to murder that obnoxious little geek?"

"That's what I said. You want to tell me what you did last night?"

"Willie and I took Dr. Popoleyev for cheeseburgers and draft beer at Wendy's Tavern in Cougar. Aloysius Daroun showed up to entertain everybody with a little hyperbole. What happened to Pollard?"

"Some people who closed the bar here found his body in the parking lot at half past one. Somebody had shot him in the face with a twenty-two."

"Close range?"

"Looks that way. We haven't had a chance to check for powder burns yet."

"Somebody who knew him, then?"

"That'd stand to reason. How much did you drink in Wendy's?"

"Everybody except Whitefeather got a bit sloshed, and she drove us all back at about midnight, something like that. No DWI for us, thank you."

"The Russian lady get sloshed too?"

"Where the Russian lady's from, they knock their vodka back cold and neat. Antifreeze for Siberian winters and so they can suffer the bureaucrats."

"How loaded was she?"

"Loaded enough to sing us some Russian drinking songs. Not loaded enough to shoot Alford Pollard in the face with a twenty-two, besides which she has no conceivable motive, and you know it."

"After which you did what?"

"Took some aspirin and went to bed. You want to take a look around, go ahead."

"If I don't have to wait for Boogie or Olden Dewlapp to hold your hand."

"Hey, be my guest, Sheriff. One of the advantages of not carrying a weapon is that I'm never tempted to use one."

"But you don't mind drilling somebody with an arrow, eh, Denson."

He had me there. I had once killed a man on a bridge over the Columbia—at the time still technically in Skamania County.

He said, "The way I hear it, you're lucky David Addison didn't have a weapon yesterday morning."

I watched as Starkey checked the bathroom, then turned his attention to the closet. His search was indifferent because he knew perfectly well I wasn't the kind of guy to kill a moron like Alford Pollard. But he had made a big show and had to carry through with it.

I said, "Maybe Bigfoot did it. I bet he's a tool user. He could learn how to shoot a pistol, couldn't he? Maybe he got tired of people charging admission to view his excrement and decided to put an end to it once and for all."

Starkey gave me a I'd-just-love-to-break-your-neck look. He opened the top drawer of the bureau and began jabbing his hand around in my sox and underwear. "This is how I earn my so-called living, digging around in other men's underwear."

I said, "The juicy socks are tied to the dirty shorts."

"God!"

"Just trying to help."

"You know, Denson, everybody is jumping up and down for me to let the Sasquatch search continue on schedule. 'How can you stop us, Sheriff?' 'How can you prevent us from going?' Whitcomb even has a lawyer waiting on his leash. But we both know who they're gonna blame if one of you damn fools murders somebody up on the mountain, don't you?" Starkey was on a roll. " 'Why didn't you stop them, Sheriff?' 'Why didn't you let them go?' 'What were you thinking of? Awful Sheriff Starkey!' 'Guilty Sheriff Starkey!' Yeah, yeah, yeah! Well, hell!" Starkey banged the bureau drawer shut to punctuate his anger. "Now just what am I supposed to do? What would you do, Sam Spade?"

It was true, there were lots of accidental ways people could die on St. Helens without anybody knowing the difference. It was also true that Starkey would be blamed if anything went wrong.

Starkey's lips tightened. "Sasquatch hunters, my behind! It's more like dealing with a bunch of kids been eating too damn many Twinkies."

"We heard two shots after we got back from Cougar. Willie and Bobby both say it was a twenty-two. It was twelve-thirty A.M., and we had just stepped into the foyer. Any time I hear shooting that late at night, I try to remember details. I took a look in the parking lot, but didn't see anything. The guard was listening to Donny Mack on the radio. I took a look around the halls too. All quiet, all empty."

Starkey took out a pad, and made a note with a ballpoint pen. "Why, thank you, Denson. I appreciate it. I really do. Half past midnight. Two shots. Think it was a twenty-two. Donny Mack on the radio."

"It was the song with the line in it about the guy who's tired of dirty sheets and wants his wife back. You know the song."

He regarded me with a suspicious eye.

"I know it sometimes helps to pinpoint things. Details. Details."

"Is that all?"

"All that I can think of."

Starkey put his pad and pen away. "I wish to hell you and your redskin pal would find some county to hang out in other than mine." He stalked out of the room, slamming the door in anger and disgust.

I got out my matchbox tape recorder and taped the details of Starkey's visit, as well as I could remember them. I used the recorder to obtain statements for the use of my clients and took it everywhere. In this case—with two people murdered—it behooved me to make perfectly clear both Starkey's questions and my answers.

Chapter Sixteen

He and Jack at the Forum

I was in the shower, enjoying hot water beating on the back of my neck, thinking about the murdered Pollard brothers and Sheriff Starkey, when the phone began to ring.

It's impossible for me to blow off a ringing phone, so I trailed water across Cascade Run's fancy tiled bathroom and over the bedroom carpet and grabbed the receiver.

It was Sonja Popoleyev, sounding distraught. "I think I need some help, Mr. Denson. I . . ." She didn't finish the sentence. Her voice didn't sound like the self-assured Dr. Popoleyev that I had come to know.

"What's the matter?" If Starkey had spooked her with his big-deal swagger . . .

"It's just that I haven't had any experience with something like this. I'm a guest in your country, Mr. Denson. I want to be polite, but I don't know what to say. They're extremely pushy. I finally told the operator to put them all on hold until I talked to you and Willie."

"I'm just finishing my shower. First tell me who the *they* is?"

"Well, the first was a man named Charles Banyon, who said he was with that awful paper, the *National Gleaner,* offering me twenty-five hundred dollars for a 'world exclusive' for my story, whatever that means. I politely told him no thanks, but he wouldn't give up. I said I was very busy; I was expected in a meeting to help plan the Sasquatch search."

"Good for you."

"But he wouldn't take no for an answer. I told him I had seen the *Gleaner,* and I didn't like it. He said fair enough, would I take five hundred dollars for a book 'option'? He said he could give me up to twenty-five hundred for an 'option' for a television movie. I told him I no idea what an option was."

"Good for you."

"He said I was 'hot property' and it would be stupid for me not to work the best deal possible. This was America, not Russia."

"I see."

"He said a television movie is as good as a done deal. He says he and Jack Nicholson watch the Los Angeles Lakers together at the Forum. What or who the Lakers or the Forum are, I couldn't tell you. Finally, he said his agent is Terry Mann in Beverly Hills, who handles Sylvester Stallone and Tom Cruise."

"Dr. Popoleyev, did I tell you Willie Prettybird's half-brother is the chief of the Comanche nation and a good friend of Marlon Brando's? The three of us fly down to Marlon's island in Polynesia every January to go skin diving and horse around."

"You do?"

"He mumbles 'I coulda been somethin', I coulda been champion,' for our benefit and tells us how it was to film that car ride with Rod Steiger. He does his Don Corleone bit, too, and shouts 'Stella! Stella!' "

"He does? Mr. Denson!"

"Heavens, no. Willie claims his relatives are all poachers, and the closest I've ever been to Marlon Brando is a videotape. A dork hustling cheapie options isn't watching the Lakers with Jack Nicholson, you can make book on that. The Lakers are a basketball team, by the way. The Forum is where they play ball."

"I thought so, but I wasn't sure. Dodgers are baseball. Rams are football. Anyway, I let him give me his number and hung up. The second was one John Ordover, if I heard it correctly. Mr. Ordover says he is a sales representative . . ."

"Salesman."

". . . salesman for McDougal, Inc., which sells packages of freeze-dried food for hikers and mountain climbers. He said McDougal wants to pay us a promotional fee for using their Tenzig Norgay Gourmet Meals that are prepared by San Francisco chefs. 'Conceived' was the word he used."

"I bet."

"Then he named several Mount Everest climbers and Antarctica explorers who had eaten this food on their adventures. Can they do that, Mr. Denson? Name a freeze-dried food after poor Tenzig Norgay? He's dead! My word! Ordover, or whatever his name is, said Roger Whitcomb and Emile Thibodeaux are being paid promotional fees by Budweiser beer, and Bausch and Lomb binoculars, and by firms selling hiking books and camping gear."

"What happened when you told him we were eating Willie Prettybird's dried and salted grub?"

"He laughed at me. Moose jerky? He said I was endangering my health, at which point I hung up. Mr. Denson, I didn't come here to make money or go to Hollywood. I came to ensure that if a Sasquatch is found, he is left alone so that we may study him properly."

"And to see if he is a match for Fred and Wilma."

"Well, that too."

"Which is good as far as it goes. But Fred and Wilma are intended to prove the validity of Stanley and Blanche, are they not?"

"The validity of our whole system—including Stanley and Blanche, yes."

Hmmmmmm. That presented us with some problems. I said, "When you tell them about Fred and Wilma, you're doomed."

"Doomed? How is that, Mr. Denson?"

"They're like a fuse to a cultural bomb. The reporters won't give up until they've got everything out of you. Questions about Fred and Wilma will lead to questions about Stanley and Blanche. And when they learn the practical consequences of Blanche's having to bear and bring to maturity these complicated cerebrums of ours, why, then, I just don't know . . ."

"Did the operator tell you how many people were on hold?"

"Yes, she did. Twenty-seven. Cascade Run is designed to handle retreats and conventions, Mr. Denson. The switchboard is computer-operated. She said most of the calls were from reporters who have already checked in to Cascade Run. She said Mr. Thibodeaux has a newspaperman friend helping him. A public relations firm is fielding Mr. Whitcomb's calls. What do I do? We're scheduled for a meeting at nine."

"You shouldn't talk about Fred and Wilma if you can help it. Tell them that if Dr. Porchnev's *troglodytidae* are at last found, and his beliefs and reputation vindicated, a Russian scientist ought to be present. It's a matter of honor. You Russians have gone through a lot in the last several years, but you still have your pride."

"None of that is lying, Mr. Denson. It's all true."

"The word 'lie' does not cross our lips. You give them part of the truth. The fat, so to speak. You keep the lean for yourself. You tell them about Porchnev and say the species should be allowed to remain undisturbed in its natural state."

"I'll do my best, Mr. Denson."

"Give me time to get dressed, and we'll talk it over. Maybe somebody will want to draft you as a Presidential candidate."

"Mr. Denson!"

"I was just teasing. But it is true that if you want, you'll very likely be able to choose from any number of offers for *Death on the Bigfoot Trail* or whatever the Hollywood high rollers want to call the television movie. The murdered Pollard brothers just about guarantee that."

"I'm a scientist."

"I know you are. But you're also a featured performer in this stretch of the parade."

She sighed.

"After the press conference, you should give public television a few extra minutes if you can. They have more viewers who are interested in science rather than freaks."

"I can just pick and choose from among them? Is that how it works?"

"Be polite to them all, but some of them count more than others.

They know that. All you have to do is be yourself. It's when you try to fake it that you get into trouble."

It was clear from the calls to Popoleyev that there was no shortage of ways for people to earn money off the search for Sasquatch. The more ways to make money—or ways to lose money, in the case of scholars who had careers resting on wrongheaded theories—the more motives for murder.

It being impossible to overestimate the lengths to which greed could propel a determined Stanley, it stood to reason that the more motives for murder, the more dangerous the company of murder suspects.

I dressed quickly and headed down the hall for Sonja Popoleyev's room.

Chapter Seventeen

The Independent Captain

We assembled in the Cascade Run auditorium at nine o'clock, team members only, so that there were no more than forty people present, including the support people who would remain at our base in the resort.

Whitcomb's eleven climbers sported large Budweiser patches on the backs of their dark green jackets. These were real men, with splendid moustaches and grizzlied, Eric the Red beards. Thibodeaux's nine colleagues—all from the famous Mazama mountain-climbing club—looked only a little embarrassed at the clutter of colorful sponsor's badges sewn on their jackets and trousers. The chief difference between the two groups of climbers was that Whitcomb's climbers were apparently wearing brand-new togs, while Thibodeaux's people wore well-used gear.

Donna McGwyre began the meeting by briefing us on not one, but two new concerns to add to the confusion and concern attending the mystery of the murders of Elford and Alford Pollard.

McGwyre's first announcement—no doubt a fact overlooked by the initial planners—was that five days remained in the Washington State deer season. She said there was nothing the state's Fish and Game Commission could do to keep hunters out of the area, but "their people in the field say the whitetail population is unusually low on the hillsides for this time of the year. Deer ordinarily close to timberline are down in the meadows, a fact that's been written about in the sports pages, so that's where the hunters will be."

Whitcomb said dryly, "Of course, there's always that ten percent who don't get the word."

Thibodeaux puffed thoughtfully on his pipe. "You've got a point there. A ten percenter carrying a high-powered rifle."

We laughed nervously. *Ha, ha, ha.* Two dead Pollards and he was talking about a ten percenter carrying a high-powered rifle? *Ha, ha, ha.*

McGwyre rolled in a screen, upon which she projected the second oopsie, allowing us to hide our dismay in the dim light.

She said, "First, the expected weather pattern as it is for this time of year." She punched a clicker.

She projected a satellite photograph of the Pacific Northwest, Western Canada, and Alaska—with the edge of the subzero Siberian air mass lurking on the left, an obsessive, if lethargic beast, ready to rumble in and freeze our behinds.

McGwyre said, "Siberian cold fronts usually don't arrive until early December. But this year—for reasons upon which no two Weather Service computers can agree—an impressive bank of frigid Siberian air started our way late yesterday."

I liked a nice snug bed at night. Screw the cold.

She clicked up a second photograph, this one of the front over the middle of the Pacific. "You see it here. The Weather Service expected the cold air to pass north of Washington State and across British Columbia, but it suddenly turned south."

She clicked a third time, and oof, Howdy Doody!, there it was, covering Vancouver Island and crossing Puget Sound.

Another click. "At the same time, out over the Pacific fifteen hundred miles west of California, you see it here, we've got a second front containing moist air pushing to the northeast."

Click. Another satellite photograph, showing the two air masses on an apparent collision course.

"If both fronts continue on their current course, we could, in three or four days, be in for heavy snow or high, gusting winds, or both."

"A blizzard?" Popoleyev said.

"That's at and above timberline where you'll be, not down here. To be honest, Dr. Popoleyev, we ordinarily don't get a storm like this until the last week of December or the first week of January, but . . ." She smiled. "Made to order for a Russian, I suppose.

"The Weather Service is now of the opinion that the the air mass off California will, in fact, turn west. The cold Siberian air could swing northeast again and resume its usual course, but it's not likely. The odds are it will be clear and cold for a few days with an outside chance of snow and high winds if the worst case comes to pass."

I was going to have to camp out on the side of a mountain in a blizzard. I knew it!

The question of the weather taken care of, Bondurant asked the team leaders and two assistants each to join him and McGwyre to discuss how the search should proceed.

Sonja Popoleyev asked Willie and me to come along, but I stepped aside in favor of Bobby Minthorn. Willie and Bobby were veteran hunters of elk and bighorn sheep. They worked in territory that made this look like a backyard stroll. They loved it, and they were good at it. I'd heard many times from Willie's Indian friends that Bobby Minthorn was a tracker without equal, and I believed it.

I didn't know squat, so I stayed back with Whitefeather Minthorn and the climbers from the other parties and eavesdropped on the conversation. We could hear most of what was being said.

Thomas Bondurant led the meeting.

Roger Whitcomb, wearing a jaunty alpine cap with "Budweiser," "Bausch and Lomb," and "Tenzig Norgay" patches on it, was forceful and expressive. Emile Thibodeaux wore his patches on the sleeve of his jacket; he mumbled, chewing thoughtfully on his pipe.

Willie Prettybird did the talking for our team, consulting with Bobby and Popoleyev. Prettybird, grinning, friendly, intelligent eyes alert, was self-deprecating and casual.

Bondurant proposed, without objection, that the teams should work from the proposition that Sasquatch was a cave dweller who came down out of his rocks to forage for food at the edge of the forest.

Consequently the search teams should establish camps below timberline, which was at 6,000 feet.

Bondurant, again without objection, suggested that we begin our trek at the 2,500-foot level at a point where Swift Creek flowed between St. Helens and the 4,116-foot Marble Mountain—located between the volcano and Swift Reservoir. From there it was a 3.5-mile hike across ash and volcanic rocks to Battle Camp Dome on the left, and about 2.5 miles to both Monitor Ridge in the center and Worm Flow on the right. All three proposed campsites were roughly at 5,000 feet.

Ape Cave, at 1,600 feet, was five miles slightly southwest of Monitor Ridge. Although Bondurant had checked and rechecked, he had found no Sasquatch sign at Ape Cave

"If we drive you to the jump-off immediately after the press conference, you should have plenty of time to settle in by dark." Bondurant glanced at Popoleyev and hesitated, then said, "Then there's the question of whether or not Sasquatch is diurnal or nocturnal."

Popoleyev spoke up. "We humans are diurnal, and the consensus apparently is that Sasquatch is diurnal as well. Since a nighttime search of the rocks above timberline is out of the question, I'm entirely comfortable with proceeding on that assumption. If he's nocturnal, we'll find him anyway."

Bondurant seemed relieved. "Good. Then I suggest we proceed according to the conventional wisdom that Sasquatch lives in caves above timberline, venturing down to forage for food early in the morning and late in the afternoon."

Thibodeaux said, "That makes sense. If Sasquatch does exist."

Whitcomb said, "He does, Emile. Living that high up is why he's rarely seen."

Thibodeaux shrugged.

Bondurant said, "From your base camps, you will work together then, concentrating on the early morning and late afternoon hours. Does everybody agree?"

Thibodeaux nodded yes.

Whitcomb said, "Fine by me."

Willie, glancing at Popoleyev, and receiving no objection, said, "We agree."

Thibodeaux said, "We should do this systematically, starting low and working to the west, say, then moving higher and searching to the east. Back and forth, back and forth."

"Makes sense," Whitcomb said.

"Yes, it does," Willie said.

Bondurant said, "If you relay your communications through Sasquatch Central, I can help coordinate things if you do spot anything."

Thibodeaux said, "You wait, Ike-like, eh, Thomas?"

Bondurant laughed. "Not much else I can do with this foot. Objections to the plan so far?" He checked the leaders with his eyes.

No objections.

Bondurant said, "If you find footprints or other evidence, you should contact me immediately so I can analyze it for the media people."

Whether a beast lumbered east or a beast lumbered west, Bondurant said, he or an assistant at Sasquatch Center would chart the pursuit with color-coded pins stuck into a three-dimensional topographical map. The pins had numbered triangular flags on them, each number corresponding to a name. Thus, the dispositions of Bondurant's Sasquatch searchers would be graphically depicted and constantly updated, awaiting the coming and going of reporters with their questions.

The leaders pledged that whoever found Sasquatch would keep his or her distance and inform the others, and everybody would cooperate in seeing to it that Sasquatch was not approached or disturbed.

From the snatches of conversation Whitefeather and I could hear, they decided to ban vehicles and helicopters from the area so as not to spook Sasquatch.

The question of who would get the middle and who the flanks was tricky. Activity on the flanks could drive Sasquatch to the middle and it was closest to Ape Cave, so that's where everybody wanted to be. Finally, they decided to draw straws to settle the question of positions.

Bondurant held the straws.

Whitcomb drew. Short.

Thibodeaux drew. Shorter. "Figgers," he said.

Whitcomb brightened.

Willie drew. Longer. In fact, longest. Popoleyev got the middle.

That chore done, Whitcomb, lowering his voice, entered an objection of some sort. This had nothing to do with the draw, but with the Popoleyev team, judging from an exchange between him and Willie. Whitcomb kept his voice low so those of us eavesdropping couldn't hear the details.

Popoleyev was momentarily nonplussed, but Willie, amiable, lowering his voice to match the serious Whitcomb, gave an answer that had Thibodeaux and Bondurant laughing.

Whitcomb was not finished. He raised his voice. He was talking about Earl.

Bobby Minthorn said something.

Whitcomb insisted.

Willie resisted.

Thibodeaux and Bondurant grew more serious.

Popoleyev spoke up.

Finally, Willie, his body language saying this was one pissed-off redskin, looked Whitcomb straight in the eye and murmured something that made Whitcomb furious.

Willie shook hands with Thibodeaux and Bondurant and pivoted on his heels, his gesture saying that the powwow was finished.

When the three of them got back, Whitefeather Minthorn said, "Okay, group. What happened?"

Willie said, "We lucked out and drew the middle."

"No, no. We picked that up. I mean at the last there. We couldn't hear a thing."

Willie said, "Oh, the son of a bitch was objecting to Earl. He said we were all sanctimonious about not harming Sasquatch, and here we were, set to run him to ground with dogs. I said dog, not dogs . . ."

Bobby said, "I told them when Earl ran sign, he stayed with me."

Popoleyev said, "I told him I would object vehemently to any attempt to run Sasquatch down, by dog or any other means."

Willie said, "He said the sound of a barking dog would carry for miles this high up."

Bobby said, "I told him Earl's one of the smartest animals he's ever set eyes on. Earl's not a casual barker. When he barks, it's for a reason. If he's told to heel, he heels. If he's told to stay, he stays."

Willie said, "He called Earl a cur, which really got my dander up."

"I could see that."

Bobby said, "Not that Earl isn't a cur, but it was an insult coming from him."

Willie said, "Then he said it wasn't fair for us to have a dog when nobody else did. I said, unfair, what the fuck are you talking about? You've got satellite photographs and Budweiser beer patches. I told him if his party came on some sign and needed help from Earl's nose, all they had to do was let us know."

Popoleyev said, "I told him Earl was an expedition dog, belonging to all three parties. It's the money that's doing it, Mr. Denson. The reward on top of everything else. It's turning people crazy."

Willie said, "Thibodeaux and Bondurant didn't object to Earl, so that pretty much ended it."

Popoleyev said, "I don't think Dr. Bondurant liked it much."

"I noticed that," Prettybird said.

"What happens now?" I said.

Popoleyev said, "We'll talk to the reporters. Then we form a caravan and drive partway on up the mountain for the start. We've got a three-mile hike up an ash flow."

Willie said, "When we reach our assigned spot just below timberline, we set up camp and savor some of Whitefeather Minthorn's special mountain grub. Then we get a good night's sleep. It's easy, Denson. No sweat."

I said, "Two murdered Pollards. It's easy. No sweat. Sure, sure."

While Sonja Popoleyev was doing her thing at the press conference, I ran quickly back to my room and dialed Boogie Dewlapp's number in Seattle. Boogie wasn't in, but I talked to his secretary, Ruth Anne, who'd tell him what I wanted.

In addition to making sure all investigator's reports were clear, thorough, and accurate, the clever Ruth Anne had the good sense to know when more questions needed to be asked. Sometimes a promising lead, unanticipated or overlooked, had to be followed then, not later. Ruth Anne was decisive and did what had to be done.

Boogie once told me that as a young man he had read Alfred T. Mahan's *Influence of Sea Power upon History* and was particularly impressed by Mahan's comparisons of French and British battle tactics.

The French captains took their instructions from the flagship, from where, theoretically, the admiral would direct the attack in a coordinated fashion. But what with shifting winds and bad luck and the inevitable confusion, well . . .

The sensible British allowed their captains to fight according to the circumstance of battle. If the wind shifted, the British captains had been taught the correct tack to take. They were expected to take it, immediately.

Boogie Dewlapp was a British admiral. Captain Ruth Anne would have been an investigator herself, on the streets like Willie and me, except that she had multiple sclerosis. Her four-master was a wheelchair.

I said, "Okay, Ruth Anne, tell Boogie I know these are questions Sheriff Starkey will be asking, but it's unlikely he'll be sharing the answers with me. Somebody should check the clips of the *New York Times*, the *Washington Post*, the *Seattle Times*, *Seattle Post-Intelligencer*, and the *Portland Oregonian*. Also *Willamette Week* down in Portland. I remember they ran a series of articles on scamming in the resort development business. Got it, Ruth Anne?"

"The biggies and *Willamette Week*. Got it, Mr. Denson."

"And you might check *The Weekly* in Seattle just in case."

"*The Weekly* just in case. I'll take care of it, Mr. Denson. What am I looking for?"

"I would like a brief financial and legal history of Cascade Run. Who developed it and when. Et cetera. Who owns it now. Also, I'd like to know more about the guy who shot the Sasquatch tape at Ape Cave. He was from California State University at Bakersfield, I remember. You never know, a little bio might trigger some kind of connection."

". . . and whoever taped Bigfoot at Ape Cave."

"Correct. Also, whatever you can learn about Dr. Thomas Bondurant."

"The man from the British Museum?"

"Yes. That might be a tough assignment, but you never know what you might find out. And I'd like a bio on David Addison, the man who offered the one-hundred-thousand-dollar reward. The usual financial data, of course. His employment history. When he was married. How many kids. That kind of thing.

"Also, here's one that will need an investigator. I know Olden's two-ace gumshoes are unavailable, but maybe he can come up with someone who can ask a simple question. The bartender at Cascadia, the bar at Cascade Run, recently made a large order of three kinds of Jamaican dark rum—Myers's, Appleton, and Overton—and one order of Puerto Rican light rum, Bacardi. We're talking multiple cases, Ruth Anne. Appleton dark is *gooooood* stuff!"

". . . Myers's, Appleton, and Overton dark, and Bacardi light."

"I want to know when the bartender placed the order. Can Olden help me out? Somebody will have to find the wholesale distributor who sells to the Cascadia bartender. Probably someone in Vancouver or Portland. What do you think, Ruth Anne?"

"Most of this newspaper stuff I can call up on my computer. I don't know what to say about the rum question. That might take some time. The bios will take work as well. I'll get right on it, but you know how it goes. Boogie's got a pile of requests waiting for me."

"Doesn't he always?"

She said, "Boogie's been grousing that he needs Willie on a cattle-rustling case down in Bend, and you to investigate a fishing-rights squabble in Bellingham. And where are you, he asks? Out chasing ghosts on some damn mountain." She imitated Boogie's sonorous, rumbling voice.

"Has he complained when he and Olden have been mentioned in the newspapers as financing Dr. Popoleyev's team? Puts them up there with Budweiser and Bausch and Lomb."

Ruth Anne laughed. "Oh no, Mr. Denson. He's quite proud. In fact, he's assigned me the job of collecting the clippings."

"I thought so. Get to this whenever you can, Ruth Anne. I'd appreciate it."

"I'll do my best, Mr. Denson, but you know how it goes around here."

"How it goes" meant that it would take Ruth Anne days at least, perhaps weeks, to find the answers to some of my questions. It was important to be patient with each step of the process. In that respect, detection was like making good elderberry wine.

"And also, Ruth Anne, as usual, do please keep your eye peeled for anything I've overlooked."

Ruth Anne said, "I'll do my best, Mr. Denson. It's fun to be in on this one."

Chapter Eighteen

A Chance to Take Pictures

All three Bigfoot parties, led by Thomas Bondurant and Donna McGwyre in a Cascade Run lead car, and trailed by a full half-mile of media vehicles, drove north on Highway 83 to Marble Mountain, a geologic bulge just south of Mount St. Helens that hardly qualified for the designation of mountain.

The flattened top of Marble Mountain blended into an ash flow that rose to become the foot of Mount St. Helens, and that's where we went.

Bondurant's car pulled to a stop at a lookout parking lot, and we all followed suit. Oblivious to the fact that one of our number was possibly a double-murderer and deer season wasn't over, we piled out of our vehicles, stretching our arms and legs. We unloaded our gear amid joking and small talk, the banter suggesting we knew what we were doing and had good sense.

In the distance, across the boulder-strewn grayish-white ash flow, the mountain loomed.

Those who believed that Sasquatch existed *knew* that he existed, and so he did. And the believers craved action, not a bunch of sniveling sissies cowering back at Cascade Run. Pushing heroically off to begin the search was part of the spectacle, and the public expected to be dealt in on the action. This mandatory ritual, a chance to take pictures, was called a "photo op."

We set about getting our teams squared away to perform a ritual media start for the benefit of cameras. This was easy enough for our team. There were only five of us, and we didn't have to worry about getting our sponsor's patches aimed the right direction.

Roger Whitcomb and his eleven Explorers Club colleagues would set off over the volcanic ash for the foot of Battle Camp Dome, their base camp on the left.

When the cameras were ready, Whitcomb and his team members started off in single file, marching manfully under what looked like incredible backpacks. They walked with robust strides, heads up, determined to triumph at all costs; lacking food, they'd eat bugs for protein and chew pine needles for vitamin C; if they got thirsty enough, they'd suck the sweat out of their socks.

Emile Thibodeaux's nine Mazama compatriots went next—stalwart figures bearing eighty-pound backpacks, including those dried meals "conceived" by San Francisco chefs. All those lean muscles and healthy blood pressures. The Mazamans were mountain-climbing nuts from all backgrounds, and probably regarded St. Helens as a mountain for teenagers and old ladies. What the Canadian and the Mazamans thought of hustling Tenzig Norgay trail grub was anybody's guess.

Thibodeaux's Mazamans were destined for the right flank of the search camping at the Worm Flow, a break in the summit where the 1980 eruption had popped through the south flank of the mountain.

As the other departing teams were being photographed, we took our places for the start. We would hike northwest, establishing our base camp in the center just below timberline on Monitor Ridge. Our backs were conspicuously bare of sponsor's patches—this lack being the mark of amateurs.

Bobby Minthorn, Popoleyev's tracker nonpareil—his long black hair woven into a single braid for the occasion—with the faithful Earl at his heel, took point, as though he were escorting John Wayne out of Fort Apache. Whitefeather had picked out Bobby's outfit, including his favorite Levi's jacket, worn nearly threadbare, and a pair of jeans with a patch on the ass. She said she wanted him to look like an Indian, which he was, but not like a movie Indian. She had tied a bit of red ribbon on the end of his braid, which stuck out from under his wool stocking cap.

I wondered if anybody thought that Sasquatch, watching from his hideout in the rocks, was going to hustle down onto the slope of volcanic ash and give us some good, clear prints so Bobby and Earl could demonstrate their stuff.

To the media, whether or not Minthorn was capable of finding the supper table twice in a row was beside the point; he was an Indian. While Minthorn was not Chingachgook or Jim Thorpe, his storied competence as a tracker—and Earl's as a dog with an incredible nose—would grow with each story filed from Sasquatch Center. There breathed not a reporter present who did not regard the pair of Bobby and Earl with the emotion of Ted Williams being served a hanging curve ball, belt-high. A form of journalistic tether ball.

At Bobby's heel, Earl, the peerless cur of amazing nose, appeared indifferent to the commotion. He had been told to remain at Bobby's heel, and so he did, ignoring the clicking of cameras.

Willie Prettybird took his place behind Minthorn. Prettybird was dressed like Minthorn, except that on the back of his Levi's jacket, he had a large, oval patch that showed what looked like a log cabin with a Douglas fir in the background. This was "Louella's Bar, Fried Chicken, Darts, Venonia, Oregon."

On the end of his pigtail, Willie had tied three gray feathers, plus the claw of a hawk or eagle, and a tuft of reddish fur. He told me this was his "Sasquatch talisman." As usual, it was difficult for me to divine whether or not he was pulling my leg.

I slipped up beside Prettybird and handed him a copy of that morning's *Seattle Times,* in which a reporter had referred to him as the "storied" Cowlitz medicine man.

A Cowlitz he was. As to a medicine man, well, maybe.

"Storied what, Willie? Pickler of barnacles? Smoker of lamprey? Vintner of elderberry wine? Cocksman?" I looked wide-eyed, disbelieving.

Willie, reading the story, grinned. "Pipe down and take your place. Dammit, man, this is the same as a war party here. Discipline is the word." Willie looked scornful. "White men. Jesus! Can't take you anywhere."

I retreated to the rear, where my lady of gray legs, Opal, waited patiently under her load.

Sonja Popoleyev, amused at our bantering, took her place behind Willie. Popoleyev wore an all-white waterproof outfit of the type worn by ski troops in the Russian army. Popoleyev charmed the reporters by telling them that the outfit was light and warm, and if it snowed and invading Norwegians parachuted out of the sky, they wouldn't be able to see her.

Whitefeather Minthorn also had her hair in a pigtail. Wearing her hunting outfit—puffy, camouflage jacket, jeans, and well-used hiking boots—she stepped up behind Popoleyev. Harold, it was said, preferred to deal with women and responded best when Whitefeather led him. Harold carried our radio gear, and Whitefeather was in charge of communications. It was her responsibility to maintain contact with Thomas Bondurant and his assistants at Sasquatch Central.

Then me, at drag, trailing Opal, and wearing a puffy gray nylon outfit that Olden Dewlapp used for cross-country skiing. Ordinarily, Bobby led Opal, and Opal liked men best. Leading her was fine by me. The weight on Opal's back—including Olden's Sony videocamera—was a load that wasn't on mine.

Bobby Minthorn, Willie, and I carried a sissy forty pounds each. Sonja Popoleyev and Whitefeather Minthorn each shouldered a womanly twenty-five pounds each. Harold packed 300 pounds, and Opal lugged 250. The mules seemed positively frisky, bless them.

Harold and Opal spent most of the year grazing in the Minthorns' pasture outside of Clatskanie, Oregon. Lugging loads into the interior was their thing. They loved it. Several times a year they had to earn their winter alfalfa and grain. Come time for the hunt, they were eager for action.

By this time, the reporters and photographers were enjoying the high camp lunacy of the proceedings.

When we were ready to roll, Bobby gave a war whoop.

Willie Prettybird, looking grave, his silly feathers rustling in the breeze, raised his right hand. He circled it twice, pointed toward the mountain, and gave a hearty yelp.

Mules are notorious for being stubborn. I thought: *Don't do it to me, Opal. Please don't. When I say go, go.*

Cheerfully and with spirit, I said, "Come on, Opal old girl, let's show 'em what kind of stuff we're made of!" Opal, without a hint of mulish balk, stepped right on along.

We were off.

Opal's hooves fell into a rhythmic, satisfying *clup, clup, clup* in the volcano ash. She was my kind of mule. I knew that from the start.

A photographer shouted, "Dr. Popoleyev, could we have you walk beside a mule for a minute? Please."

I stepped back to make way for Popoleyev, who took Opal's rope, but when she did, Opal flat balked. Quit moving.

Everybody laughed, including Whitefeather, who said "Oops! Forgot!" and quickly gave her Harold's rope.

The studly Harold was most pleased to be led by Popoleyev.

I took the rope back, and Opal resumed, *clup, clup, clup* beside me. I said, "Atta' girl, Opal. Loyalty's the thing. Never let 'em tell you anything else. They'll give you all kinds of stories, but don't listen to 'em."

Hearing that, Popoleyev turned, grinning, and raised one eyebrow.

I said, "Just listen to me, Opal, and you'll go far."

Chapter Nineteen

The Odds on
Bobby and Earl

A scant half hour after we set out, we heard the distant popping of gunfire in a ravine to our left, lower down where the deer were located, and presumably, the hunters would stay there. As we climbed higher, the trees got smaller. And as the sun sank lower in the west, the air got colder. I thought, well, I'll get used to it.

But no. It got colder.

And colder yet.

"The cold front has hit us, right, Willie?"

Willie stopped, looking back. His breath came in frosty puffs. "You'll know it when it hits, Denson. This is just plain old mountain air. Air out them nuts of yours, man. Good for what ails you."

The first time we stopped for a break, I gave the appreciative Opal's velvet nose a couple of comradely pats. The second break, I gave her some more pats. She liked it. She snorted, I thought, rather demurely for a mule—demulely?—and blinked her large brown eyes.

Willie, seeing this, raised his eyebrows. He gave me a suggestive look. My, my!

"Asshole," I said. I gave Opal another pat on the nose. She was a hard worker and deserved it.

After three and a half hours of hiking, and with maybe forty minutes of daylight left, we arrived at Monitor Ridge, the agreed-upon site for the Popoleyev base camp. We were just below timber-line.

"Cold enough to f-f-freeze the b-b-balls off a b-b-brass monkey," Bobby said.

Monitor Ridge was steep, but not impossible for a campsite. I helped Whitefeather Minthorn and Sonja Popoleyev set up camp, using a string of six huge boulders as a windbreak. We erected our communal tent while Willie and Bobby scouted the rocks above us for Sasquatch sign. One tent required just one stove, and five bodies meant five sources of body heat.

Whitefeather started our fire. As dusk descended, we watched the lights come on in Portland, some forty miles to the south as the crow flies. The arterial boulevards and highways leading out from downtown Portland, bisected by side streets, looked like a huge, eerie spiderweb. We could see the interstate highways leading into the city, and the lights on Portland's bridges. It was a lovely sight.

A few minutes later, darkness was fully upon us, and a vicious, icy wind kicked up from the north, slipping over the boulders of our windbreak and knifing through our camp. Nobody had to be told: the mass of frigid Siberian air, one half of the recipe for truly bad news, was upon us.

Willie and Bobby returned from their reconnoiter bearing bags of ice chiseled from the snow pack that—tucked under the shadow of protective rocks—had survived summer. Melted ice would give us water to rehydrate and cook Willie's dried food.

Willie said if wolverines and Sasquatch could turn that trick, so could we. Whitefeather dumped dried vegetables into an aluminum pot of boiling water, and added shredded, dried elk. She had good, strong coffee ready to drink while we waited.

Given the length and breadth of the terrain that Sonja Popo-leyev was assigned to cover, the prospects of the enterprise didn't look good to me. While we drank coffee and waited for our supper to cook, I said so to Willie. "Frankly, Tonto, there's a lot about this so-called search that just doesn't make a whole lot of sense to me."

"How's that?"

"Well, suppose, tomorrow morning, Popoleyev and I search, say, area A in the morning. And we move to area B in the afternoon." I pointed to an imaginary A and B on the map. "Maybe A was Sasquatch's regular hunting territory. Entirely by chance, say, he was off somewhere relieving himself or on a lark the day we searched his favorite spot. But we wouldn't know that, would we?"

"Wouldn't have a hint," Willie said.

"But in an attempt to be systematic and methodical we'd proceed through the drill of checking each area in order. One by one, we'd search them all. All the while there is no chance, none, that we'd ever bump into our beast. While we pointlessly work our butts off, Sasquatch could be kicked back in his favorite haunt, sucking the brains out of a chipmunk."

"Chief, Chief, what if you came up with sign here, at G, say, that led back to here." Willie poked at an imaginary G, then the A.

"Well, there's that too," I said.

"That's why we've got Bobby Minthorn. He can follow sign across the bottom of a shallow river or over bare rock. You have to anticipate how your quarry thinks, and from that you deduce his habits. But if Sasquatch is making trips back and forth to his snowpack deep freeze getting ready for winter, he'll most likely take the easy route. I think you and Dr. Popoleyev should do the same."

"You do?" Well, there was some good news after all. I was beginning to wonder.

"Why should Sasquatch want to break his neck any more than you? I'd check the arroyos and draws where a trail or path would seem likely, and save the steep stuff for last."

He unfolded his map, studied it for a moment, then pointed with his finger. "Since Bobby and I will be working up here looking for caves and food caches, why don't you and Popoleyev check out this draw down here?" He pointed to a draw several hundred yards below where he and Minthorn would be searching. "We'll slowly work our way west, toward Whitcomb."

"Looks okay to me."

"When you check this draw, leave room in your daypacks. And stay alert."

* * *

As her last chore before supper, Whitefeather Minthorn called Thomas Bondurant to report the lack of Sasquatch sign at Monitor Ridge. With both Whitcomb and Thibodeaux on the air and listening in, Bondurant reported two other interesting bits of information.

First, Alford Pollard's RV had been found near Chehalis, Washington, minus the Pollard brothers' collection of Sasquatchiana. "The police say they are checking the RV for clues, but as yet don't have a suspect."

Then, Bondurant said, for whatever it was worth, Las Vegas bookies were taking bets on which party would actually find Sasquatch. "Dr. Popoleyev, you'll be interested to know that your camp, at seven to three, is the favorite. This is because of Bobby Minthorn's reputation as a tracker, which I unintentionally boosted by mentioning his performance with my photographs yesterday, and because of Earl, who has captured the affections of dog lovers everywhere. Mr. Minthorn should be warned in the event Hollywood calls."

"All right!" Minthorn raised his fist and wiggled his hips, then gave Earl an affectionate slap on the ribs. "You good old dog, you."

"Mr. Thibodeaux, your Mazamans are listed at eleven to two, based on your knowledge of the Cascades, and the fact that your men are from the area. Any comment, the reporters want to know?"

Thibodeaux said, "If the odds were a thousand to one, it'd probably still be a safe bet on their part, but we'll do our best."

"I'm afraid the betting is seventeen to one for you, Mr. Whitcomb. Your team is being called 'imported California adventurers.' That's the bookies' phrase, not mine. They're saying you look like you stepped out of a casting studio." Bondurant sounded amused. "Did you hear that, Mr. Whitcomb?"

Laughter on the radio. Whitcomb's. He said, "The bookies must be from Oregon or Washington. If I were you, Dr. Bondurant, I'd bet the north forty on these imported adventurers and then some."

We had no sooner finished with that fun when, slightly to the west—in clear contravention of our agreement—we heard the chopping of helicopter blades. *Whuff-uf-uf-uf-uf!*

A helicopter?

What the . . . ?

We listened as the helicopter circled our position and went down the mountain.

Did it land somewhere to the west of our camp?

We thought so, but in a few minutes we heard it again, circling back again, up and over the summit.

Whuff-uf-uf-uf-uf.

Whitefeather called this in to Bondurant, who said Whitcomb's camp had heard the helicopter too. Bondurant said the U.S. Forest Service was checking it out.

Bondurant said there was one other thing. He sounded uncertain as to how to proceed.

"What's that?" Whitefeather asked.

"It seems that word is out in the academic community concerning Dr. Popoleyev's participation in the search . . ."

Popoleyev put her hand over her mouth, repressing a giggle.

Whitefeather, looking at Popoleyev, said, "And? Dr. Bondurant?"

"Well, Mrs. Minthorn, would you . . . ? Would you, please? Are you there, Dr. Popoleyev?"

"I'm here."

"The wire services yesterday ran profiles of the team leaders, and what has happened, Dr. Popoleyev, is that we've received something of a firestorm of calls today protesting your inclusion in the search. I bet you could even guess a few of them." He sounded amused.

Popoleyev said, "I could try, but better that I should be diplomatic, I think."

Bondurant laughed. "Professor Bernadette Simmons was particularly incensed."

"And what did you tell her?"

"I told her no favoritism was involved, which was true. Outside of myself, you were the only scholar of primate evolution who asked to participate. The others no doubt thought it was beneath them."

I said, "Whoever gets there firstest . . ."

". . . gets the mostest," said the pleased Sonja Popoleyev. "Dr. Inskeep used to say that. You Americans!"

Chapter Twenty

A Fancy,
Faraway Table

The question for Dr. Sonja Popoleyev that first night around the campfire, posed by Whitefeather Minthorn, was how, in the past, Blanche had dealt with Stanley, as the monster stood revealed in her team's researches into primate behavior.

"I have to deal with the monster Bobby Minthorn, and I thought I might learn something," Whitefeather said.

Popoleyev said, "As you can probably guess, Whitefeather, smart women, those likeliest to survive, eventually came to understand that sex is a commodity. If he wanted it badly enough, Stanley had to pay."

"It's true, you wind up putting a price on it," Whitefeather said.

"Whitefeather was quick that way," Bobby said.

Whitefeather gave him a look.

"Well?" Bobby turned up the palms of his hands.

"If Stanley doesn't have it, he wants it. If he has it, he wants more of it. Blanche has it, but won't give it up without a price. No intelligent woman gives sex away.

"Furthermore, the computer tells us, whoever enjoys sex the most holds the least power. You can see that. When a couple first marries, the wife holds the power."

I said, "It's called PW in the vernacular."

"PW?"

"Pussy-whipped."

"Mr. Denson!"

"Sorry."

"Unfortunately, as Blanche learns to enjoy sex and gets better at it, she's also growing older."

"I think my old lady's gonna be an old, old woman before she learns how to . . ." Minthorn, choosing not to end the sentence, leered at his wife.

"Bobby!"

Popoleyev continued with aplomb. "As Blanche nears menopause, she begins to lose her edge, and the power shifts to Stanley. Stanley's evaluative mechanism for female beauty is based on a single fact: he can only reproduce himself by having sex with women who are able to bear children. If human brains matured as quickly as those of squirrels, women would remain sexual objects until they died."

I said, "Then, again, if you had the brains of squirrels, you'd be stuck with estrus again, wouldn't you? No sex for fun or an extra piece of liver."

"Always remember the unpleasant evolutionary rule, Mr. Denson. Always. Sexual strategies evolve to ensure fitness of a species, not personal happiness."

"Speaking of personal happiness. If we're all sufficiently recovered from last night's exertions." Willie got up and disappeared into our tent, returning momentarily with a bottle of Stolichnaya.

Popoleyev's eyes lit up. "Stolichnaya. Oh, Mr. Prettybird, aren't you the thoughtful one! Good for you. Last night was last night, I say."

Whitefeather Minthorn said, "I agree. And besides, I don't have to drive tonight."

As Willie poured for us all, I said, "Whitcomb and Thibodeaux have each staked out Sasquatch as their private territory. Would that be cause enough for murder, do you think?"

"Of the Pollard brothers? Almost certainly. Males demonstrating their prowess commit murder every day. It is the burden of your genes. While you Stanleys kill one another off in various forms of competition over our charms, we Blanches sit back and watch the action in safety—as if it were a movie. You're all such eager performers, although a little predictable."

"You choose from among us."

"Of course. You have shorter lifespans because you work yourselves to death giving us what we demand. I'm sure the baby-boom women felt they earned their divorce settlements fair and square. Prime value received now for prime sex given earlier, and for the probability of loneliness in the future. What is it your bankers call it, a 'balloon' payment?" She gave me a cockeyed, crooked grin.

"Dr. Popoleyev, when we bumped into Alford Pollard in the hallway yesterday, did you notice the petite woman he was with?"

"His brother Elford's widow."

"A grieving brother-in-law comforting the distraught widow. The lady's husband, his brother, has been murdered. Now, he himself has been killed, and his collection of Sasquatchiana has been stolen by some vile bastard. The outrage! Is that what you saw, Dr. Popoleyev?"

She thought about her answer.

"Did you see his hand on her waist? A little moral support. Did you notice that? An overly thoughtful Stanley, perhaps?"

"Oh, you are the suspicious one, aren't you, Mr. Denson?"

"The Bible admonishes us to covet not our neighbor's ass, but I don't remember it saying anything about the ass that belongs to our brother."

"Mr. Denson!"

I loved it when Popoleyev admonished me, a fact of which she was surely aware. "But if Alford murdered Elford, who murdered Alford, right?"

"Exactly."

"So much for that theory." I held up my cup of vodka. "To men and women. May we all muddle through with as much good intention and humor as possible, and with as little pain and disappointment as we can manage."

Popoleyev tapped my mug with hers. "Well put, Mr. Denson.

We do the best we can. I drink to Bobby and Whitefeather Minthorn. You'd think they were natural pair bonders."

Bobby drank to that, giving his wife a hug. "It's true, I do like the old lady."

Whitefeather said, "My brother speculated that I was scraping the bottom of the barrel when I plucked Bobby out, but he's been okay."

"You don't say that when I let beer farts."

"Bobby!"

Willie said, "I've got a couple more bottles stashed away. The first night out, and with a wind like this, a little antifreeze will do us good." He refilled our cups. "With thanks to Harold and Opal."

We toasted Harold and Opal, who were, perhaps, lucky in their way; born of horses, sired by donkeys, mules, with a reputation for being strong but stubborn, were sterile and so had no species to worry about.

Which is when my cellular phone rang. It was Ruth Anne in Seattle.

"Well, I'm sorry, Mr. Denson, I haven't had time to do much in the way of the questions you asked. I did call Phil Sanford at the *Oregonian.* Phil tells me the word, second-hand, is that Sheriff Starkey had brother Alford at the top of his list as a suspect in Elford Pollard's death. Alford's murder slowed that line of reasoning, Phil says."

"The motive?"

"Elford's wife, plus the collection of Sasquatchiana. The Pollard brothers' exhibit has been a real money-maker on the circuit of county and state fairs in recent years."

"So now who's Starkey looking at, Elford's widow?"

"That would be Judy Pollard. Unfortunately, Mrs. Pollard has an airtight alibi in both cases. Phil says Starkey's plain stumped."

"They found the RV, but the Bigfoot stuff was gone."

"That's it."

"Well, everything counts, Ruth Anne. There's an explanation there somewhere."

"I'll start checking newspaper references to David Addison tomorrow, Mr. Denson. Maybe I can come up with something more helpful there."

* * *

Later, snug in the sleeping bag I had borrowed from one of Willie's friends—listening to the wind go *whuff, whuff, whuff* against our tent—I thought about what Sonja Popoleyev had said about Stanley and Blanche.

Popoleyev was a fellow logician and in my opinion sensational because of it. She looked the consequences of human genes straight on. She did not bitch or whimper or whine. Of course, with a face and long legs and a behind like hers, Popoleyev was perfectly aware of the handsome price she was capable of exacting on the hormonal market.

Whuff, whuff, whap, whap, went the tent. *Whuff, whuff, whuff, whap, whap, whap.*

I lay there unable to sleep. Were the others asleep? I didn't think so.

Popoleyev's voice said, "Cheer up, Mr. Denson. Tomorrow's another day."

It was nearly pitch-black in the tent, but I could see the silhouette of Popoleyev in her sleeping bag. She was on her side, resting her chin in the heel of her hand. She was looking my way.

"Hard to sleep," I said.

She said, "The news is only bad if we let it be. In my opinion, it is far, far worse to proceed out of ignorance."

Whuff, whuff. Whuff, whuff, whuff.

She stirred in her sleeping bag. "Our imaginations enrich us women, Mr. Denson. As we imagine, so we are. Even if we cannot be, so we imagine. It is why we are readers and such romantics. We escape. We transport ourselves. It's that or go slightly mad in our separate, private ways."

"The Russians love poetry. I bet you write poetry, don't you?"

"It must be the vodka. It was so good. A touch of home. Do I write poetry? Give me just a moment, Mr. Denson."

I waited, knowing by the tone of her voice that she was translating in her head.

Finally, she said, "Here's one, which no doubt won't come off as well in English as the Russian, but I'll do my best. It's called 'On Walking to Finland':

> *It is cold and gray*
> *on the shores of the Baltic Sea*
> *where I go to watch sea gulls fly.*
> *I tell myself that I will one day*
> *walk across this water*
> *to a cafe in Finland*
> *and have lunch.*
> *I will drink real coffee, rich and strong*
> *and eat a different kind of bread.*
> *I can only imagine that I will like this lunch,*
> *having never sat at such a fancy, faraway table.*

"It may not be the best poem there ever was, especially translated into English. But if a squirrel could write a better one, I would be disappointed. Are you not a dreamer too, Mr. Denson? Or are you satisfied as a frustrated Stanley?"

The wind kicked up again, changing the *whuff, whuffs* to a slapping *whap, whap, whap.*

She said, "You know, Willie, we cannot allow Sasquatch to be found by people who sell space on their hats to beer advertisers. What if it is *Troglodytes recens?*"

We were silent, listening to the wind buffet the tent.

Finally, Popoleyev said, "Good night, Mr. Denson."

Willie giggled. "Would you listen to that? A special good-night for Mr. Denson. Did you hear that, Bobby?"

"I heard it," Minthorn said.

"Willie!" Popoleyev was embarrassed.

Willie crooned, "Good night, Mr. Denson!"

I said, "Shut up, Tonto."

"I agree," Whitefeather said.

Whuff, whuff, whuff.

Whap, whap, whap.

Chapter Twenty-one

Willie Goes for a Stroll

I felt nice and snug in the sleeping bag, a kind of mint-green mate to the one they had loaned Sonja Popoleyev. For a while, I thought, well, Denson, this is not going to be so bad.

I couldn't shift back and forth from hip to hip as easily as in a bed. Still, as long as my teeth weren't chattering, I would make it.

I imagined myself back on my soft couch in Seattle. I flipped off the television with a remote. The Mariners had won. Life was good. The pillows and the quilt my mother had made for me were warm and soft. The Mariners were in a pennant race. Could life be better?

I started down the stairs, counting gold numbers on purple carpet:

Twenty. I looked down at the couch. The pennant! Took a step down . . .

Nineteen. The quilt was so soft. Took another step down . . .

I can't remember the number when I went to sleep, but I woke up at three A.M. having to take a pee. This was the part I hated most about the whole outdoorsy gig. I couldn't just swing my feet off the bed and head for the john. First, no john. Second, I had to climb out of a cocoon on the floor.

Next, I had to put something on my feet because it was cold out there and because, for aesthetic reasons, I felt compelled to go some distance from the tent. Then it was fumble, fumble, fumble to find everything and not wake everybody else in the tent. I didn't want a reputation as an inconsiderate tentmate.

I put my boots on, then realized that long johns weren't going to cut it outside. I took my damn boots off. I put my pants on and zipped the fly and buckled the stupid buckle. And a shirt. Buttons to deal with. And a coat. More buttons. And a stocking cap. Then the boots again, this time with socks. I even tied the laces. In the end, I felt like Admiral Perry. All for what I knew would turn out to be a couple of miserable ounces of urine. Evolution had somehow failed me when decent bladders were passed out. It was to weep.

I took a deep breath, quietly, and quickly unzipped the tent and hopped outside . . .

. . . into the jolting frigid air.

The cold! *Yeaaahhhhhh!*

It was also beautiful.

My feet *ker-unched* on the frost that glittered like crushed diamonds as I walked down the trail that Willie and Bobby and I had started making from camp. I did my thing and stood for a moment enjoying the clean air and the awesome silence. When . . .

Something in the distance caught my eye.

Something coming up through the forest. Coming toward the camp.

I squatted and pulled my stocking cap lower over my ears.

Whatever it was disappeared.

I'd forgotten my gloves. Damn. I put my hands under my armpits to keep them warm. I was starting to get cold. In a few minutes I'd really be feeling it.

I waited, watching.

I shifted my weight from foot to foot to keep my feet warm. Left foot. Right foot. Left foot. Christ!

A sound, and then another sound.

It was getting closer.

I squatted.

Movement.

One shape. Two?

There.

A man! Huge.

Willie, stopping to take a piss himself.

Where had he been?

Out looking for the nocturnal *Troglodytes recens?*

Wait a second. Willie was not alone. There *was* a second. A big fucker! He loomed over Willie, looking down at him.

Or was there?

No, just Willie Prettybird. Willie walking up the hill by himself, seemingly oblivious to the frigid air.

But a few feet earlier. A shadow? At the time, I thought I saw a man.

Willie slipped back inside the tent. I stayed low to give him time to go to sleep. The shadow didn't reappear. I gave Willie twenty frigid minutes before I went back inside.

I eased out of my clothes and slipped into the sweet, sweet sleeping bag. I hoped it didn't take forever to get the old sack toasty and cozy again. I wanted it all warm and nice. My toes felt like blocks of ice.

In the darkness, Willie whispered, "This ain't no time for reading, Denson. The light's not good for your eyes, and it's gotta be five below zero out there."

I whispered, "Who was that with you down there?"

"Oh, for Christ's sake."

"I saw somebody."

"You saw diddly."

"You had been farther down the mountain. You stopped to piss on your way back. There was somebody with you."

"We both know you can't see at night, Denson. Go to sleep."

"Bull too."

"If I told you the truth, you wouldn't believe me."

"Try me."

"Sasquatch. I was out for a walk with Sasquatch."

"Liar."

"Okay, have it your way. Bear, then. You saw Bear. We were

down there palavering. Crow was down there too, but your eyes aren't good enough to see him at night."

"Oh, for Christ's sake."

"I got the call, Denson. The animal people said I was supposed to take a hike and meet Crow and Bear, and so I did." Willie giggled.

"Jerkface."

"I tell you the truth, and you won't believe me. So predictable."

"Bear. Sure."

"Nobody down there but me, Chief. You know how I am."

Willie Prettybird was the closest thing to a nocturnal that I had ever met. But still, I lay there wondering. Crow? Bear? No.

Finally, to get my mind off the incident, I forced myself to repeat the counting of sleep's blessed stairs, my imagination locked onto my goal.

Twenty. I looked down at the comforting couch. The pennant! I took a step down.

Nineteen. I looked down at the couch. Pennant? The Mariners? Impossible.

Eighteen. I imagined the couch.

Talking to the animal people? Crow? Bear?

Crap too!

I got as comfortable as I could and took two deep breaths.

Twenty. I looked down at the comforting couch . . .

Chapter Twenty-two

Big Feet,
Big Dreams

Willie Prettybird and Bobby Minthorn began their pursuit of Sasquatch shortly before sunrise, when, without fuss or commotion, they slipped quietly out of their sleeping bags, but not so quietly that they didn't wake us all up as they dressed.

They had assigned themselves the arduous and risky job of searching the treacherous rocks and cliffs above timberline for signs of Sasquatch's cave. Bigfoots had to live somewhere, and the consensus—as suggested by Dr. Porchnev's name, *troglodytidae*—held that it was in a cave.

"You be careful," Whitefeather Minthorn whispered to her husband.

"Good luck, Willie," Popoleyev said.

"If you break your neck, I get your food dryers and the elderberry wine," I added.

"Figgers," he said, unzipping the tent for Bobby. He followed Bobby through, and as he was zipping the tent closed, I shouted, "And the blackberry brandy, Willie. I get all the blackberry brandy. The caviar and smoked salmon too. Mine, all mine."

From her sleeping bag, Whitefeather Minthorn said, "Pipe down, white man."

I wiggled back into the womblike warmth of my sleeping bag, thinking about the day ahead, and the assignment given to Sonja Popoleyev and me.

I remember when I was a kid and my parents went to the mountains, I always wanted to find a cave. Caves were romantic, and in the movies, the hero and heroine, driven to desperation by the weather or the forces of evil, or both, always managed to find a handy cave nearby. You want a cave? The script writer provideth: here's a cave, a real dandy, just waiting to shelter you from the raging storm— and with no parking lot or ticket booths or popcorn wagons outside.

In real life caves were rare. I had driven up and down the Columbia River gorge hundreds of times, and although the geography would seem made-to-order for caves, there were in fact precious damned few of them.

From a distance, the rocky flanks of St. Helens looked like they ought to have caves, but how many would Willie and Bobby really find?

Not very many, I bet. Certainly not as many as city dwellers had been led to believe from depictions of nature in the movies.

A cave suggested a beast that stayed put. Caves were not tepees. One did not casually strike off confident of finding a hip, cozy cave come sundown. If Sasquatches did migrate the length of Washington State to avoid bad weather, as one theory had it, they'd have to stay in caves they already knew about—in the manner of line shacks and permanent campsites used by cowboys scouring the back country. Why had none of these Sasquatch caves been found?

Although the lava tube they called Ape Cave was a splendid specimen—running for hundreds of yards—it remained for a logger to discover it in 1946. I'd have thought a cave like that would have been a regular Bigfoot apartment building.

Why had no Sasquatch artifacts been discovered there? Were there no rocks worn smooth from Sasquatch buttocks past? Thomas Bondurant said he had double-checked Ape Cave and found nothing.

Dr. Popoleyev and I were assigned to search what was considered the critical threshold of cave country, to use Whitcomb's term.

Some of this was sane terrain. Steep, yes, but a person could get around okay if he took his time.

In other stretches, the "threshold" belt of thinning, stunted evergreens was a 60-degree slope of loose and sliding rock, a form of lethal banana peel for the unwary or unlucky.

Big feet, big trails, the logic went.

Big dreams.

Just what the hell did Sasquatch eat? There were grubs, but not much real grub, to be found at timberline. A few mice maybe. Squirrels lower down. The stands of berries were ordinary farther down too.

And finding them was easier said than done. In fact, the easy availability of wild nuts and berries for movie heroes and heroines was a romantic fiction that ranked right up there with the surfeit of caves. Willie knew his wild food. He knew where to go and when, but he and his friends had learned to forage when they were kids. I bet Willie and the Minthorns could live off what they could hunt and fish and gather at the coast. But they'd have a damned hard time surviving off what they could scrounge at timberline.

Whitefeather Minthorn was the lucky one. She got to sit back in camp by the stove with a hot drink and take messages, monitoring conversations between the other camps and Sasquatch Central. This was officially to help Bondurant and his helpers coordinate the search, and unofficially to ensure that the Popoleyev team didn't get screwed.

At Cascade Run, the flagged pins bearing colors assigned to Whitcomb, and Thibodeaux, and Popoleyev, plus a number for each participant, were presumably being moved about on the Bigfoot Bigboard, or whatever it was the topographical master map was being called. Ten pins for Thibodeaux. Twelve for Whitcomb. Five for Popoleyev.

Whitefeather also took care of Harold's and Opal's needs. She was as good at cooking as Willie was, if not better, a fact which even he admitted. Her special soup, made of several varieties of salted fish and dried seaweed, wasn't half bad. And her invigorating tea, made of boiled Douglas fir needles and wild rose hips, was positively of the gods.

As I lay there, I wondered: if Sasquatch only came out early in the morning or late in the afternoon, and was not nocturnal in the biological sense, what did he do with all those hours inside his cave? It was unlikely that he had yet invented pinochle or mah-jongg.

Chapter Twenty-three

What
Frenchmen
Like

Sonja Popoleyev and I didn't know exactly why we were to leave room in our daypacks, but we did what we were told. Be wary, Willie Prettybird had said. With map, water, lunch, and warm clothes, we set off, tacking downhill to the southwest.

To the inexperienced, knowing how to read the closer-together, farther-apart elevation whorls on a topographic map did not mean you could actually envision the terrain. I also knew the difference between a whole note and a quarter note, but I couldn't read music, sing, or play an instrument.

The map made far more sense when you could compare the elevation whorls to the real thing, which we were able to do after more than an hour of hard, downhill going. When we reached our assigned draw, we tried to get our bearings by matching names and lines on the map with what we could see below us.

The narrow, steep draw had scattered, stunted evergreens on both sides, and a dry streambed at the bottom, strewn with rocks and boulders. Each year the draw was etched deeper by runoff from the snowpack that accumulated over the winter. The runoff started in early spring and continued well into June and July. Come August and September, the snowpack was depleted, and the dry streambeds awaited the next cycle of snow and thaw.

What began as a trickle in a rainstorm or at the edge of a melting snowpack, ended up in the Columbia River on its way to the Pacific Ocean. Now, in October, the Cowlitz River flowed north; two forks of the Toutle River flowed to the northwest; the Kalama and the Lewis rivers emptied to the southwest; and the Wind and White Salmon rivers ran to the south. We couldn't see Cascade Run, which was blocked by Devil's Ridge and Marble Mountain.

Popoleyev said, "I just thought of a poem."

"Let's hear it."

"It's my first poem in English, so if you'll bear with me. It's called 'Only Lately Mountain Water' ":

> *As it grows larger,*
> *faster goes the water,*
> *fast'r, fast'r,*
> *and then . . . slower,*
> *ss-low-wer*
> *slow-goer when it's low-er,*
> *until, see-date-ly,*
> *(Only lately*
> *mountain water),*
> *it slides softly*
> *into the sens-sual sssea.*

"All right!" I said. "What goes around, comes around."

Popoleyev and I set forth down the steep side of the draw, aiming for the bottom. By the time we got there—finding a rocky gash that must have handled a torrent during the spring runoff—we had been gone more than two hours from camp.

The worst part, we both knew, would be going back. That was uphill, hard work.

We decided, for our first day's assignment, to make a careful sweep at least two hundred yards downhill at the bottom of the draw Willie had selected for us, taking time to rest along the way.

"Are you ready, Dr. Popoleyev?"

"After you, Mr. Denson."

I took my side of the draw, and she took hers. We eased slowly downhill. There was no evidence of a Sasquatch trail that I could see, but then again I wasn't Bobby Minthorn.

At the bottom of the draw, where the rocky bed of the runoff stream split, and with the trees growing taller and a carpet of moss at their bases, we found . . . Awwww, that clever Willie. Leave room in your daypacks, he had said.

Chanterelles.

Chanterelles everywhere. Those beautiful orangish-yellow, trumpet-looking mushrooms—so firm and delicately flavored—were just everywhere.

Stay alert, Willie had said.

If we loved chanterelles, Sasquatch had no doubt discovered them too. A place like this should be fat city. Did Sasquatch spend most of the winter thawing out frozen chanterelles?

I grabbed a quick handful and held them up for Popoleyev to see, but she had figured it out for herself. She was squatting, staring intently downhill, her heart no doubt thumping like timpani.

I did the same thing. Dammit, I wanted Popoleyev to find her Sasquatch. I'd been wrong before. And I could always buy myself another bus.

We searched the area carefully, and then I sat down, contemplating chanterelles beyond count. The draw was a regular freeway leading up to cave country. This had to be something in the order of a Sasquatch supermarket. Had to be.

But . . .

Nothing.

After a while Popoleyev came over and plopped down beside me.

We waited.

And we waited.

Still nothing.

Finally, she said, "All of these beautiful mushrooms just waiting to be picked and stored by a *troglodytidae*. No Sasquatch. No foot-prints. No trails. Nothing."

"This is just the first day."

Popoleyev was not cheered. "Shall we eat our lunch now? I'm hungry."

"Now's as good a time as any," I said, slipping my daypack over my shoulders.

We sat in silence, eating dried apples and jerky and drinking cold water out of our canteens.

Finally, I said, "Dr. Popoleyev, did you hear the story about the guy who went to heaven and bitched to Saint Peter that he'd never won a lottery. Saint Peter said, 'Well, did you buy a ticket?' At least you bought a ticket, Dr. Popoleyev . . . As far as I'm concerned it's TT for those morons back there bitching because you're part of the search."

"TT?"

"Tough tittie. Expression of my cousin Bill who raised turkeys for a living. Was one himself, I always said."

Popoleyev laughed. "When I get back, I'll add it to Stanley's memory. Dr. Inskeep loved the vernacular."

High noon and it was too cold for me. As the sun got lower, the cold would settle into our bones. We finished lunch and filled our backpacks to bulging with prime chanterelles, and started the long, hard uphill hike back to our base camp and a warming fire.

On the way, in order to keep my mind off the hike, I told her about the summers I spent helping Bill with the artificial insemina-tion of hen turkeys. Bill managed the turkeys' sexual strategy himself, with the help of pamphlets written by professors at Oregon State University.

When new kinds of low-fat, all-turkey lunch meat and hot dogs became popular, Bill's turkeys developed bigger and bigger breasts and smaller and smaller brains until they were so stupid that if one of them looked up in a rainstorm and opened its mouth, it'd drown.

Popoleyev said that was a perfect example of what happens when reproductive strategy is left entirely in the hands of a male.

When we got back, Whitefeather Minthorn was bent over the radio listening to Thomas Bondurant trying to calm an incensed Roger Whitcomb.

Whitcomb said, "We all have detailed topographical maps, Dr. Bondurant, and we have an agreement. We shook on it."

Bondurant said, "Yes, yes, I know we did, Roger."

"We agreed that we would begin low and systematically move higher. A coordinated search aimed at producing results."

Thibodeaux, listening in, said, "Jesus H. Christ."

"Your people are all Mazamans, Emile, experienced climbers. They know how to read a topographical map. They knew perfectly well where they were, and yet they continued."

"We felt we were on a trail. We were following what we thought could be sign. Under the circumstances, you don't spend your time fiddling with a map. You stay alert."

I understood Thibodeaux's annoyance. For one thing, his climbers couldn't be seen from Whitcomb's position. The terrible transgression of the Canadian's team could only have been spotted by an outsider with binoculars.

Whitcomb said, "Did you report this 'sign' and 'trail' of yours so we could share the information?"

If Whitcomb was monitoring Thibodeaux's team, he was almost certainly watching us as well. I could hear a faint *pf, pf, pf.* I couldn't figure the sound for a moment, then it hit me: Thibodeaux's pipe.

Whitcomb said, "Nobody in my camp heard anything about a trail. I asked everybody. Double-checked, in fact."

Pf, pf, pf.

"This is supposed to be a joint expedition, is it not? I ask you, Dr. Bondurant, did Emile report finding an alleged trail?"

Pf. Pf.

Bondurant cleared his throat. "In the future, Mr. Thibodeaux, if you find what you think is a Sasquatch trail, be kind enough to let us know immediately. It would help us avoid hurt feelings and confusion."

Whitcomb said, "If we work together, Emile, who knows what we might accomplish?" He had a sarcastic, self-righteous edge to his voice.

"Jesus H. Christ," Thibodeaux repeated.

"In retrospect, did you think it was a trail, Mr. Thibodeaux?" Bondurant asked.

"What does that mean? At the time we thought it might have been a trail, and that's what counts," Thibodeaux said.

"Bullshit too," Whitcomb said. "Had to freelance it. Just had to. We need to work together, Emile. Cooperation."

What a boy scout!

Pf. Pf. Thibodeaux said, "Perhaps we could have altimeters sent in, Roger. My climbers could tie them to their peckers, so they wouldn't forget to check them."

Politely, as though Thibodeaux had said nothing at all untoward, Bondurant said, "Mrs. Minthorn, are you listening in up your way?"

"Oh, sure," Whitefeather said. "Everything's fine here in the center. We maybe had too much vodka last night, but we were up and at 'em this morning."

"Have any of your party found anything that might be interpreted as sign, or anything that might assist Mr. Whitcomb and Mr. Thibodeaux in their efforts?"

"No, they haven't, but John and Dr. Popoleyev brought back a good mess of chanterelles. They're coming on up here."

Thibodeaux said, "We collected a bunch of 'em ourselves, Mrs. Minthorn. They're just delicious."

Whitcomb didn't like it that Thibodeaux and Whitefeather Minthorn were being cordial—especially after the crack about altimeters. "Chanterelles. Sasquatch, man! Sasquatch. We're after Sasquatch here."

Mildly, Thibodeaux said, "If a Frenchman likes his chanterelles, Roger, did it ever strike you that Sasquatch might like them too?"

I was eager to see what Whitefeather Minthorn would do with the chanterelles.

She stood over me grinning as I emptied my daypack full of mushrooms. "You think you're pretty smart, don't you? Mr. Fancy Stuff."

"They're beautiful, aren't they?" Popoleyev said.

"They're in their prime," Whitefeather said.

Popoleyev and I set about cleaning them as we watched Whitefeather dig into her larder. She came up with some slabs of

Bobby Minthorn's salted, dried salmon, a bag of dried onions, and small dried chilis.

Sound seemed to travel farther in the thin, quiet mountain air.

We all heard a fragment of laughter. Bobby Minthorn.

Another snatch of laughter. Willie Prettybird.

"Ah, they'll be here in a few minutes," she said. She crushed a handful of chilis in her hand and dumped them into the hot oil. She added the dried onions. When the onions were plumped and golden, she dumped in hunks of salmon, frying them until they were crisp; this rehydrated the salted fish with oil that was peppery and contained plenty of onion.

Then she set the fish and onions aside and replaced them with heaping handfuls of sliced chanterelles.

We heard more laughter. Then Prettybird and Minthorn's conversation became clear. They were getting closer.

Whitefeather sampled a slice of chanterelle to see how the 'shrooms were doing.

"And?" I asked.

"Just right. Just short of done." She dumped in the crisp chunks of salmon and the onions and began reheating them.

A branch popped.

Minthorn said, "Of course they scored. And I bet that's what Whitefeather will do with them. I know she brought the salmon, and she'll want to please Dr. Popoleyev. Believe me, it all adds up."

"I hope so."

Whitefeather's timing was perfect. When Prettybird and Minthorn stepped into camp moments later, the fish and mushrooms were both done just right.

Seeing the salmon, Minthorn said, "See, didn't I tell you!"

This dish of Whitefeather's, I knew, was one of Willie's favorites. "Okay!" Willie said.

Whitefeather was pleased. "We heard you guys making bets. Oughta make you good-timers chew jerky tonight."

"I know what I'd like to chew on tonight," Bobby said. He leered at Whitefeather. *"Mmmmmmmm!"*

Whitefeather giggled. "And you, Mr. Hot Damn Tracker, pipe down! What do you think, Sonja? Should I feed him or not?"

Popoleyev grinned at Bobby. "I don't know whether I would, a guy like him."

Bobby sniffing the air, said, "Aren't you forgetting the rest of it?"

"Oh, oh. Almost forgot." Whitefeather opened her fireside oven, a homemade metal contraption, and removed a baking dish containing pear cobbler, the biscuits on top a light, golden brown.

Chapter Twenty-four

The Coolidge Effect

That night, Ruth Anne called. "You know, Mr. Denson, every once in a while I get to feeling sorry for myself being in a wheelchair and everything. But when I put together a string of newspaper clippings like this, I sometimes wonder if I'm not just as happy as a spectator as I would have been as a participant. David Addison, who is now fifty-seven years old, has been married and divorced seven times. Laraine Adams Addison, wife number eight, is twenty-two years old and was a student at Clark College this time last year."

"Children?"

"He has seven. From four of the wives. All the children are still minors, so we've got college coming up with a vengeance."

"And the cost of all this?"

"Boogie thinks it must surely exceed the GNP of Uzbekistan."

"How does he pay for it?"

"This is more difficult, Mr. Denson. Addison's been in and out of a lot of enterprises. He was at the top of his game ten years ago when he was wheeling and dealing as president of the Fort Vancouver Savings and Loan Association, which was the original developer of Cascade Run."

"Well, well. Little flag there."

"Fort Vancouver went under at a cost to the taxpayers of tens of millions of dollars. Addison made an unseemly bundle, but I can't find a clip that says he was ever indicted for anything."

"What happened to Cascade Run?"

"The government took it over and sold it to something called the Great Pittsfield Mining Corporation, of Vancouver, Washington. I can't find anything that suggests that Great Pittsfield actually mines anything."

"Except Cascade Run."

"Olden says the word in Portland is that Great Pittsfield bought it for almost nothing because people don't want to buy expensive vacation chalets at the foot of an active volcano. I'm still working on this. I'll do my best to see if there's any connection between Addison and Great Pittsfield, because I know that will be your next question."

"It certainly is. Thank you. Say, Ruth Anne, did Olden say if he could have somebody check that question about the rum for me?"

"He said yes he would, Mr. Denson. I hope to have the answer tomorrow or the next day."

I told Sonja Popoleyev about David Addison's many failed attempts to find happiness with a woman. "And I bet he's got girlfriends on the side. Dr. Popoleyev, based on your knowledge of Stanley, what do you think would account for Addison's behavior? Frenzied mating? Does that describe it? Surely there's something basic at work here."

Popoleyev thought. Then she brightened, smiling. "Here's a story I got courtesy of my American colleagues. It features your President Calvin Coolidge and his famous chickens. Chickens, like us, are a tournament species, so in this instance, the rooster's strategy, not to mention his frustrations, should be roughly identical to Stanley's."

"Calvin Coolidge?"

"Yes. It seems President Coolidge and his wife once visited a model chicken farm. Mrs. Coolidge and her party toured the farm first, and her husband and his aides went later. When Mrs. Coolidge asked the farmer how many times a rooster performed in a day, the farmer said twelve.

"Mrs. Coolidge said, 'Oh? Tell that to the President.'

"The farmer did.

"Coolidge asked, 'Same hen?'

"The farmer looked surprised. 'Oh, no, Mr. President. Different hens.'

"The President said, 'Tell that to Mrs. Coolidge.' " Popoleyev laughed. "Yes, your President Coolidge! Isn't it a wonderful story? My colleagues in the United States refer to the excitement of variety experienced by males of a tournament species as the Coolidge Effect. The phrase is commonplace in the literature.

"Stanley is like Jason chasing the Golden Fleece. Whereas the frustrated Jason always crashes on the rocks, just missing the Fleece, Stanley actually finds it. Or thinks he has. He finds Her. The one. She is shining. Golden. So sexy his head spins. But to a tournament male, familiarity is a form of evolutionary oxidant, and in a couple of years, the fleece that was golden becomes ordinary. Gilt! It was all gilt! The luster is gone. What happened to the gold?

"Blanche slowly loses the provocative sexuality of youth, so Stanley is condemned to a life of eternal frustration. What he thinks he wants, he can't have. Never. It is impossible. If Blanche is doomed to lose her sex appeal, Stanley is condemned to retain his sexual desire. In time, the more or less civilized Stanleys come to understand the nature of their dilemma even if they can never really come to terms with it.

"As long as Stanley's success with Blanche is determined by tournament, which is what various forms of competition is all about—from the athletic field to the workplace—the Coolidge Effect will remain with us, Mr. Denson. You may be sure we will get eternally frustrated Stanleys like David Addison who pursue the phantom of the impossible no matter what the consequences."

Chapter Twenty-five

A Visitor at Midnight

The cold crept into my bones after I got up to take my usual midnight leak, but I fought it off, trying to get back to sleep. It would have been hubris to believe I could defeat the rising tide within me.

The wind knocked against the tent, *wuh-whap, wuh-whap! Fap, fap, fap! Wuh-whap, wuh-whap! Fap, fap, fap!*

In the darkness, I saw that Earl had abandoned the warmth of his nest atop Bobby and Whitefeather and was standing up listening.

I whispered, "What's the matter, Earl? Little insomnia?"

Earl glanced my way, then flopped back down on Bobby and Whitefeather.

Then his head popped up, listening again.

Then I heard something in the woods to the west, in the direction of Whitcomb and his party.

Or did I?

Earl leaped to his feet.

I wiggled out of the sack. Earl looked at me in the darkness.

Should I go outside and take a look?

In the darkness, Willie said softly, "What do you think, Denson? Earl hear something?"

I said, "I thought I heard something. A branch breaking maybe. Heard it twice."

Bobby said, "What did you hear, Earl?"

Earl growled.

"Easy, Earl." Bobby began abandoning his warm spot alongside Whitefeather.

Willie crawled out of his sleeping bag and started grabbing for clothes.

Earl was getting agitated.

"Easy." Bobby squatted, his arm around Earl.

Popoleyev whispered, "What do you recommend we do, Willie?"

Everybody was awake now.

Willie, his voice soft, said, "I think we should go outside and have a look around."

Popoleyev said, "Good idea."

"We'll each take a flashlight. We'll ease on outside and give our eyes time to adjust to the darkness. If we hear something, we give ourselves time to get a fix on it. On my command we do our best to pin it with five beams at once, which is when you, Chief, do your thing with Olden's camera."

"Got it," I said.

Willie and Bobby went first with Earl, then me, then Popoleyev and Whitefeather.

Willie and Bobby squatted low in the shadows, and we did too. We listened, waiting for our eyes to adjust to the darkness.

Earl growled softly, hardly more than a rumble in the back of his throat. He had been hunting with Bobby Minthorn many times, and he knew noise was not in order.

One of the mules snorted.

Earl growled again, slightly louder. His growl said: it's getting closer, dude.

Bobby held him by the snout. "Easy, Earl. Easy does it."

Earl tensed.

A branch snapped.

We could hear whatever it was moving around maybe twenty or thirty yards below our camp.

Willie put a hand on my shoulder. He whispered in my ear. "Watch me. When I give the word, we'll pin him with our light, and then you do your thing with Olden's camera. If he runs, stay right with him, Bobby and I will be right beside you with our flashlights."

"With your flashlight? Tonto! What if it gets pissed or something?"

He gave my back a reassuring pat. No problem.

"It could come back our way. What if it attacks, for Christ's sake?"

"You're the cameraman, Kemosabe. Your job to capture all the action."

"Willie, dammit!"

He whispered instructions to the others, and we waited some more. Whatever was making the noise was slowly, no doubt warily, approaching the camp, easing closer and closer.

The mules stirred.

Whitefeather moved noiselessly past me on her way to them.

The mules settled down.

Whatever was down there moved closer. Something down there. Some animal-thing.

Closer still.

Then stopped.

Bobby held Earl firmly by the snout. Earl was crouched, muscles tensed, ready for the chase.

I could see Willie's finger at his lips, signaling everybody to remain as quiet as possible. Then he motioned for us to get ready.

"Now," he said softly and evenly.

We rose as one, beams on . . .

A Sasquatch! Or something huge and hairy and two-legged.

Reflecting bright, piercing pink eye shine.

"Heel!" Bobby said.

I pulled down on the beast with Olden's camera and pulled the trigger. I had him in the lens. Yes!

The beast put one arm up, as if shielding his eyes from the lights, then turned, and started running. He might have had big feet, but he sure could move.

I was pumped. I took off after him with Willie, Bobby, and Earl cruising on either side of me. I had longer legs than Willie or Bobby, but that didn't count for diddly.

Willie said, "Run, run, run, Denson, keep 'em moving."

Bobby said, "Watch-it, watch-it, watch-it, John. Watch your feet. Heel, Earl. Heel."

Willie said, "Move, move, move, John."

"Watch your feet. Watch. Heel, Earl."

Awww-ooof! Awww-ooof! Action. Earl loved every second of it.

"Quiet, Earl. Dammit. Heel. Heel."

Awww-ooof!

"Quiet!"

I ran as hard as I could, carrying Olden's camera like a football, but it was hopeless. After about sixty yards of dangerous lurching and stumbling through the darkness—my lungs raw from the cold air—I tripped over something and pitched forward. Using my knees and elbows to protect Olden's camera, I tumbled into a roll on the frozen ground, skidding to a painful halt.

I lay there, my bruised knees and elbows throbbing, thinking Sonja Popoleyev could take this job and shove it. It was bad enough slamming my elbow against the wall at Cascade Run, but this was worse. Ay!

Earl came up and gave me an excited slurp on the side of my face with his tongue. A real dog-to-man show of affection. Yuch! I said, "Dammit, Earl!"

Willie and Bobby, gasping for air and laughing at the same time, helped me to my feet.

Bobby said, "He just loves you, Denson. He wants to kiss you."

Willie said, "Man, Denson. You surprised me, you bastard. Crazy legs! I could hardly keep up."

"Sure, sure."

"You were moving, ain't no doubt," Bobby said. He rested the heels of his hands on top of his knees and scooped in a lungful of air.

"I should have dropped the stupid camera and protected myself."

Popoleyev caught up with us. "Are you okay, Mr. Denson?"

"I'm fine," I said. "Be a little sore in the morning."

"Mr. Denson, you should have seen yourself run!"

"Ooof!" I swear it even hurt to grin.

Willie said, "Crazy legs!"

I said, "The worst part was getting licked by Earl. God! Would you tell him to keep that damn tongue of his in his mouth, Bobby?"

Bobby said, "You'll hurt Earl's feelings, talking like that."

"No telling where he's had that tongue of his."

Bobby nuzzled Earl behind the ears. "He didn't mean to say bad things about you, Earl."

I said, "The hell I didn't. What was that we were chasing, Willie?"

Willie looked into the darkness. "To tell you the truth, John, I don't know. Big furry thing. Sasquatch maybe. Bobby?"

"It was big and furry and fast, I'll give it all three," Minthorn said.

Popoleyev said, "Did you see the eye shine?"

"I have to admit," Willie said.

"I saw it," Bobby said.

"Me too," Whitefeather added.

Popoleyev said, "No human's eyes reflect light like that. Not at that distance. Well, Mr. Denson, what do you say now?"

"Something reflected light, I can't deny that."

"He's a nocturnal. *Troglodytes recens.* We must not tell the others of this. We must not. Please."

"See what?" I said. "You see anything, Willie?"

Willy looked confused. "See what?"

"What are you talking about?" Bobby said.

"I didn't see anything," Whitefeather said.

"Thank you all," Popoleyev said. "Human eyes do not reflect light that brightly. I know we have an agreement with the others, but until we find out for sure that the creature who looked back at us with those eyes is somehow bogus, we owe our loyalty to his right to be left alone. If it is a *Troglodytes recens,* we are, thank goodness, precisely where we ought to be."

Chapter Twenty-six

What Crow
Saw

None of us could sleep.

One by one, we each sat up, our sleeping bags wrapped around our hunched shoulders.

All the talk of footprints and diet and habitat had juiced our imaginations. Then, Earl's restlessness . . .

Somebody was either funning us big-time, or a large, curious beast was out there roaming around.

Sonja Popoleyev was especially excited because the intruder's eyes had reflected light. Pink eye shine. He was nocturnal. He was *Troglodytes recens*. Popoleyev's monster. She was sure of it.

I could understand her excitement. She was reserved if anything. If it had been me, I'd have been out of control.

Willie turned up the kerosene stove to give us a little heat. His eyes were great hollows of darkness. He said, "What do you think, John?"

"I think I'm sore."

"You, Whitefeather?"

Whitefeather, petting Earl, said, "I'm worried that thing will come back on Harold and Opal. They can't run when they're tied up like that."

Bobby said, "They'll be okay. Earl will give us plenty of warning if he comes back."

Popoleyev said, "That was my monster out there. *Troglodytes recens.*"

Willie said, "Denson?" He was getting his weird voice. Señor Shaman, or whatever.

"Yeah, Tonto."

"I think I feel the pull coming on. I may be about to travel. Would you explain the drill to Dr. Popoleyev, please?"

"Sure, Willie." Willie Prettybird, aka Coyote, never went into one of his trances when a person could get a good look at his face. Whether his communication with the animal people was genuine shaman business or Prettybird's jive, I noticed he never did it under direct light.

I said, "Willie thinks he's being called to the world of the animal people, Dr. Popoleyev. We'll have to give him a few minutes of silence to see if he can make contact."

"Of course," she said.

"He may reach them. He may not. If he does, they may talk. They may not."

"Understood."

"I've talked to the animal people through Willie many times before. I have become a skeptical guide, which they seem to prefer to true believers. Whatever they are, you should know these are real people, some of whom, you could say, have become my friends. You should pay attention to what Willie says because he won't remember any of it later."

"Got it, Mr. Denson."

And so we waited. A séance at six thousand feet.

Willie was sincere when he said he couldn't remember his visits. He had as much fun as anybody else in trying to interpret the oftentimes mischievous conundrums offered by the animal people. Some of their messages were enigmatic in the extreme, but Willie seemed capable of divining meaning out of anything.

It was my theory that Willie jacked himself up on these occasions with secret hits of dried psilosybe mushrooms. In the fall, a tiny variety popularly called liberty bells covered the fields and meadows of Western Oregon and Western Washington like a nearly invisible light-brown down. Just about anybody who had grass in their yard had a crop. Fields with cow-pies were fields of bounty come October.

I knew Willie kept an envelope of dried liberty bells in the tool box of his pickup, and I bet it wasn't there now. It was either that or some form of self-hypnosis that I didn't understand.

At length, he said, "I'm Crow, sitting in the top of a Dougie fir, and I'm taking questions. It's cold up here. I gotta get my ass flying or freeze to the branch, so ask away."

I said, "Crow, if you've been watching this Sasquatch business, will you tell us what you saw, and what you make of it? We're entertaining a guest from Russia, and she'd like to know."

> *I saw a man on the moon*
> *sing a lonely tune.*
> *I saw two purple penguins flying in the*
> *moonlight, brighter than the starlight.*
> *I saw one penguin covet the other penguin's plum.*
> *I saw a swallow fly over the Pole.*
> *I saw a goose fly down from the north.*
> *I saw a rat fly up from the south.*
> *I saw a hawk float in from the east.*
> *The first purple penguin was killed with a spoon.*
> *The second purple penguin fell to a loon.*
> *Watch the great horned owl.*
> *Beware the kildeer.*

Willie fell silent. Crow was gone.

We waited.

Willie said, "I'm Crow's friend, Bear. Crow might be right about kildeer, I'm not sure. I say watch for the ouzel . . ."

Earl sat up, alert.

Bobby jumped to his feet.

Whitefeather Minthorn was out of her bag and at the zipper, yelling, "Harold, dammit! Opal!"

We all scrambled out of the tent, but heard nothing. After his initial excitement, Earl quickly relaxed.

By the time we got back from checking the mules, Willie had lost his zone. As usual, he couldn't remember anything.

But Sonja Popoleyev, it turned out, had written down what Crow and Bear had said. We lit the main lantern so she could read her scrawled notes, and we could try to figure out what it was Crow and Bear had meant.

Popoleyev read the statements, then asked, "Anybody want to take a guess?"

I said, "Crow said he saw a man on the moon. Some of us look at the moon and see only the moon. Others see a man on the moon. Not only that, but this one sings a lonely tune. He's a solitary. We're talking about Sasquatch."

Popoleyev said, "Okay!"

"That's it. I agree," Willie said.

"The purple penguins both get killed. They're Elford and Alford Pollard." I waited.

Popoleyev said, "The first penguin was killed with a spoon." She waited for me to tell her what I thought that meant.

Should have kept my mouth shut. Real smart I was. "A spoon is something you need to eat. It's an instrument of consumption. I say spoon in this context means something like 'greed.' He was killed by greed. The swallow that flew over the North Pole is you, Dr. Popoleyev."

"I believe so."

"Slender and elegant. Swift. A beautiful bird."

"Mr. Denson!"

"The goose that flew down from the north is a Canadian honker—Emile Thibodeaux. The rat that flew up from the south is a sea gull, Roger Whitcomb. Willie always says if a white rat had wings it'd be a sea gull."

Willie said, "A sea gull and a rat'll both eat anything. The only difference is rats don't have wings."

Popoleyev said, "That's awful, Willie."

I said, "The hawk that floated in from the east is Thomas Bondurant, come all the way from London."

Popoleyev said, "Crow said 'floating' in from the east. What do you make of that, Bobby?"

Minthorn said, "Hawks have good eyes. Some of them are able to float on updrafts of warm air with their wings outspread, nearly stationary. A shadow sweeps by, and you'll look up, and, high above, there one will be, floating."

I said, "Bondurant rides the currents of hot air, more like it. The second purple penguin, Alford Pollard, was killed by a loon. That is, somebody crazy. I'll leave the great horned owl and the kildeer to you, Bobby."

Bobby said, "A great horned owl is a large, skillful predator with a voracious appetite. The kildeer draws an intruder away from its nest by faking injury. It flaps its wings and says 'Kildeeeeeer! Kildeeeeeer!' Then it flip-flops a little farther away from its eggs, and goes through the routine again. 'Kildeeeeeer! Kildeeeeeer!' "

Popoleyev said, "Bear said we should watch for the ouzel. What did he mean by that, Bobby?"

"An ouzel is a bird that lives around swift, clear mountain streams, so you'll find them in this area. They look like finches or sparrows. Just little guys. They blend in with the rocks, and they're quick so it's hard to see them. But their big surprise is they can use their wings to swim underwater. They fly underwater."

Popoleyev said, "Well, there's one to test your powers, Mr. Denson."

I said, "It could mean something, and it could mean absolutely squat, thrown in there for the hell of it: hey, Bear, why don't you give the Russian lady something fun to think about? She likes evolution. Do they have ouzels in Russia? Ouzels fly underwater. That'll get her."

Willie said, "Come on, Chief!"

"Their riddles are fun, though, I have to admit. I like puzzles. Purple penguins and stuff. A spoon that may or may not be a spoon, depending on whether it is or is not a spoon. Too much Lewis Carroll for the animal people."

"Aw!"

Bobby said, "Denson's got a point, Willie. Tell the nice Russian lady the whole truth."

"Well, okay, Dr. Popoleyev. Once in a while the animal people get bored, it's so. Most of the time, when I ask them a question, they do their best to be helpful. But sometimes . . ."

Popoleyev said, "They express their sense of humor in what manner, then? In addition to riddles."

"You should hear some of the outrageous tales they try to palm off on me. It's like Paul Bunyan time, or Pecos Bill. They just love to see how much they can get away with."

Popoleyev laughed. "Once in a while they 'have you on,' I believe is how an Englishman would put it."

My buddy, the shaman, or whatever he was supposed to be, gave Dr. Sonja Popoleyev a big, good-hearted grin. Coyote smiling.

Or a smart-as-hell screwball having a good time.

I didn't care either way.

Chapter Twenty-seven

Opal Earns
Her Oats

By the time I got up at six-thirty, Willie, Bobby, and Earl were already forty-five minutes gone, hot on the trail of our nocturnal visitor. I had no sooner dressed and joined Whitefeather and Popoleyev for a morning cup of coffee than they were back, looking frustrated.

Willie plopped down, dejected. "Lost him."

Popoleyev said, "What happened?"

Bobby said, "He went west until he came to a large bench, then cut straight up the mountain. If Earl could climb rocks, we would have found him by now, but there's no way to take a dog up that terrain outside of carrying him."

"What'll you do now?"

"We try again after breakfast, but we leave Earl here with Whitefeather. Sorry, old partner." Bobby gave Earl a hug.

Willie unfolded his topographical map and, with Bobby, Popoleyev, and I standing over his shoulder, tapped his finger on the representation of a large, flat landform, a geologic bench that lay to the west, clearly closer to us than Roger Whitcomb.

Willie said, "The mountain is nearly perpendicular above the bench—prime geography for caves. If all the suppositions about Bigfoot's habits have any merit at all, this spot"—he tapped on the map again—"an isolated bench in prime cave country, ought to be Sasquatch Junction."

"You and Bobby will check the rocks above the bench, while Dr. Popoleyev and I check the bench itself. Is that the idea?"

"That's how Bobby and I see it."

I studied the map more carefully. There wasn't an easy way to get from our camp to the promising bench. The shortest path, due west, was also the steepest. The pitch was civilized at the base of a cliff farther down, but that meant a time-consuming descent and maneuvering, plus climbing up again on the far side. I said, "How did the Sasquatch get there? He was headed west, not downhill."

Willie said, "He continued straight across. He obviously knows this part of the mountain."

Bobby said, "He's either nocturnal and can see well at night, or he turned on his flashlight after he ditched us. You'll have to take your time if you go straight west, it gets steeper than a bitch in places and is littered with shale."

Willie said, "What do you think, Dr. Popoleyev?"

"I think I couldn't sleep all last night for seeing those eyes shining back at us and thinking *Troglodytes recens*. It would be fun if Dr. Inskeep were still alive. On the trail of Popoleyev's monsters. He'd love it."

Willie said, "If you do take the high route, you'll eventually come to a rocky nub that sticks out. Good place for a breather. The bench is about a hundred yards beyond that. But remember, be careful."

I carried Olden Dewlapp's Sony videocamera in my daypack so I'd have my hands free to grab things in an emergency. Sonja Popoleyev brought our lunch of jerky and dried fruit in her pack, and we each carried a canteen of melted snow on our hips.

Thus provisioned, we headed straight west. We wanted to spend our time checking the bench, not getting there and back, so we proceeded, slowly, straight across the treacherous slope.

I suppose a 90-degree drop was required for a cliff, but this slope looked just as dangerous, if not more so. Here, once loose, a rolling stone gathered no moss, that was a fact, just gained speed bounding downhill.

It was difficult for me to imagine that a Sasquatch would want to spend much time in such terrain. I suppose Popoleyev and others felt that human failure of the imagination was the reason for his survival.

If Popoleyev or I slipped, the only thing to stop us from hurtling all the way to the bottom were occasional Douglas firs, which, at this elevation, were so stunted as to be a joke. The trees that survived here at the top edge of the timberline were no more than six or seven feet high, nature's own *bonsai*. At lower elevations the Douglas fir wide-bodies, rising to seventy feet high, were highly prized timber, much sought after by loggers bent on making every dime possible.

Besides being short, skinny little things at this elevation, there weren't very many of them. Why the silly trees bothered to take root in such an inhospitable area was beyond me, but these gritty evergreens were to be admired for their perseverance in surviving.

I tried to avoid looking downhill, telling myself that if I could negotiate stairs, get in and out of bed, and climb into my VW bus without falling down, it should be no different here. I concentrated on each step, testing it before I put my weight on it. That didn't leave me a whole lot of time to look for Sasquatch, but I didn't care.

If Popoleyev wanted to find Sasquatch that badly, *she* could peer ahead as she progressed. Not me.

We hadn't gotten more than thirty yards when I cheated. I looked down, down, down. If there was more level terrain down there, I couldn't see it. The pitch got steeper and steeper until, nearly perpendicular, it disappeared into the trees. Somewhere down there was the cliff.

I stopped, my mouth dry. "Maybe we should just find one place and sit. Have you taken a look down there?"

"I've been trying not to." Popoleyev looked downhill and took a deep, anxious lungful of air. "Perhaps if we go extra slow, Mr. Denson. Slowly and carefully."

"I'd have thought Sasquatch would have evolved small feet for this kind of terrain."

"Watch your step, Mr. Denson."

We went slow, and slower, picking our way, selecting and testing each step. Still it was spooky. There was a good reason for people to have a fear of heights, just as there was for them to avoid snakes.

After about a hundred and fifty yards, a nearly level patch of large boulders protruded from the steep pitch in front of us. This was the nub Willie had mentioned. We were inching toward this civilized terrain when we both froze in place.

Behind me, Popoleyev whispered, "Mr. Denson?"

"I see him," I whispered back.

In the rocks, watching us. Sasquatch. Or some moron dressed up like Sasquatch.

"A hominid."

"Steady," I whispered.

Keeping an eye on the beast, which peered over the top of a rock, I reached around to retrieve Olden Dewlapp's camera from my daypack.

"Sasquatch," she whispered.

"Easy. Easy. Look at the ground, not at him." I wasn't worried about being wrong, only about the truth. Bogus or real, I wanted to get the damn thing on tape. I felt for the zipper tab on the daypack. Got it. I started to pull. Stuck. The zipper was stuck.

Aw!

Popoleyev, seeing my problem, freed the tab.

I yanked again.

I also slipped.

Ahhhh!

And went plummeting down the slope, belly-surfing sideways on loose rocks.

Whack! I hit one tree. Caught it across my legs.

Kept going.

No!

Bam! Another tree. Ribs this time.

Bounced away.

Sliding.

Gaining speed.

Crunch! Another tree.

I grabbed. Got something. Held tight.

I spit blood and dirt from my mouth. The side of my face stung from scraped hide.

I looked back up at Popoleyev.

She called, "Are you okay?"

"Until I start sliding again. But don't mind me. Go for Sasquatch."

"Don't move."

Such roots as there were to the tree had been very nearly ripped out by my impact. "The tree is coming loose."

Above me, Popoleyev had her binoculars out, studying my predicament.

Looking up at her, I swallowed. "What do you think?"

"Stay perfectly still."

"What's below me?" I didn't want to call too loudly for fear the exertion would jar me loose.

"Quiet."

I took a quick peek downhill. About six feet below me there was nothing—the top of the cliff.

She said, "I'm going to return the way we came. If I circle to the east and take it over to you from that side, maybe it won't be so dangerous. That's the way we should have gone in the first place."

"The way we should have gone. I'm glad we had Ike at Normandy."

"I'll be right back. Don't wiggle around or try to go anywhere. Just hold on."

"Do you think I'm going to let go?"

"Shush."

I waited. And waited.

My tree's roots were moving. It hardly had any roots to begin with, and those it did have were pulling away from the shallow, rocky soil.

In the grip of the gentle hand of gravity, I was slowly . . .

Slowly . . .

Beginning to move . . .

Ooof!

When, not if, I popped free, I knew, that would be it.

I waited for what seemed an eternity, but was maybe only twenty or thirty minutes.

Finally, above me and to my right, Popoleyev and Whitefeather Minthorn approached me from the relatively safe southeast.

Seeing me, Whitefeather said, "Oh, God!"

Popoleyev tied a length of wood to a rope and threw it out onto the slope above me. The wood slid downhill, headed my way. It got caught on a rock. She swore in Russian and yanked at it until it was free.

"Hold on."

The roots moved a little.

"The tree's coming loose." I was scared. Real, real, scared.

Whitefeather, holding on to a small tree, leaned out to help jiggle the rope and guide the wood. She said, "Don't talk, John. Listen to me. Listen to what I'm telling you."

I shut my mouth.

The wood got stuck again. Popoleyev jiggled it free, swearing in Russian.

Whitefeather said, "It's going to be all right, John. Relax. Just relax."

Just relax. Sure. Down it came, lower and lower . . .

The roots were coming out.

Christ!

Four feet away . . .

"Hurry."

"Steady, Mr. Denson."

Was there enough rope?

Two feet . . .

"Do it, please."

Popoleyev gave the rope another flip.

Inches away. Inches!

The length of wood hung momentarily, then kept sliding.

The roots pulled free.

I grabbed for the wood.

Got it!

I hung on, wondering if I had the energy, with my ribs throbbing, to pull myself up. But I didn't have to.

Popoleyev and Whitefeather, together apparently possessing the strength of three or four Sasquatches, hauled me right on out of there. Damn near yanked me, skidding, beak first, up the slope.

It was not until I got to the top, hands trembling, that I found out that my brown-eyed ladyfriend, Opal, was the one who had done the pulling. Harold had been put off by the slope, but Opal, sweet thing, had chanced it.

Ms. Twinklehooves.

Unembarrassed, wincing from the pain of bruised ribs, I gave the lady a kiss on her velvet nose. With Popoleyev and Whitefeather laughing, I promised Opal that when I got home I'd buy her a hundred-pound sack of rolled oats spiked with the sweetest molasses money could buy. I'd stir in some nuts if that struck her fancy. I could get a price on hazelnuts in Oregon. Exotic grains. Anything.

I didn't imagine the forces of evolution had given Opal any particular motive to pull me out of there, but she had done it. She was the second female who had saved my life. The first, a *Homo sapiens sapiens* named Pamela, had blown a man's brains out in the middle of a rainy night in Seattle, thus preserving for another day John Denson's most precious bacon.

No amount of oats or molasses or grain was too good for Opal. Whatever the nature of her mulish strategy, when I needed her, she was there. No fair price could be placed on such steadfast and comforting loyalty.

I took care of Opal. She took care of me. She earned her oats. Reciprocity was life's basic deal. Human to human. Human to dog. Human to mule. Surely our genes understood that.

Chapter Twenty-eight

A Bare Patch
of Rock

When we got back to camp, I couldn't shake the episode from my memory. Mountain climbers could have it.

I said, "We got a beast with eye shine last night. Now this. Maybe that was a Sasquatch watching us, and maybe it was foolishness. Either way, I'd like to hear what Willie and Bobby have to say before we call Bondurant and the others."

"So would I."

The incident had reminded us of the fragility of our mortality. It wasn't like we were skiers and could brake ourselves with a neat twist of our skis. Once you got started, as I had, it was *mo-men-tum*, Big Mo, all the way to the bottom.

Just one slip or false step and we were gone, which was no doubt the thrill of climbing mountains.

Popoleyev shook her head, grinning. "You should have seen yourself slide, Mr. Denson. It was truly something."

"It was something all right."

"The last tree. The very last tree." She giggled.

"If you could call it a tree. Hardly had any roots."

She shook her head again, grinning. "I'm sorry to laugh, but now that you're okay, it's funny. Slapstick."

Ha, ha, ha. "Proof that the fear of heights has a logical basis."

We were camped on reasonably civilized terrain, however, and it was possible to go for a walk without pretending to be Edmund Hillary, so I went foraging for some extra goodies for Opal's supper.

After the mules were taken care of, I had a cup of coffee. A couple of minutes later, Willie and Bobby showed up, hungry for a little camp stew themselves.

Willie and Bobby listened, amused, as Popoleyev and I told them what had happened.

When we were finished, Willie said, "Man, you've outdone yourself this time, Denson. You know, they don't run an Olympic downhill without snow. No sense practicing on rock and bare ground. You have to use snow, man." Willie unfolded our topographical map and studied it. "Let's see, you were closing in on the rock nub when you saw him and lost your step."

Popoleyev said, "He was peering over a boulder. Although it's hard to say, to be honest. It all happened so fast."

"Let's go back and take a look. We've got time. It stays light longer up here than in the valleys."

Bobby and Willie could have picked up our trail and found the spot by themselves, but Popoleyev, her imagination inflamed by the promise of *Troglodytes recens,* was eager to return.

There was no way, none, that I was going to stay back in camp with Whitefeather and nurse the bruises on my precious wrists and elbows. If Popoleyev was going back, so was I.

When we got to the edge of the steep slope, we queued up, our waists joined by a single nylon rope, to retrace the path of disaster. Bobby went first, followed by Willie, Popoleyev, then me.

As we set out, Willie said, "The purpose of this line is so Denson can kill us all at once without meaning to or even half trying. This is the disaster-in-waiting that Boogie and Olden have been predicting for some time."

My accident hadn't taught me more fear or more acceptance of the danger of the hillside. Being afraid of heights was inside me, like snakes and Popoleyev's monsters. It was a logical fear. The farther you fell or tumbled—or slid—the more damage you risked, starting with broken wrists and ankles and working up the disaster ladder to budget-busting fractured skulls, full-body casts, and worse.

When we got to the spot of my accident, Bobby stopped. He unhooked himself and climbed uphill several yards.

Willie, who could then see what Bobby had seen, said, "Oh ho!"

Above us, Bobby said, "Isn't that something?" He went downhill six or eight yards past Willie and took another look. Shaking his head, he returned to his place.

Willie unhooked himself and did the same thing as Bobby. Uphill, then downhill. "Amazing," he said. "Wait'll I tell Boogie and Olden about this one. This'll give us ammunition for years."

All Popoleyev and I could see was Willie's back, or Bobby's. We were dying to see what the fun was all about.

Willie and Bobby knew that, and so made us wait.

Bobby said, "Tell me, Dr. Popoleyev, after Denson slid down the hill, what did you do?"

Popoleyev looked back at me, puzzled.

Bobby said, "You started downhill after him, didn't you?"

"Yes, I did. Out of instinct. Then I knew it was impossible."

"Did you glance back to see if Sasquatch was still there?"

"A quick look, yes. He was gone."

"Take a look now."

Bobby and Willie hunched down so Popoleyev and I could see over them, and what we saw were boulders. However, several of the rocks were piled in such a way that, with the sun just so and a little imagination, they could be mistaken for the silhouette of a large beast or man.

Popoleyev and I groaned nearly simultaneously.

Bobby said, "If you go uphill or downhill a few yards, all you see are rocks. You have to see them from the right angle."

Willie said, "It's like you told Emile Thibodeaux, Dr. Popoleyev. You see what you want to see."

Popoleyev said, "What you are psychologically prepared to see, yes."

Both Popoleyev and I, still excited about seeing the Sasquatch the previous night, had been momentarily convinced we had encountered another such beast. It was this mountain Rorschach, a suggestive combination of rocks, no more, that had gotten me so excited I had nearly slid to my death.

We continued to the Sasquatch rocks where we took a break, laughing at the screwup that had nearly cost me my life. Then we pushed off for the geologic bench that lay about 150 yards dead ahead.

Willie was right. The rocks, boulders, and pock-marked cliffs immediately above the bench looked like nothing if not cave country. In the movies, there would have been a cave up there, guaranteed.

The flat bench, following the curve of the mountain, was about 150 yards long and 20 yards wide. It was covered with whitish-gray ash, and littered with rocks and volcanic debris. In addition, rocks and boulders tumbling down from above had accumulated at the base of the bench—where the landform butted up against the mountain.

We spread out, looking for Sasquatch sign. But before we got a chance to look at much, Sonja Popoleyev stopped and called us over. She had found a large circle that was devoid of ash, exposing bare rock.

The four of us gathered around the spot and knelt. No ash. Why?

Popoleyev said, "What do you make of it, Willie?"

Willie retreated to the edge of the circle and blew on the whitish-gray ash, exposing more rock. "Remember the helicopter we heard the first night?"

Bobby said, "I see. I think you're right, Willie."

Popoleyev said, "You're thinking the ash was blown clean by the wash from helicopter blades."

"I say it landed here," Willie said.

Chapter Twenty-nine

Fruit Salad
Woman

As we gathered around our campfire that night, loading up on biscuits and honey while Whitefeather made supper, Ruth Anne called. She was in a cheery mood.

"I did it for you, Mr. Denson. Thomas Bondurant. I got you the dope on the man from the British Museum."

"You did? How?"

"Isn't the telephone wonderful these days? I can punch you up on Mount St. Helens or I can call London, all without leaving my wheelchair. I knew if I called the museum all I would get would be polite evasions, so I called the editorial offices of the *Daily Telegraph.*"

"You gave 'em your sexy telephone voice, I take it."

"Of course, Mr. Denson. Let 'em imagine, you always say."

"Lower registers. Sultry."

"I purred, Mr. Denson. I asked for someone who wrote about science, but more specifically anyone who knew about the politics of the British Museum. I was turned over to a certain Clive Pepperton."

"Well, ta-ta Clive."

"No, no, Mr. Denson. He was relaxed and lot of fun and told me everything I wanted to know. The English are especially curious about the Sasquatch search because of Bondurant's connection. In fact, Pepperton wrote a Sunday feature on the search."

"All right. Let me have it."

"On a happy note, you'll be pleased to know Dr. Bondurant has numerous citations in the scholarly literature and is very well liked."

"On the not-so-happy note?"

"A number of his colleagues in the British Museum are annoyed that Thomas scoffs at Yeti. They have a patriotic stake in Yeti and Nepal because Edmund Hillary's expedition found Yeti sign there. When Bondurant wrote a Bigfoot book that zinged Yeti but said Sasquatch maybe, some of them got miffed. They accused Thomas of sucking up to the Americans as a way of cadging free trips to the Northwest. He likes to go trout fishing, and they know it."

"It must be a bitch trying to find a place to fish in England without belonging to some club or other."

"Pepperton said what it really comes down to is that Bondurant has been a fixture at the British Museum for years, and younger scholars are waiting to edge him out of his chair. They've been trying to get him sacked for years."

"Did your man Pepperton know anything about Bondurant and the footprint controversy?"

"Yes, he did. Bondurant's colleagues claim he only talks about a fraction of the many thousands of alleged Sasquatch footprints that have been discovered. They say comparing prints from Bluff Creek, California, to those from Bossberg, Washington, is arbitrary. The Bluff Creek prints appear to be anatomically impossible, making the Bossberg prints seem more authentic than they actually are."

"Say, they are sore, aren't they?"

"They claim he ignores the majority of the footprints, which don't represent anything that a zoologist would recognize. And they would never, ever accept anything that crossed Emile Thibodeaux's lips, for example."

"No amateurs need apply."

"They're very snooty, Pepperton says."

"You don't suppose Thomas Bondurant brought his curriculum vitae with him when he caught the plane to Portland?"

"Ah, ah, Mr. Denson. One last bit of sweet gossip. But gossip only, Pepperton said."

I said, "Come on, quit teasing, Ruth Anne. Give me the rest of it."

"One of Bondurant's former girlfriends told Pepperton that the great man had worked out some sort of retirement position in the Northwest."

"Having to do with Sasquatch, I bet." I thought of Bondurant's chumminess with Donna McGwyre.

"Yes. That's the sweet part, if it's true. I told him if he could think of anything more to please call me collect, and I promised to let him know if anything happened to Bondurant that would make a good story for the *Telegraph.*"

"Transatlantic back-scratching. International wheeling and dealing. Good for you, Ruth Anne."

"I also have a juicy bit of gossip about Mrs. David Addison that might interest you. Sort of a postscript to my call last night. It seems that Laraine Addison, née Adams, was voted Miss Nude Yakima Valley last year. Isn't that fun? Old capitalists never die, I suppose. Remember what they say happened to Rocky Rockefeller!"

"An entirely honorable way to go, Ruth Anne. Miss Nude Yakima Valley? Really?"

Ruth Anne laughed. "That's right. Miss Apple Knockers. Sweet and crisp, just the way you men like 'em, eh, Mr. Denson?"

I said, "No, no, Ruth Anne. Miss Canteloupe Buns. Ripened in the sun."

"Five years ago, when she was seventeen, Ms. Adams was one of a party of teenagers in an outing—this was sponsored by the Church of Christ—that reported seeing a Sasquatch just outside of Cougar."

"She what?"

"That's right. At the time, the *Seattle Times* and the *Oregonian* both ran features on it. The computer hopped on the name Adams. Laraine Adams, Vancouver, correct age. Has to be the same one."

"The reported sighting caused enough of a fuss to interest the checkout rags, do you think?"

"I'd say almost certainly. Give them something to work with at least."

"Is it possible she met the Pollard brothers in her moment in the limelight?"

"That would take more work to pin down, I'm afraid. Nobody wastes their time keying the contents of the *National Gleaner* into any information retrieval system. Just the national biggies and the principal metropolitan papers, although the selection is getting bigger and more useful."

"Mmmmmm. Watsons aren't what they used to be, are they? Nifty piece of work, Ruth Anne. Thank you."

"You're welcome, Mr. Denson. I knew you'd like it."

I liked it, yes. But I didn't know what the hell to make of it just yet.

In the tent before we went to sleep, Whitefeather Minthorn asked Sonja Popoleyev whether the members of her research team could actually "see" Stanley and Blanche. Were the simulated humans represented physically? Did they have some sort of body, or did they simply reply to questions keyed into their memory?

Popoleyev said, "We have three-dimensional models we can examine on our screens. For example, Stanley's teeth are determined by the fact that he eats both plants and animals. His hands enable him to use tools. Blanche is about eighty-five percent as large as Stanley, but he has roughly twice the apparatus for aggression. In a state of nature Blanche chose the male who could best defend and provide for her, so we wound up with large, aggressive males."

"What about the apples and canteloupes?" I said.

"Among pea fowl, the hen, who has for some reason fixated on fancy feathers, chooses from among the males, and so we get the splendid peacocks one sees in the zoo. Stanley and Blanche respond to the same laws of inheritance, except that Stanley selects. If successful Stanleys in a state of nature chose Blanches with substantial breasts, their daughters likely had similar breasts. Monkeys and chimpanzees nurse their young just fine with mere nipples up front; they don't need breasts that bounce around on their chests.

"Likewise, the rumps Stanley preferred were passed on to his female offspring. Blanche doesn't need a butt that large to sit on. Look at Stanley. He weighs more, but his butt is smaller."

"Stanley just liked 'em."

"That sums it up nicely, Mr. Denson. Both breasts and rumps started small. Because Stanley liked 'em, over time they got larger and larger."

It was clear David Addison liked 'em. From my sleeping bag I imitated Marlon Brando. Or tried to. "Stella! Stella!"

Dr. Popoleyev said, "You sound like Don Corleone, Mr. Denson. It's Stanley Kowalski we're talking about here."

I gave Stanley another try. "Stella!"

The moist air had arrived.

Snow.

And not a little snow either. Real snow. The arctic air and the moist air were doing a meteorological tango. Light, dry snow twisted and billowed and swirled, snaking around and about rocks and trees.

There was not a hint of moon or star; still, the snow was eerily beautiful rushing through the blackness.

A blizzard. Or close to it.

And cold? Thought I'd freeze my precious weapon before I finished my duty.

This was not that wishy-washy wet snow that swooped over Portland a couple of times a year, getting the radio deejays all excited but melting by late afternoon.

If Sasquatches survived storms like this every year, they had to be some tough hombres!

I returned to the tent and the comfort of the sack, knowing that overnight my scrapes and bruises would cool and knot up properly so I could really suffer in the morning.

Chapter Thirty

Whitcomb
Finds
Footprints

I woke. I started to move. The pain! *Ay!* I was paralyzed. Or close to it. The bruises on my chest and stomach and thighs had had a chance to cool off.

The others were already up and out of the tent. I had slept late because my body needed time to recuperate from the beating it had taken. Once I started moving around and got my muscles warm, I knew I'd feel a lot better.

Was it still snowing as well?

I dug my wristwatch out of my boot. Ten o'clock. Whoof!

I forced myself to get up. *Ay!* The pain!

First came the pulling on of the pants, which meant bending over. *Yeaaahhhh!* Getting into a shirt meant raising my arms and hitting the holes of the sleeves. *Ouchhh!* Putting on my heavy wool socks and lacing my hiking boots meant more bending over. *Ohhhh!* But the worst, the very worst, was the sweater: I had to raise my arms over my head and straighten them out. *Awwwwwww!*

I finished off with gloves and heavy, hooded coat, unzipped the tent and stepped outside into an eerily beautiful world in which the snow twirled, and whirled, and swirled in lazy, *lap-si-doodle, lisssst-lesssss* whorls and sworls without making a sound. In absolute, total, awesome silence. I couldn't see more than fifteen yards.

Trees and tent were shrouded with snow, which was already knee-deep and rising. Popoleyev and Whitefeather were tending the campfire, which was now sheltered by the tarp that had formerly belonged to Harold and Opal. The mules were gone.

Seeing me, Popoleyev said, "Well, good morning, Mr. Denson, did you have a good sleep?"

"All this snow. You must feel at home."

"Isn't it beautiful?"

I headed for the fire and sheltering tarp, and Whitefeather poured me a cup of coffee. I sat stiffly down on my favorite rock and said, "Where are Harold and Opal?"

Whitefeather said, "Willie took them back as soon as it got light enough for them to see. If the snow gets too deep, it'd be a real struggle for them to get out."

"And Willie'll be back when?"

"He figures dark or a little after."

"Willie's got more energy than brains. You can't see ten yards in this stuff, much less watch out for two mules."

Whitefeather said, "I wouldn't worry about Willie if I were you."

"I know. I know. A little old snowstorm is no big deal for Coyote."

Whitefeather took a sip of coffee and shrugged her shoulders. "The world's loaded with people who believe in virgin births."

"And Santa Claus and *Troglodytes recens*," I said, glancing at Popoleyev.

Popoleyev said, "Willie seemed to think he'd have no problem, Mr. Denson. By the way, how are your muscles this morning?"

"A little tight, I'm afraid." Wincing, I shifted my weight on the rock. "What about our chief tracker and his faithful cur? Where are they?"

Whitefeather said, "Oh, they're out for a hike. They both just love the snow. The more miserable the weather, the happier Earl is . . . Listen, do you hear that?"

I didn't hear anything for a second, then, a buzzing downhill and to the west of camp. Snowmobiles. Two of them, sounded like. The snow acted as a muffle and dampened sound, so they couldn't be too far away. The agreement among the teams had been clear: no snowmobiles.

Who were these intruders?

I said, "Did Bondurant say anything about snowmobiles being sent up here?"

"No. Not a word. He called this morning wanting to know whether or not we wanted to retreat because of the weather."

Popoleyev said, "I told him we were doing fine and would remain in place."

The buzzing stopped.

The camp transceiver popped to life. "Base camp, base camp, this is Roger Whitcomb calling to report Sasquatch footprints on our left flank. I say again, we have found fresh Sasquatch footprints to the west of our position."

Thomas Bondurant said, "Heavens, tell us more, Mr. Whitcomb!"

"We have found Sasquatch spoor in the form of fresh footprints. We have thoroughly photographed the footprints, and have protected several from the accumulating snow. We urgently request confirmation."

"I understand, but Roger, until the storm lets up, I can't imagine any helicopter pilot would agree to fly me in there. We've got wind and zero visibility. You see the problem."

"Yes, I see the problem. But if the prints aren't confirmed, they'll be lost."

"Hmmmmm. Well, you have them well photographed, I take it."

"Oh sure, we have plenty of pictures, but evidence from me is considered tainted before I start. We both know that. A footprint is a footprint, it shouldn't make any difference whether I have a Ph.D. in physical anthropology. But it does. What I need is independent confirmation that I have, in fact, found Sasquatch footprints in this snowstorm." Whitcomb was starting to get sore.

"Say, Roger, what if we had Bobby Minthorn and Dr. Popoleyev do the confirmation? Bobby's a respected tracker, and Dr. Popoleyev's credentials are as good as or better than my own. Surely nobody would quarrel with their opinions."

Whitcomb hesitated.

"The Russians will get pretty damn sore if we conclude her word isn't good enough. And justifiably so."

"Okay. As long as it is clearly understood that this trail is ours. This is our assigned territory. We found the prints. We'll follow them out."

Bondurant said, "Are you listening up there, Whitefeather?"

"Yes, I am."

"Is Dr. Popoleyev in camp this morning?"

Popoleyev said, "Yes, I am, Dr. Bondurant. I've been listening to the conversation. When Bobby Minthorn returns from a hike, we'll be glad to confirm the sighting. I heard Mr. Whitcomb's concern, and he may rest assured that we'll respect the spoor as his team's find, and his team's to follow."

Whitcomb said, "Thank you, Dr. Popoleyev. We would appreciate it if you could come as soon as possible. There's no telling how long we can protect the prints in this storm." He gave her map coordinates for the location of the prints.

Whitefeather said, "Bobby should be back in a few minutes, and then they'll be on their way, Mr. Whitcomb. It may take a while in this weather."

Below us on the mountain, the two snowmobiles started in and headed downhill and slightly to the southwest.

Whitefeather, gesturing to the transceiver, mouthed "snow-mobiles?"

I shook my head no. Don't tell him.

Popoleyev agreed.

Whitefeather signed off.

Minutes later Bobby Minthorn and a frisky, floppy-tongued Earl returned to camp. Bobby said the snowmobiles that we had heard had stopped briefly just below the bench.

Nobody had to be reminded that the bench was where Popoleyev had found the spot that had apparently been cleaned by the wash of helicopter blades.

"I bet Whitcomb heard the snowmobiles, too, but you'll note he's not saying anything either."

Sonja Popoleyev told Bobby about Roger Whitcomb's request for an independent confirmation of the tracks his team had found, and they began to get ready to go.

Chapter Thirty-one

A Buzzing Below the Bench

Earl and I stayed behind with Whitefeather while Bobby Minthorn and Sonja Popoleyev went to check out the prints found by Roger Whitcomb's team.

Bobby reasoned that Earl and I might both be needed in the event that *Troglodytes recens,* hungry, but not wanting to dig up a precious cache of frozen grub, was driven mad by the smell of Whitefeather's coffee and camp stew—such odor wafting up the mountain and into his cave.

In Bobby's scenario, which he told with the addition of imaginative sexual details—calculated to make his wife giggle—Sasquatch, stomach growling, might come down, enter camp, and ravish Whitefeather, reveling in her succulent human parts before he chowed down on her good grub.

Bobby said, "To be honest, I'd hate to count on Denson to protect you, the shape he's in. But with Earl, you've at least got a fighting chance."

Whitefeather said, "Shush. Go do your thing so you can get back before dark."

Bobby said, "If Earl starts barking, strap on your snowshoes and move your butts. Okay, John? You up to it?"

I said, "In the event Earl starts barking, my muscles will loosen up damn fast, guaranteed."

"Whitefeather?"

"I'll give him a goose if he doesn't get a move on."

Bobby Minthorn gave the faithful Earl a scratch behind the ears and was off, closely followed by Sonja Popoleyev, who worked her snowshoes with the easy, practiced stride of someone who had spent most of her life at longitude 60 degrees north.

There was nothing Whitefeather Minthorn and I could do but wait and hope nothing went wrong. We sat huddled around the campfire as the billowing whorls of snow continued to accumulate around our camp at the nape of the mountain's broad neck.

Whitefeather tuned her radio to a country and western station, and we drank coffee, listened to music—and watched the violent beauty of the blizzard as the dry snow swirled around us.

On the radio that ol' Carolina racer, Delbert Fenster, a sometime stock car driver, sang his current number four hit, "Winchester .22." Fenster's voice, fueled by imitation high-octane emotion, coasted in woe-is-me overdrive:

> Francine said, Bye-bye, ba-by!
> Bye-bye, ba-by!
> I'm just a-walkin' right ou-hout on yoooou
> Boo, hoo, hoo, hooooo
> I said, Bye-bye Fran-cine!
> Bye-bye, Fran-cine!
> I'm just a-checkin' on ou-hou-hout toooo
> Win-ches-ter twenty-twoooo

I said, "Heavens! Sounds like Sonja Popoleyev's notion of conflicting sexual strategies, doesn't it, Whitefeather?"

Whitefeather laughed. "I was thinking the same thing."

"She can get more for it from the guy down the street, so she's left the poor bastard Delbert Fenster."

She giggled. "Good thinking on her part."

A few minutes later Ruth Anne Weston called. "Got a little circumstance, got some good poop, Mr. Denson. You said to let you know as soon as I get it, and it's coming quick."

"Call anytime. Lock and load and fire at will, Ruth Anne."

"Circumstances first. I found out Ralph Mactan was an assistant trainer at the University of Georgia before he became head trainer at California State, Bakersfield, which didn't mean anything as far as I could tell. The computer didn't have any matches either. Then, while I was home fixing myself a pot of tea, I remembered something. A delayed flash."

"Densonian in nature, I see."

"I remembered a feature story in the *Oregonian* about Cougar on the eve of the search. The Seattle Seahawk defensive end Aloysius Daroun was mentioned as being among the folks gathered in the local tavern. Dr. Popoleyev was mentioned too."

"We were there that night, introducing her to the wonders of cheeseburgers cooked for loggers. Daroun was drinking beer and bragging about the size of his feet."

"Daroun played for the University of Georgia, didn't he? Do you suppose Mactan was wrapping Bulldog ankles while Daroun was becoming an all-American?"

"That's a definite maybe, Ruth Anne. Has to be. Where did Addison go to school?"

"Sorry. Not the University of Georgia. The University of Arizona."

"How about Mactan?"

"Where did Mactan go to school? One moment, Mr. Denson . . . Mr. Denson?"

"Yes?"

"You're very good, Mr. Denson. The University of Arizona. In the morning, I'll find when Daroun played at Georgia."

"Ahh circumstance, sweet circumstance. Wouldn't any of this cut much cheese in a court of law though, would it, Ruth Anne?"

"No, I'm afraid it wouldn't, Mr. Denson, but keep in mind two men have been killed."

"You said you had some good poop."

"Your hunch about the rum was a good one. The Cascade Run bartender ordered twenty cases of Caribbean the rum the day before the Sasquatch was videotaped at Ape Cave."

"My, my." As I suspected, if they ordered Caribbean rum, they had to order early. They could have ordered perfectly good, inexpensive rum from the distillery in Hood River. Their Bigfoot Banger wouldn't have tasted a bit different.

Sasquatch was a favorite subject of commercial promotions from Northern California through British Columbia. It was possible, but unlikely, that the Cascadia bartender had legitimately been planning a Bigfoot Banger special before the sighting at Ape Cave.

I said, "They had to get fancy, didn't they? Going for the California trade, I suppose."

Ruth Anne laughed. She was from Los Angeles.

"I say that's better than circumstantial evidence, Ruth Anne."

"Far better. You be careful up there, Mr. Denson. Willie Prettybird too."

Fifteen minutes later, Whitefeather and I heard the faint buzzing of a snowmobile downhill and to our southwest, that is, roughly below the bench.

Bobby Minthorn and Sonja Popoleyev would have crossed the rock bench on their way to check the footprints found by Whitcomb's team, and they'd cross it again on their way back.

Whitefeather Minthorn began chewing on her lower lip.

I said, "Would you feel better if I took a look, Whitefeather?"

"Oh, I don't know. There's nothing we can do except wait, I suppose."

"What if I went as far as the rock bench, then came right back? It shouldn't take more than an hour or so round trip."

"I'd appreciate it, John."

"Remember, if Earl barks, you beat it out of here."

"Got it, John. Thank you."

I strapped on my snowshoes, and leaving Whitefeather in camp with Earl, I took off to see what I could find.

The trail left by Bobby and Popoleyev was still clear in the falling snow. In a few minutes my muscles were loosened up, and I was striding right along as though I knew what I was doing. My chore was made easier because Bobby and Popoleyev had mashed the snow for me. Bobby had led the way—the hardest part—with Popoleyev in his steps. Now me.

It took me about forty minutes to reach the bench, during which time no more snowmobiles were to be heard. But the trip was not wasted because I found a set of perfectly incredible footprints crossing the trail of snowshoes left earlier by Bobby and Popoleyev.

I knelt down and studied the footprints, made by large bare feet. They looked like human prints, only far larger. If labels were required, they were definitely more Bossberg than Bluff Creek. I photographed the prints with Olden's camera, and followed the trail to the pile of rocks and boulders that had tumbled down the mountain and accumulated at the base of the bench.

The owner of the prints had scrambled up and over the jumble, disturbing a lot of snow in the process. The accumulating snow would cover the footprints overnight, so I built a knee-high pyramid of fist-sized loose rocks to mark the site where the Sasquatch, real or pretend, had gone up the mountain.

My chore complete, and having found no evidence that Bobby and Popoleyev had run into trouble, I headed back to camp to do the best I could to relieve Whitefeather's anxiety.

Chapter Thirty-two

A Snootful to Remember

The snow had eased by the time Bobby Minthorn and Sonja Popoleyev returned a half hour later. On their return from Roger Whitcomb's camp, they had spotted the same footprints I had found, and had followed the impressions made by my snowshoes as I trailed the prints to the base of the rock bench.

"What do you think?" I asked Bobby as he poured himself a cup of coffee.

He considered the question over the steaming cup. "Whitcomb's men found a large footprint they think belongs to Sasquatch. In my opinion, they weren't Sasquatch prints. They were made by a human. The prints you found on the rock bench are both longer and wider, closer to something Sasquatch might leave."

"What did you tell Whitcomb?"

Bobby said, "I told him I wasn't sure what his prints were, and asked him if he needed any help. If he hadn't been such a jerk about everything, I'd have told him the truth. I figured a little exercise might do him good. Besides, it'll get him farther away from the bench."

"And he said?"

"He said, 'No, no. We'll handle it by ourselves.' I said, 'Are you sure? I'd like to help.' He said, 'We've got it under control, thanks.' He was real, real cool, wasn't he, Dr. Popoleyev?"

"He sure was."

"He interpreted my volunteering to help as a sign the prints belong to Sasquatch. I knew that's what he'd think, which is why I did it."

"Clever redskin."

Bobby grinned. "Once he was convinced he had found Sasquatch prints, he wanted me out of that camp pronto."

I grinned. "And what happened then?"

"We started back for our camp, and Whitcomb and his team took off in pursuit of whoever had made those footprints."

Popoleyev said, "It's true, Mr. Denson, the footprints Whitcomb found did look kind of small to be *Troglodytes recens.*"

I said, "An adolescent *Troglodytes recens,* perhaps?"

"I don't think so," Bobby said.

"Whitcomb wanted to believe he had found Sasquatch prints and so did."

Bobby said, "When I saw the footprints you found on the bench, it occurred to me that whoever left the prints Whitcomb found might have been trying to lure Whitcomb away from the area."

"And with your help, it worked?"

Bobby laughed.

Mmmmmm. The story grew curiouser and curiouser. "Did Whitcomb or any of his team mention anything about hearing snow-mobiles between here and there?"

"No, they didn't. Of course, the bench is far closer to us than it is them. We were on our way to see Whitcomb, about halfway between the bench and his camp, when we heard the snowmobiles."

"But they could have heard them as well."

"The way sound carries up here, they probably did."

Popoleyev said, "What do you think, Mr. Denson?"

"It's got me stumped, to be honest."

Popoleyev said, "I don't know what to think about the snowmobile or the footprints. All I know is that the beast we chased Monday night had eyes that reflected light."

Bobby said, "The prints you found on the bench were made by something mighty big, that's a fact."

Earl who had returned, stretched out beside the fire, now scrambled to his feet, alert.

From below the hill, the brief call of an owl. *Hooo! Ho-hooo! Ho-hoo!*

Bobby cupped his hands around his mouth and blew his reply: *Hooo! Ho-hoo!* He said, "Willie's back."

A few minutes later, Willie Prettybird stepped into camp, pooped from his daylong trek on snowshoes. But he had completed his mission; Harold and Opal were on their way back to the Minthorn farm. Willie was looking forward to Whitefeather's evening meal.

There was still a few minutes of daylight left as we settled around the fire with mugs of hot coffee to fill Willie in on the day's events: We had heard snowmobiles somewhere below the bench. I had hiked to the bench and found huge Sasquatch-looking footprints that appeared headed straight up the mountain. And finally, Roger Whitcomb had discovered large footprints—which Bobby believed to be human—headed west, away from the bench.

Willie didn't know what to make of this any more than the rest of us.

Suddenly, Earl, who had been listening to our palaver with doggish indifference, scrambled to his feet and stared down the mountain.

Bobby said, "Ooops. What have we got here?"

Earl had heard something. He was frozen, listening, his brown eyes unblinking.

The *snap, snap* of a .22 automatic and Earl's yowl came simultaneously as he jumped about three feet high. I grabbed the startled Popoleyev by the nape of the neck and threw her to the ground, joining her in the process.

Earl came back to earth and started charging down the mountain, but Bobby Minthorn, on the ground beside his wife, yelled, "Heel! Heel! Heel!"

Earl did as he was told, but he didn't like it. The end of his tail was bleeding. He had been shot near the tip.

"Sorry if I was rough," I said to Popoleyev.

"No need to apologize for that, Mr. Denson. I don't want to get hit either."

We waited, flat on the ground.

A couple of minutes later, we heard the *varoom, varoom,* of two snowmobiles starting up.

Bobby jumped to his feet and began strapping on his snowshoes, joined by Willie.

Bobby said, "Come on, Earl. Let's go have a look."

Whitefeather said, "Let me tend to his tail first, Bobby. It's bleeding."

Bobby said, "We'll fix it when we get back. We've only got a few minutes of light." Without another word, he was off, followed by the bloody-tailed Earl, and by Willie.

It was dark and once more snowing hard by the time they got back, and Whitefeather set about cleaning and disinfecting Earl's wound. Unlucky Earl had gotten hit not quite square about a half inch from the tip.

Bobby, who held Earl's muzzle while his wife applied healing goo on the dog's wound, was furious. "But at least Earl got a snootful of those motherfuckers."

Popoleyev said, "Do you suppose Earl really knows why you took him down there?"

"The sound of the twenty-two and the pain were simultaneous. Then I take Earl down the mountain where the sound came from. If you think he's too stupid to put two and two together, Dr. Popoleyev, you've been studying monkeys and apes too long. Earl knows, don't you, Earl?"

Popoleyev patted Earl on the head. "Poor, poor Earl."

While Earl's tail no doubt throbbed with pain, his misfortune was earning him extra attention, and he reveled in the affection. The sympathetic petting and scratching from Popoleyev and me—coming from somebody other than Bobby and Whitefeather—were obviously special.

Earl didn't wag his tail; that would have agitated the painful wound. But he smiled a drooling dog's smile, tongue flopping—charming payment for our ministrations in his time of distress.

Bobby said, "You should have seen Earl's eyes while he savored the smell on the bushes where those bastards stood when they tried to kill him. They had a license plate and didn't know it."

"A license plate?" Popoleyev looked puzzled.

Bobby Minthorn said, "Their smell. Earl was memorizing their odor."

Chapter Thirty-three

The Meaning
of Cuff Links

As we talked, Whitefeather Minthorn tended a pot of water that was presumably the beginning of supper. She brought out plastic bags containing shreds of dried venison, dried potatoes, dried onions, and more than a dozen of the best varieties of dried mushrooms, which she dumped into the pot along with a garnish of wild herbs.

The simmering stew smelled wonderful.

After I shared the news about Ruth Anne's detective work, I added that, in my opinion, the odds were good that at least one of the snowmobiles belonged to David Addison. I still had no idea what to make of all the footprints or why Addison would want to kill Earl.

Sonja Popoleyev said, "Mr. Denson, do you expect Addison to actually pay you that reward if you can prove some kind of fraud?"

"No," I said. "Especially since the odds are he's part of the fraud himself. He's playing a form of a game called 'make-believe.' "

"Make-believe?"

"We 'make-believe,' as kids do. In this case, we all pretend that

Addison will give us the money. It adds to the fun of the chase. A big reward, then the credits roll."

"But we know he won't pay any reward?"

I said, "He was dressed casually, but he looked ill at ease. Question: who or what made him dress the way he did?"

"His wife?"

I cocked my head. "Maybe. Maybe not. What does he ordinarily wear?"

"A suit and tie."

"Right. Why?"

Bobby, eyeing the venison stew, said, "How about now, Whitefeather, looks ready to me. How long do we have to wait?"

Whitefeather said, "Just hold your horses. Give it a few minutes."

"Willie's hungry."

"You can say that again," Willie said.

"Drop the con, both of you," Whitefeather said.

Popoleyev said, "A conservative business suit connotes membership in the upper classes, Mr. Denson. In your case, I would venture you never wear a tie." She smiled. "Those with the most power, that is, those with the most to conserve, dress the most conservatively. And they demand that their subordinates dress the same way."

"His wife could have told him to loosen up," I said, "But it could also have been a public relations man. 'You gotta loosen up, big guy, be one of the gang.' Did you note that he was wearing fancy cuff links? Cuff links, for Christ's sake. I say a guy who loves to waste money like that doesn't offer a one-hundred-thousand-dollar reward for anything if he think's he's going to have to pay off."

"Densonian logic?" Popoleyev asked.

"Denson's mother once bought him a collection of Sherlock Holmes stories," Willie said. "He likes to watch the little things."

Bobby said, "How about now, Whitefeather?"

"Oh, sure, go ahead," Whitefeather said, passing out stainless steel spoons and aged Tupperware bowls.

We went for the venison stew.

Popoleyev, finished with the ladle, gave it to Willie, who filled his bowl with quick scoops and took a quick sample.

I said, "Buttons would hold the cuffs of Addison's shirt together just as easily, and wouldn't waste gold or his bank account. I watch big things too," I added quickly. "For example, consider his wife's sensational butt."

"*Uuunnnhhh!*" Willie said.

Bobby groaned pleasurably too. Whitefeather gave him a pretend cuff on the ear.

"Women with butts like that are likely to cost more than women built like bowling pins. Isn't that right, Dr. Popoleyev? That is, according to your own reckoning of the evolution of all God's children."

"Women with rumps like that and with standard imaginations ordinarily require an interested male to demonstrate superior prowess, yes," she said.

"In this case, the prowess is measured in the form of dollars accumulated. Did she look like she had extraordinary imagination to you?"

"Well, no," she said.

"You don't bet big unless you think you have a winner. Addison expected to make even more money by offering the reward, not less. Only by pursuing profit at all costs and keeping nobody in mind but himself has he wormed his way into a position to have a blonde with a butt like that hanging onto his arm."

"You have a point."

"I rest my case. Keep in mind, I'm not skeptical about all things, Dr. Popoleyev. Some things I do know are true. For example, I can assert with certainty that Whitefeather Minthorn makes a venison stew that is truly memorable. By my standards, this is eatin' pretty damn high on the hog."

Willie, licking his lips, finished the last of his stew. "Say, this is good stuff, isn't it? You got her well trained, Bobby."

Whitefeather said, "Shoot too."

I said, "My compliments to the chef." I gave Whitefeather a hand, and my companions joined in the round of applause.

Willie wiped his mouth with the back of his hand. "Tomorrow I think we should find the marker Denson left and check out the cliffs above that bench. See what's up there." He glanced at Popoleyev. "You're thinking *Troglodytes recens,* eh, Dr. Popoleyev?"

"I can't forget the eye shine."

Earl, watching us clean our dishes, got to his feet, nose twitching. He was confident that the pot contained savory dribbles, and that in his case—whatever the prohibition against begging at the Minthorn table—seconds were in order. His tail hurt something awful. He was deserving. If the Minthorns really cared for him and were sympathetic to his misfortune, they'd give him more.

Earl's mournful con was easier to pull when there were visitors. Whitefeather, glancing at her husband with resignation, scraped the dribbles of stew from the pot into his dish. Earl was nothing if not grateful. He attacked it with relish, his long tongue slurping.

As we settled into our sleeping bags that night, we knew intuitively that the next day we would, in all probability, get to the truth behind the eye shine, footprints, snowmobiles, and the shooting of Earl—or much of it.

Before he snuffed our gas lantern, Willie said, "When Mouse told the animal people about Dr. Popoleyev's poem the other night, they all got excited. They think of themselves as poets because they've got nothing better to do than sit around playing with the sounds of words. Mouse wrote one especially for you, Dr. Popoleyev. The title is simply 'To S. Popoleyev from Mouse.'

"First, Mouse says, you have to imagine the snow-capped mountains of Wigglin-Swamplin." Using the light of the lantern and his knuckles, Willie made a series of jagged mountains on the wall of the tent.

"And below the high mountains lies a terrible swamp with gloomy trees." Willie turned his fingers up. He undulated his fingers slowly back and forth. The gloomy trees. "Okay, Mouse, let's hear it."

Mouse-Willie recited the poem:

> *Down to Wigglin-Swamplin.*
> *dimplin-domplin, hippy-hompin we go,*
> *enjoying the show,*
> *catching the freaks*
> *until, their beaks*
> *turned just so,*
> *eyes aglow,*

we see fancy birds dressed in hot-damn boots
smoking big old willow roots.
They got six-guns hanging from their feathered
hips
and easy smiles upon their lying lips.
Between their legs, their mighty nub
is well burnished by frequent rub,
this organ said by those who cry in vain,
to do the work of this bird's brain.

Chapter Thirty-four

A Bloody Trail

The snow had stopped during the night. The next morning it was bitter cold, and a gloom of fog had descended over the mountain.

We talked over the mission of the day, namely to see if we could find out where whoever or whatever it was who had made the Sasquatch prints on the bench had gone. To a cave somewhere higher up the mountain? In view of the snow and Earl's misfortune, we decided he would remain in camp with Whitefeather; if he was needed to help Bobby with his tracking chores, one of us would return to pick him up.

Bobby said, "Whitefeather, remember, because of Earl's ears and nose, you can see other people in this fog, but they can't see you. If Earl says you have an unknown visitor coming up the hill, or if you hear shots from our direction, head directly east to Thibodeaux's camp, and tell them what happened. Thibodeaux seems all right, don't you think, John?"

"I think so. But Whitefeather, do not, I repeat do not, tell any of this to Bondurant or his helpers."

"The shots, the snowmobiles . . ."

"Any of it. If you can somehow talk to Sheriff Starkey directly, that's okay."

"But not Thomas Bondurant?"

"Not Bondurant or anybody else down there. For them, it's business as usual up here." I didn't know if Bondurant was guilty of anything, but it was hard to forget Ruth Anne's reported British Museum gossip. Did Bondurant have a retirement position lined up in the Pacific Northwest? Where? As part of the Tom and Donna show?

Willie said, "If you head south for base, you're at the mercy of those fucking snowmobiles. If these jackasses are crazy enough to shoot a dog, you don't know what they might do. We can always catch up with you."

"Got it," Whitefeather said.

Bobby said, "And if for any reason there's a screw up or a surprise, and you wind up with someone right on top of you, you know what to tell Earl. You know what the word is."

Earl, hearing his name, perked up, as if to say, word? Word? What word?

Bobby scratched Earl behind the ears. Bobby's hand said, yes, Earl, we're talking about you.

Whitefeather said, "I heard you in the back yard teaching him. I know the command. Believe me, I'll use it if I have to."

Bobby said, "Practice, practice, practice. Maybe all that practice will pay off, eh, Earl? Get a chance to show what you can do."

After breakfast, we strapped 'em on and headed west, destined for the rock bench. We were about ten minutes out when we heard the *snap, snap, snap* of a .22 up ahead, followed shortly by snowmobiles that sounded headed down the mountain.

When we got to the bench, we found that the footprints I had seen the day before were covered by snow, replaced by fresh prints. Whatever or whoever had left the prints had fallen, leaving the bloody imprint of a huge body. The footprints were the same as I had seen the day before. The imprint of the body was surrounded by the impressions of two pairs of snowshoes.

Out of this mess, a trail of huge footprints, trailing blood, headed straight up the rocks.

Bobby Minthorn squatted, studying the bloody, disturbed snow. He looked up through the fog at the dim flank of the mountain. "What happened was this: somebody shot a large man or Sasquatch. Then two men on snowshoes came up to look at him. They stood above him. You can count the snowshoes. One knelt and checked him, you can see the imprint of his knee there. Then they left the bench, going downhill. After a while, the man, or Sasquatch, got to his feet and headed uphill, bleeding, as you can see."

Popoleyev said, "That's an awful lot of blood."

Bobby looked south through the gloom in the direction the snowmobiles had disappeared. "It looks like they left him for dead."

It didn't take Geronimo or Bobby Minthorn to follow the blood and huge footprints up and over the rocks at the base of the bench. Fifteen yards above the rocks, we found a trail that zig-zagged up the bluff. Our quarry, trailing blood, had taken the trail.

Twenty minutes later, we came upon a cave.

Chapter Thirty-five

These Eyes
Don't Shine

This wasn't just a rock overhang of the sort that might be called a cave by an enthusiast given to hyperbole. It was a real cave with a proper mouth and an apparently spacious interior. Genuine shelter.

The bloody footprints led into the blackness of the cave.

Willie Prettybird and Bobby Minthorn, our official cave hunters, had flashlights in their daypacks—just in case—as did the optimistic Popoleyev. Would a wounded Sasquatch explode upon us? Or was some clown of a human in there bleeding to death? We stood to one side of the cave mouth.

Willie looked at me. "Well, Chief?"

I leaned toward the darkness and said, "Hey, in there. We're friends. We want to help you."

Silence.

Popoleyev said, *"Troglodytes recens* would hardly be expected to speak English, Mr. Denson."

I shouted, "We saw the blood down below and followed it up

here. We've got a first-aid kit and a radio at our camp. All kinds of stuff. You need us."

No reply.

"You've obviously lost a lot of blood already. If you don't get help, you'll bleed to death."

Nothing.

"Well?" Willie said.

"I suppose we go in. Dr. Popoleyev?"

"I agree. Here, Mr. Denson, you take my flashlight, and I'll follow you. There are times when it's logical for Stanleys to flex their muscles."

Willie and Bobby went first, then me, flexing ordinary muscles, then Popoleyev, gripping my belt with her left hand.

We slowly explored the cave with the beams of our flashlights. After the narrow entrance, the cave widened into an egg-shaped chamber maybe twenty feet wide by twenty or twenty-five feet long.

It was empty, save for some large rocks—or small boulders— around the edges. Some of these were two or three feet high and just as wide. The bottom of the cave was covered with animal droppings, bones, some sticks, and miscellaneous feathers.

The trail of blood led directly to one of the large rocks, then . . . The blood disappeared under the rock.

We gathered around the stone.

Bobby Minthorn knelt beside the blood. "What the hell?"

I yelled, "Goddam it, open up in there! We're trying to help."

Popoleyev said, "Mr. Denson! Have you taken leave of your senses?"

Even louder, I shouted, "I said open up! We want to talk to you before you bleed to death."

Willie knelt and studied the stone. "By God, I think you're right. Sherlock Denson." He tapped the stone with his finger.

"If you want to sack any more quarterbacks, you better wise up in there. I'm a Seahawk fan. I want you back on that field where you belong, knocking the piss out of those strutting little bastards. Isn't that what you call them?"

No reply.

"You cost the Seahawks a number one pick, dammit! They have a hard enough time as it is without guys like you fucking up."

As if by magic, the rock suddenly rose, moved left, and settled. It was artificial, and the hand that moved it was large and covered with reddish-brown fur.

Sasquatch's head, not covered with fur, belonged to Aloysius Daroun. He staggered back from us, holding one side of his blood-drenched Sasquatch outfit over his ribs. The Sasquatch head lay on the ground beside an inflatable couch that was slimy with blood.

Daroun knelt stiffly and fumbled with the furry head. "Awwwwwww!" Disdainfully, he flipped the head away and flopped on the couch, draping his feet over one end. "I think you're right. I need help real, real bad." He grimaced. "Too weak to get outta this monkey suit. Fuckin' thing's filling up with blood, I can feel it."

"We'll get you out of it," I said.

"A person'd hate to die like this, dressed up like a damn fool going trick or treat. One thing though, my grandkids'll be able to say I died with my big feet on." Daroun's laughter was cut short by a groan.

"Easy, big guy," I said. His big feet were flexible, molded soles on the bottoms of his boots, the tops of which became the legs of his costume. I could see that the soles, which added about three quarters of an inch to the length and width of each foot, would bend with his stride and so leave a believable set of Sasquatch footprints.

Popoleyev, Willie, Bobby, and I set about getting Daroun out of his reddish-brown fur suit, now soaked with blood. As we struggled to remove his arm, Daroun said, "They paid big money for this damn thing, and it wasn't bad, really. It was nice and warm inside."

The entire cave was shaped something like an hourglass; that is, it had two egg-shaped chambers joined by a narrow passage. This inner chamber, which Daroun had blocked off with a plastic rock covered by pulverized lava to make it look real, was the smaller of the two.

The artificial rock was so realistic it was astonishing. There was no way, on an unsuspecting glance, that the fake could be distinguished from the other lava boulders and rocks around the edges of the cave. If it hadn't have been for the blood . . .

In the inner chamber, Aloysius Daroun had established all the comforts of home. He had a heater, cooking stove, and refrigerator that ran off three large propane tanks. The propane also ran a generator that supplied Daroun the juice he needed for his television set.

He had a table, chair, and bunk, in addition to his inflatable couch. The works.

He had been hit three times in the stomach and twice in the chest by a .22, and he was still bleeding.

After we got him out of his Sasquatch outfit at his request, we stretched him out again on the inflatable couch. The blood was still flowing. We covered him up with a sheet and blanket from his bunk.

His face was pale. He said, "I ain't going to make it, am I? No way."

"You got a radio up here?"

"I can't talk to nobody but Addison on the thing he gave me. Didn't think anything of it at the time. Ain't no use anyway. Can't bring a helicopter 'cause of this fog."

"Did you call him when you got up here?"

"I tried to. He didn't answer, but he knows I called because I left a message on the machine. It's rigged so I can do that. He ain't gonna do shit, is he?"

I retrieved my matchbox recorder from my coat pocket and turned it on. Holding the football player's hand and looking him straight in the eye, I said I was taking a statement from Aloysius Daroun on the facts that led to his being shot five times with a .22 automatic—such statement being witnessed by Willie Prettybird, Bobby Minthorn, Sonja Popoleyev, and me.

I gave the location, date, and circumstances.

"Do you, Aloysius Daroun, swear on your honor that what you're telling us is the truth, the whole truth, and nothing but the truth, to the best of your knowledge?" I didn't believe in invoking deities. Honor covered the territory.

"Yes, I do."

"Please tell the officers of the courts what happened, Aloysius."

"They hadn't counted on the dog."

"Would you explain that, please?"

"They anticipated everything but the dog."

"Who? Who anticipated everything?"

"Addison and Bondurant."

"David Addison and Thomas Bondurant?"

"Yes."

"Tell us what you know from the beginning. In your words."

"It ain't easy, but I'll do my best. Addison has this young wife with tits and this amazing ass, see. The way I understand it, a few years ago she was on a church picnic when they all saw what they thought was a Sasquatch. She was interviewed by Elford Pollard, who told her he'd heard there was a cave with two chambers above a rock bench somewhere on the south flank of St. Helens.

"She tells her new husband about the cave. Addison owns the controlling interest in the outfit that owns Cascade Run just down the mountain, and he gets the idea of using a Sasquatch reward as bait for California buyers."

"Addison decided to stir the action by rigging a Sasquatch hunt?"

"That's right. He went to a Sasquatch talk by Bondurant in Canada and introduced himself, telling Bondurant about the cave. He took Bondurant down to Cascade Run, and Bondurant got a thing for the blonde who runs the place, Donna McGwyre. I can just feel it leaving me, you know. I wasn't a bad ball player. Not half bad."

"You were all-pro. Can't get any better than that. Keep going, Aloysius."

"Bondurant agreed to help pull the Sasquatch scam in return for his own Bigfoot museum at Cascade Run."

"Where the blonde is."

Daroun grinned. "Them Britishers like to fuck, same as you and me. Addison knew from the papers that I was on a one-year suspension on account of the coke, and his fraternity brother, Ralph Mactan, had been on the Georgia staff when I played ball there. Ralph got hold of me and said Addison would pay me fifty thou for having a little Bigfoot fun.

"The idea was, I would run around leaving big footprints. Finally, I'd be seen up in the rocks. You folks would come after me, but I'd duck inside the cave and hide inside my chamber. You'd retreat in the name of science, and before you could regroup to watch the place properly, I'd scoot, taking my stuff with me. No problem that I could see."

"Leaving a real rock where the fake one had been."

"Sure. Let you find the inside part yourself. The only problem was, Elford Pollard remembered telling Addison's wife about the cave, and he and his brother leaned on Addison to use their Sasquatch collection as the basis of the museum. *They* wanted to run the museum, or else they'd expose Addison and Bondurant as con men and frauds.

"I think Addison told them yes, trying to buy time, and the Pollards got all excited about the deal. Bondurant once hinted that Alford had a thing going with Elford's wife. Tiny little thing, if you've ever seen her. It's my bet that Alford murdered Elford for his woman and his half of the Sasquatch crap."

"So Addison, seeing his chance, killed Alford, and tried to make it look like a suicide. Remorse for having murdered his brother.

"I don't have direct proof of it—Addison certainly didn't tell me—but I'm convinced that's what happened. Only thing was, Addison got two surprises. The weather, which wasn't impossible to overcome. But he hadn't counted on the dog. The fake rock wouldn't fool a good dog for a second. He'd smell me back there, and that would be the end of it.

"So yesterday morning, Addison met me on the bench and told me everything was off. I should pack my gear and clear off the mountain before you folks got to the cave. I said fine, I'd be down to pick up my money. He said what money? I hadn't finished the job. I said it wasn't my fault you had a dog. He said it wasn't his fault either. He tried to kill the dog, but he missed. Said it was too risky to try again.

"I said fuck you. I had food. I had heat. I had my TV. I wasn't going anywhere until I got paid. If the dog found me, he found me; I didn't give a fuck. I hadn't committed any crime that I knew of.

"He called again today to say okay; he'd give me my money. I went down to get it, and we got into another argument, and this is what happened."

"Be specific, please, Aloysius. What do you mean by 'this happened'?"

"Addison shot me with his twenty-two automatic. I fell down in the snow, and I remember him standing over me saying how the snow was just getting started. It would eventually get ten or twelve feet deep at this altitude. They'd have plenty of time to get my body off the mountain. You know what saved me? At least for a while anyway."

"What's that, Aloysius?"

Daroun grinned weakly. "My Bigfoot outfit. I had my Bigfoot head on, so Addison couldn't see my face. He reached down to see if I had a heartbeat, but he couldn't feel anything underneath all that fur and stuff. That's why he thought I was dead.

"Addison'd already killed Alford Pollard. I should have known better than to argue with him. If the forward pass is the girl what brang a quarterback to the big game, you gotta expect he'll call her number first time he gets in trouble. Does that about cover the territory?"

"It'll burn their butts, Aloysius."

"Dammit, I wanted to play in the Super Bowl. I wanted to earn me a Super Bowl ring."

I said, "You're going to make it, man."

Nonsense, and he knew it. "Yeah, man."

"I want you to picture it. Picture it now. A Sunday afternoon in January down there in New Orleans, and you're waiting with the rest of the Seahawks back in the tunnel, and one at a time you step forward, waiting to be introduced, and finally your turn comes."

He smiled. "Yeah, man, I can see it."

"At defensive end, number eighty-nine-ine-ine, Aloysius-ius-ius Daroun-oun-oun."

"I'm gonna stomp me up a fancy little white-pecker Super Bowl quarterback."

Popoleyev, who had been examining the half-man/half-ape Sasquatch head beside the bloody costume, said, "Aloysius, you must tell us how you made your eyes shine."

Daroun looked puzzled.

"Monday night. Your eyes shone when we got you with our flashlights. How did you do that?"

I picked up the Sasquatch head. I had expected reflectors mounted above the eyes, but there were none, just heavy, Neanderthalish eyebrows.

Daroun shook his head weakly. "I ain't been out at night. Been in here watching ball games and old movies."

Popoleyev said, "Monday night, Aloysius. You came poking around our camp in the middle of the night, and we ran after you with flashlights."

"No, ma'am. It was not me. First, I'm not going to be messing around with you folks knowing you got a dog in camp. Second, it's downright dangerous roaming around there in the dark. No, no. Not me."

It was nearly impossible to tell whether Daroun was lying or not. Maybe he was. Maybe he wasn't. He'd had plenty of time to learn the terrain. All he needed was a flashlight and a head start. I wondered what he'd done with his eye-shine reflectors.

Popoleyev said, "Please, we must know."

"Lady, you're talking about a sure way for a man to break his fool ass. I may not be Einstein, but you have to believe me when I tell you I ain't that damned dumb either."

Popoleyev gripped his hand. "Swear it wasn't you, Aloysius. Swear it."

"It wasn't me. No, ma'am. You got my word on it. I spent Monday night here in my cave like I have all week. Made me some popcorn and watched the Jets and Miami, then went to bed."

"And you don't have eye-shine reflectors for your costume?"

"Eye-shine reflectors? No, ma'am. Fact is, I don't know what you're talking about."

Popoleyev said, "You cannot lie to me, Aloysius. You must tell the truth. This is very, very important. If Addison hired you to play Sasquatch, he must have told you what to do. Did Thomas Bondurant talk to you about *Troglodytes recens?* I want the truth."

"*Troglo* which?" Daroun furrowed his brow.

Aloysius Daroun, the master leg-puller, glanced at Willie then me. He was about to give me a conspiratorial wink—I know damn well he was—but he didn't get a chance to pull the trigger on his eyelid. He never saw the cheapshot artist who blindsides us all.

If, as Aloysius Daroun had said, David Addison assumed the accumulating snow would cover his body where it had fallen, Addison thought he was in the clear as far as evidence of his murder was concerned. In a few hours, Daroun's body would have been a shapeless form under the snow—a log, a boulder. The higher the snow, the less obvious the form. By March it would be all but invisible. Addison would have to make a quick trip to the cave to retrieve the big man's gear, but if he had to, he could leave Daroun on the bench until May or June when the snowpack on St. Helens began to thaw.

We had a tape for the replay officials. In the morning, we would begin the complicated hassle of seeing to it that David Addison drew the maximum penalty for fouling the Seahawk's defensive end. In Washington State, a deliberate, fatal foul could draw a lethal injection at Walla Walla, taking Addison out of the game for good. No more apple knockers or canteloupe buns. No fancy cuff links or show-off automobiles. None of it.

We decided that Sonja Popoleyev and I would spend the night in the cave with Aloysius Daroun's corpse. He had been a member of the human community and, despite his failings, I had liked him. I had admired his high spirits and love of life, and the zest with which he talked about playing football. To leave him alone seemed, somehow, to lack honor.

Willie Prettybird and Bobby Minthorn helped us move Daroun to the outer chamber, a natural refrigerator, then headed back down the mountain to rejoin Whitefeather and Earl before it got dark. They would call the cops and return first thing in the morning.

Chapter Thirty-six

The 3.2-Second
Fleece

Aloysius Daroun's propane stove kept the inner chamber of the cave warm and cozy. Sonja Popoleyev and I cleaned the blood off his inflatable couch, then settled down to relax, she at one end, me at the other, a blanket over our legs.

After nearly a week of air mattresses, the billowing, soft couch felt wonderful. We sort of floated together, luxuriating in the warmth and comfort. I liked Popoleyev a bunch, and the warmth of her legs was driving me nuts. I wondered if I could actually spend a night with her on the couch without doing something stupid and uncivilized. The rules of behavior that governed we Stanleys was necessary, I knew, yet still—Sonja Popoleyev was something else!

Under the circumstances, sleep, for me, was probably out of the question. I wondered: was the business of slowly driving Stanley out of his mind part of Blanche's tactics?

Wiggling her toes, which I would have gladly grabbed and massaged for her pleasure, Popoleyev said, "What do you think, Mr.

Denson? Was Aloysius telling the truth about not being out on Monday night?"

It didn't seem fair to Aloysius Daroun, now in the process of freezing solid, to tell her the truth. I don't have any idea," I said.

"He was having fun with me, wasn't he?"

"It's possible."

"Tell me the truth."

"I don't know. Maybe he was lying. Maybe he wasn't."

Mmmmmm. She looked thoughtful. She wanted to believe Daroun, but. . . . She let it drop.

I said, "If you were a detective, Dr. Popoleyev, I take it you'd bring almost everything down to a search for a satisfying screw. That certainly appears to be the case with regard to the figures in Daroun's story. Addison. Bondurant. Alford Pollard. Am I getting close?"

"Well, yes, with qualifications. Based on what we know of Stanley's motives—and without speaking directly to the facts of any of those Stanleys that you mentioned—it seems foolish to maintain that we're somehow immune to the competitive sexual urges that inform the progress of other primates."

"In other words, orgasms fuel the competition that results in fitness of the species."

"More like evolutionary cocaine than a fuel, I would think, Mr. Denson. Orgasms are physically addicting to Stanley, an untidy fact nobody wants to put in so many words. Men who go for long periods without sex go through withdrawal symptoms. They get cranky and nasty. They can't help it."

Addiction? I blinked.

"You look surprised, Mr. Denson. It's entirely logical. In mating with Blanche, Stanley both satisfies his addiction and duplicates his genes. If his addiction is thwarted, he'll kill if necessary, as in the case of Alford Pollard murdering his brother."

"The addicting physical high lasting how long?"

"Contractions at climax last eight-tenths of a second in both Stanley and Blanche. After four or five of these, maybe three and two-tenths to four seconds of satisfaction, Stanley goes flaccid, and loses almost all interest in Blanche, who's by then just getting warmed up."

"This is one thing Blanche would change."

"She doesn't like it, but that's the way it is. Once he's finished his mission, he couldn't be bothered."

"Let me see if I have this straight, Dr. Popoleyev. The other night you likened Stanley's eternal quest to Jason pursuing the Golden Fleece. Jason runs onto the rocks just short of getting his hands on the Fleece. But he re-rigs, steadfast glint in his eye, determined as ever. The heroic, but doomed quest. But Stanley's really is a different story, isn't it? He actually gets his hands on the Fleece, triumphant, only to have it lose its gilt."

"Three or four seconds, depending on the number of contractions. If you call that triumph. The oxidation of familiarity begins at once." Popoleyev grinned. She had a hint of dimples that I much admired and could not imagine oxidizing.

By Popoleyev's account, it didn't matter if Stanley understood the process intellectually, he was a sexual druggie. All we Stanleys were. Me. Willie. Bobby. The jerks who had murdered Aloysius Daroun. All of us. Addicts. Some had it under control, others didn't.

Was Popoleyev's story the origin of "fleece" as in swindle? Short hair. Fleeces. Were men born to be fleeced? A sexual fix that could grow into decades of affection and companionship or degenerate into a lifetime of hatred and recrimination. Ooof!

"The mere sight of skin starts Stanley's motor. That's why he likes pornography and *Playboy* magazine. Blanche's response is far more complicated. She is programmed to be both physically and emotionally responsive to a permanent mate. Studies show that married women or women with permanent, committed partners are more responsive sexually and enjoy it more.

"Blanche knows what's in her best interest. Women with foolish genes go out of business. There are prostitutes who have scores of encounters in a day and have no physical reaction at all."

"But under the right circumstances . . ."

"Under the right circumstances, and with an imaginative, thoughtful Stanley, Blanche can be an extremely open-minded and skilled lover. When Stanley gets Blanche's circuits lit up, she can go just about forever before she gets pooped."

"Rat-a-tat-tat! Less than a second each contraction."

"Mr. Denson!"

I loved her playful admonitions. "I feel compelled to say I hardly believe it, Dr. Popoleyev. By the way, does Blanche have orgasms? Her profile, that is. Or whatever. Her simulation, in your computers." I did everything I could to keep my eyes above Popoleyev's admirable chest.

"Blanche is multiorgasmic, I am pleased to report. She even goes 'ooh' and 'ahh' when stimulated with the proper data. She, uh, writhes, I believe is the English word."

"Dr. Inskeep's idea?"

"Why, yes it was. Dr. Inskeep said he liked his computer simulations to be responsive."

"I bet." There were times when I was flat-out proud of one of my countrymen. I liked Inskeep's sense of humor.

"Remember the conflicting strategies, now, Mr. Denson. The indiscriminate Stanley wants to reproduce himself as many times as possible in his lifetime. The selective Blanche is after a few superior fathers."

"What do you think? Do I show potential?" I raised my eyebrows.

"Please, Mr. Denson. We're being neutral here, value free." She suppressed a grin.

"I know we select partners by tournament and that Stanley is compelled by his genes to be restless, but in the last week we've both enjoyed the company of Emile and Sally Thibodeaux, and Bobby and Whitefeather Minthorn. They're both long-standing and apparently successful unions. How do you account for that?"

She smiled. "A triumph of the human spirit in both cases, and aren't they fun to watch? Please don't misunderstand me, Mr. Denson. I'm not saying we shouldn't persevere, but the truth is in most cultures marriage is regarded as an overtly economic union, based on a division of labor, and has little or nothing to do with Western notions of romance, much less making anybody happy."

"But you do like romance? You don't think it's a waste of time?"

"Do I like it! A waste of time? No, no, no, Mr. Denson. Heavens no! It's a wonderful gift of the human imagination, and I can't think of anything more grand. I love it!" She wiggled her toes.

Later, as we lay in bed in the darkness, me on the bunk, Sonja Popoleyev on the couch, I told her that I had recently had the engine of my Volkswagen rebuilt and that the carburetors were now tuned to perfection. I could go anywhere, Mexico or Central America if I wanted.

Popoleyev said, "What are you getting at, Mr. Denson?"

I said, "Well, when you first arrived, you said you loved the field—observing primates in action."

"Yes, I did."

"As I understand it, if a scientific experiment is considered valid, it must stand the test of empirical duplication. Is that not correct?"

"Exactly what assertion do you find questionable, Mr. Denson?"

"I can accept some of what you've had to say about Stanley and Blanche in the last few days—or even most of it. I realize the temptation is great to think that we're such a special case, so smart and everything, that we're immune to behavior common to our primate cousins. But I'm not so sure about one figure you gave tonight."

"And that would be?"

"The eight-tenths-second contraction."

"I see. And just what is your objection, Mr. Denson? Do you predict that the figure is too long or too short? And for what reason? Imprecise measurements by William Masters and Virginia Johnson?"

"I haven't postulated a precise theory as yet, but I'm working on it. I'm sure I can come up with something."

"I'm sure you can."

"Theories come first, do they?"

"Ordinarily."

"The reason I mentioned the carburetors, is that if I have to, I can push my bus to start the engine, and Mexican mechanics know their Volkswagens. This is off-season at the ocean, so we'd have it pretty much to ourselves. There are mating sea lions to observe, and redwoods, in Northern California. Plus there's San Francisco with all that good food, and then Hollywood and Beverly Hills to walk around in, and fishing in Baja. All within easy reach of my bus."

"And along the way, you propose to test the eight-tenths-second figure using me as your Blanche?"

"In the name of science. I could not advance such a proposition without honorable motive. Surely, mere lust is insufficient." My heart thumped. Would she say yes? Jubilation time. Hot damn time! Yes, yes, yes!

Or would the answer be no? I had not demonstrated sufficient prowess; she could not imagine me as the sire of her offspring. Also, I didn't own anything; I offered zero security.

Popoleyev said, "As long as you understand, Mr. Denson, that the second you take a stopwatch out of your pocket, I'm taking the next plane back to Russia."

"I did it! I demonstrated prowess!"

"Prowess?" She sounded surprised. "Of what sort? A questionable proposition at best, I would think."

"Some form of prowess. You said it yourself, clearly. Blanche demands a demonstration of prowess, otherwise it's not in her best interest to . . . Say, you don't mean . . ." I leered.

She cut me off. "Good night, Mr. Denson. We'll need our sleep."

"Sleep?" I couldn't help laughing.

"We've got a long day ahead of us tomorrow."

"Maybe I could fly too, if I flapped my arms hard enough."

I could imagine the sexiest of sexy Blanches there on her couch, grinning, knowing she had jump-started my imagination. What a Russian! What horseshit the cold war had been!

The only way I was going to sleep was to try my stair-counting routine. I imagined my own comfy couch in Seattle. The couch was at the bottom of the stairs. The stairs were maroon; the old-fashioned numerals were gold. It was important to get a mental picture of the details, and let the details put me to sleep.

Twenty. I imagined the maroon stair with the ornate gold number twenty on it. I saw myself unbuttoning Popoleyev's blouse. Start over.

Twenty. I saw the twenty stair. I felt Popoleyev's breast under my hand. Awwwwww! Repeat the beginning.

Twenty. The twenty stair. I saw the comfortable couch. I was going to make it, yes. I had my hand on the zipper of her jeans.

Twenty. Twenty stair. I saw the couch. So warm. So good to sleep there.

Nineteen. I made the nineteen stair. Sleep would come. I imagined the nineteen stair. The couch. I ran my hand over Popoleyev's bare ass.

Twenty? Nineteen? Where was I?

Twenty. I imagined the stair with twenty on it. I saw the couch at the bottom of the stairs. Sonja Popoleyev was naked, and I was holding her tightly. She was so smooth and warm and comforting, it was positively incredible.

Twenty-schmenty. Nineteen-schmeinteen. I opened my eyes, knowing there would be no sleep for me that night. If ever a surge of chemicals sent a hapless Stanley positively bananas with craving, it was me. Sonja Popoleyev was the most desirable woman I had ever met. Had to be. No close seconds even. Or thirds.

I knew this feeling was a form of temporary, chemically induced insanity, urging me to do whatever it took to obtain that .8-second hit of bliss to which we Stanleys were ultimately addicted. In the grip of an amnesia that erased all objections—the mental eraser that un-hooked large portions of the cerebral cortex—I gave no thought at all to Jason's misfortunes or Stanley's delusions.

Having established her likely value in my eyes, Popoleyev, an expert on Blanche's strategy and tactical skills, and hip to Stanley's many weaknesses, had made me twist like the damned-fool idiot I was. After setting me up with the business about the stopwatch, she had cut me off and doubled me over with a wry "Good night, Mr. Denson," a nifty form of left hook. Perfect execution. Textbook stuff.

Knocked me senseless.

Chapter Thirty-seven

Out of Fog and Snow

Come morning a thin fog hugged the ground, joining the snow, which was still coming down although at a less ferocious pace than the previous day.

Ahead lay the chore of moving Aloysius Daroun's corpse from the cave to the bench. This was not an easy proposition, since Daroun was now dead weight, a six-feet-ten-inch, 315-pound block of ice. There was no way that the two of us were going to wrestle the board-hard corpse out of the cave, down the steep, zigzagging trail, over the accumulation of boulders to the bench. With Willie and Bobby Minthorn helping, yes. By ourselves, no.

While we waited for Willie and Bobby to arrive, I poked around looking for the eye-shine reflectors, but couldn't find them. Then I remembered that Daroun had knelt and fiddled momentarily with his Sasquatch head before he flipped it away and crashed on his couch. A man with five bullets in him would ordinarily head straight for the couch, to hell with the head. I checked the Sasquatch head. Nothing.

Did Daroun have the presence of mind to lift the reflectors while our attention was riveted to his wounds?

I searched every nook and cranny of the inflatable couch where we had laid him, and where Popoleyev had spent the night. No reflectors.

Then I checked his corpse. His hamlike left hand, resting on his massive belly, fingers down, was clearly clutching something. His hand looked large enough to conceal a baseball if he wanted, so what was in there was impossible to determine. I couldn't move his arm, much less his fingers. I could have solved the mystery by breaking his fingers and forcing them apart, but I didn't have the stomach for it, besides which Popoleyev, correctly, would have objected.

Daroun had been murdered; in most jurisdictions, a coroner's report is mandatory in homicide cases. My solace was that in time, the Skamania County coroner would open the hand to find what evidence he was holding.

Thomas Bondurant was the technical advisor behind the whole scam. He must have told Addison and Daroun about the nocturnal habits of *Troglodytes recens.* But until the coroner did his thing, the question of whether or not the dying Aloysius Daroun was about to give me an ain't-this-fun-foolin'-the-pretty-Russian-lady wink, would remain unanswered.

Popoleyev and I set about tramping the snow on the zigzagging path leading down from the cave. I say path, or trail, but either word applied only if you used your imagination and were generous with definitions. With the bad spots covered by snow, it was even more treacherous.

A few minutes after seven o'clock, while we were hard at our work, two bullets zinged off the rock a few inches from my head.

Popoleyev and I flattened ourselves on the path.

The shot had come from directly below us, on the bench.

From our left, that is, from the direction of our camp, came a sharp yelp.

I yelped twice; we were both okay.

Popoleyev said "Willie?"

"Willie and Bobby."

"They don't have any weapons. What are they going to do?"

I said, "You're talking Willie Prettybird and Bobby Minthorn. I bet they'll come up with something." I eased my head up and peered over the snow. About thirty yards below us, on the bench, barely visible in the thin fog and falling snow, were David Addison and Thomas Bondurant. For whatever reason—possibly because they feared the second chamber of the cave would be discovered—they had chosen to retrieve Daroun and the incriminating evidence now, rather than later.

After having missed me, they had been about to climb over to the rocks to the bottom of the trail when Willie had yelped. Addison was a determined murderer, but a fucked shot.

From my left a yelp.

From below the bench, a yelp.

I gave a yelp myself, to let them know I heard, and understood what they were doing. Bobby was staying on our left, Addison and Bondurant's right. Willie was circling south and west under the bench. They had something going, although I couldn't figure what.

Meanwhile, Addison and Bondurant didn't like the sound of a yelp coming from their rear. They were uncertain what they should do next.

Another yelp. Willie again. Farther west.

On our left, Bobby replied.

So did I. Were Willie and Bobby expecting me to know what to do? I couldn't figure it. I said to Popoleyev, "We need to get closer."

"What?"

"We need to push lower toward those rocks. If we stay beneath the snowline we'll be okay. It's hard for him to see to begin with."

"What are we going to do?"

"I'm not sure, to tell the truth. But I suspect the closer we are, the more use we'll be when the time comes. We'll figure it out."

That said, I started downhill on my stomach, pushing my way through the snow.

We had gone maybe ten yards when the action started, first from Bobby on the left, a high barking, *yip-yip-yip-yip-yip!*

Then the right, *yip-yip-yip-yip-yip!*

I eased up to take a peek. Below me in the fog, Addison and Bondurant stood back to back, facing the commotion on either side.

Then I started, *yip-yip-yip-yip-yip!* It was Willie and Bobby's gambit. If they wanted yipping, yipping they'd get.

Popoleyev joined in, *yip-yip-yip-yip-yip!*

The yipping got higher and more frenzied below us.

Popoleyev and I did our best to match the intensity.

Then, quiet.

We stopped too, watching the figures in the fog.

Seconds later, out of fog and snow, a form, leaping . . .

. . . straight at Addison's throat, hurling its body, teeth locked tight, rrrripppping.

Bondurant turned . . .

. . . stunned.

The form was on his throat too . . .

. . . and was gone, back into the fog.

Addison and Bondurant were clearly down for good.

Popoleyev and I pushed our way through the snow and started climbing over the slippery, snow-covered rocks and boulders. When we got to the bench, Willie and Bobby were there, with a happy Earl, wagging his wounded tail as Bobby finished scrubbing his face with snow. Bobby said, "There you go, Earl. Don't want any dog of mine running around with a bloody face."

On the snow, Addison and Bondurant lay dead, their throats ripped wide open. Their severed arteries had squirted and pumped loops of blood on the snow, the result looking like a painting by Jackson Pollock.

Willie said, "By God, Chief, you and Popoleyev make pretty good redskins up there, yelping and yipping. Scared the piss out of these fuckers."

Bobby said, "They didn't know whether to shit or go blind."

I stared at the bodies on the bloody snow. "Jesus!"

Bobby said, "Like I told Earl here. I said Earl, old pal, these motherfuckers shot your tail. Go for the sons of bitches. Do it." Willie laughed. "You should have seen him take off."

Willie said, "Earl didn't forget their stink, did you, Earl?"

Earl, his tail still wagging, went over to take a sniff of Addison. Sternly, Bobby Minthorn said, "Heel!" Earl did, reluctantly. Bobby said, "I don't want him to think killing people is fun."

Chapter Thirty-eight

The Amusement of Tricksters

It started snowing again, picking up intensity, and it took the four of us nearly two hours to get Aloysius Daroun's massive body off the bluff and onto the bench with the corpses of David Addison and Thomas Bondurant.

Sonja Popoleyev was grateful for the snow, for it meant, she hoped, that the trail to the cave would be covered. We returned to camp and fueled up on one of Whitefeather Minthorn's good meals.

Whitefeather radioed base camp and told them the gist of what happened and that we were coming out. Then we strapped on our snowshoes and began the long trudge down the mountain. It was quits with our search for Sasquatch, so we only took daypacks; we could zip back up in snowmobiles to retrieve the rest of our gear.

Ahead, we faced the hassles of explaining three dead bodies and David Addison's scam. Whether this could be done without revealing Popoleyev's cave remained to be seen.

The person in front did the most work, so we rotated positions.

When the point got tired, he or she took the easy drag where the snow was well tramped. We trudged along, each of us alone with our thoughts.

The way I saw it, David Addison was the real Bigfoot, as were most of the developers, bands of predators who tromp-tromp-tromped through the Pacific Northwest, bent on wringing every nickel possible from its gorgeous wilderness. These determined Stanleys would put powerboats on quiet lakes, motorbikes on peaceful trails, and buzzing snowmobiles on winter landscapes of silent, awesome beauty that could be enjoyed by cross-country skiers with no harm done. Bigfoot Bangers. Sasquatch scams. Nothing was beneath them. Without a hint of guilt at the consequences, they'd do whatever it took to make another buck. Winning the tournament was the thing; everything else be damned.

I was born here. I grew up here. To develop the wilderness was to consume it. The way I saw it, when out-of-control Stanleys consumed the wilderness, they consumed my birthright, and I resented it.

As I followed Willie, eyes on the small of his back, I got to wondering about the phantom form that had leaped from the shadows at the throats of Addison and Bondurant. I said, "You know, Willie, that snow was awful deep for Earl to be moving that fast."

Willie said, "Who else but Earl, for Christ's sakes?"

"What if it was a coyote?"

"Chief! Chief!"

"A coyote has bigger pads on its feet, doesn't it? Better for the snow. I can see Coyote moving that fast, but not Earl."

Whitefeather giggled.

Behind me, Popoleyev said, "What are you saying?"

I said, "That business of cleaning blood off Earl's face could have been staged for my benefit. I didn't see any blood."

Bobby said, "Hey, give me a break, Denson. I didn't want him running around with human blood on his snout."

"He might develop a taste for it," Willie said.

"Sure, sure," I said.

Willie, turning so Popoleyev could see, grinned and bared his teeth, raising the end of a forefinger to the tip of each cuspid. He said, "Evolution provideth, Denson. Isn't that right, Dr. Popoleyev?"

"Willie!"

"Love that hot, salty blood," Willie said. "Women's throats are especially delicious. Soft and tender, and I like the smell." He leered at Popoleyev.

A few days later we viewed my tape of our early morning Sasquatch visitor at Olden Dewlapp's house in Portland, where we had dinner with Olden and Boogie and their wives.

There wasn't much to the tape. The camera was bouncing up and down as I ran, pointing this way and that, and the viewer only got fragmentary glimpses of the beast.

As I watched the action, I couldn't help thinking that the fleeing Sasquatch—such as we were able to see—looked remarkably like the huge, shadowy figure I had seen, or thought I had seen, palavering with Willie on the first night.

Willie had said it was Bear.

The more we looked at the tape, the more I thought the figure in fact looked bearlike. Willie always said the animal-people were great jokers. They loved to tease and razz. The put-on was one of their favorite pranks. Was Sasquatch an elaborate animal people joke on gullible humans? Something Bear and his pals did to spook little kids and tourists. A trickster's idea of a good time. *Ho, ho, ho!*

Did animal people laughter ring in the high mountains from Mount Baker to Mount Shasta as Bear spread the story? *The Russian woman bought it completely, Mole, you should have seen her face. And the fool with the camera almost totaled himself.*

Did Beaver add his toothy grin to Loon's merriment? Did Coon double up with laughter as Bear related the details of our happy chase? Did Squirrel guffaw at the idea of Coyote's partner tripping and banging his knees and elbows on the frozen ground? Great sport! *Ha, ha, ha!*

That's not to mention Coyote's amusement at being a fifth columnist in the human camp—an animal-people spy whispering our plans into Mouse's ear in the dead of night while we were unconscious in our tent.

Willie, watching the tape, said, "Well, what do you think, Denson?"

The thing could be mistaken for a bear. No. Couldn't be. Could not. It'd have to be a grizzly. There were grizzlies in northwest Montana, but we didn't have them this far south.

"Looks like Aloysius Daroun in a Sasquatch costume," I said. I said this with certainty, although the Skamania County coronor, having dug into Daroun's body to retrieve five incriminating .22 slugs, had lacked the curiosity to open his closed paw. As near as I can figure it, Aloysius Daroun went to his grave holding two Sasquatch eye-shine reflectors in his left hand.

He must have, right? There was no other explanation except . . .

No, no, no. That was out of the question. Until proven otherwise, no *p*s were *q*.